Nearly Departed

Nearly Departed

An Eve Appel Mystery

LESLEY A. DIEHL

CAVEL PRESS

Seattle, WA

Epicenter Press
6524 NE 181st St.
Suite 2
Kenmore, WA 98028

www.epicenterpress.com
www.camelpress.com
www.coffeetownpress.com

For more information go to: www.lesleyadiehl.com

Cover design by Dawn Anderson

Nearly Departed
Copyright © 2019 by Lesley A. Diehl

ISBN: 9781603818230 (Trade Paper)
ISBN: 978194189882 (eBook)

Library of Congress Control Number: 002019945153

Produced in the United States of America

ACKNOWLEDGMENTS

The ongoing adventures of Eve Appel Egret, her family and friends would not have been possible in another setting. Rural Florida is unique, and its wildlife and wild places make for an exciting locale for Eve's adventures. I cannot imagine creating either the characters or the plot of the Eve Appel Mysteries outside of the swamps, grasslands, canal, lakes and sabal palm growths of the land around the Big Lake. So, thanks to Mother Nature for creating this wonderful setting where humans find life challenging but have learned to live in one of the most intriguing places on the planet. There is no other like it.

Also by the author from Camel Press:

A Secondhand Murder

Dead in the Water

A Sporting Murder

Mud Bog Murder

Old Bones Never Die

Killer Tied

Short Stories in the Series

"The Little Redheaded Girl is my Friend"

"Thieves and Gators Run at the Mention of her
Name"

"Gator Aid"

PROLOGUE

———

WITH ONE LAST loving look at the picture, Angus MacAngus lifted it from its hook on the wall and added it to the cardboard box he planned to place in storage while he rented out his house in Scotland. The other artwork on the walls of his study might be worth more in dollars than this small handmade picture of a grinning cat, but he loved it more than all the expensive objects in the house put together. The cat was a decoupage of rice, beans, seeds and other natural items glued onto a linen canvas. The ears were of different sizes, and the face was lopsided, rounded on one side and flat on the other. His grandson, Dylan, had made it for him.

Angus and his wife, Carolyn, had been separated for over a year, and he was closing the house to travel. His wife now lived in the United States in a Naples, Florida condo she filled with new possessions. When she left, she turned down his offer of the furniture in the house as well as her share of his extensive art collection.

"Pay me my half," she had said with a dismissive flap of her hand. "Everything here reminds me of us, and I want to begin again. Besides, how would all this dark, heavy furniture fit into a sun-filled place on the beach?"

Once she settled into her new home, she wrote to him—he knew she wanted to rub his nose in how happy she was without him—to brag about how much she was in tune with the Florida coastal style. "It's so me," she said in her letter. He knew the breezy, beachy lifestyle in Florida was only part of the reason why she loved her move there. The other was her love affair with Angus' best friend from college which blossomed when the friend came to Scotland the year before last. His friend Bruce hadn't visited for many years, not since Angus' son Mickey was young. Now Carolyn was off leading her new exciting life. If he was honest about their relationship, he had to admit there hadn't been much between them these last few years. He wasn't happy she had left, but he didn't miss her either.

Angus loved the house in Edinburgh and didn't consider anything in it dark or heavy and certainly not the picture he held in his hands. He ran his fingers over it, feeling its bumpy texture. His grandson, Dylan, had made it from the seeds gathered from the gardens and fields surrounding the villa the family had rented one summer in Italy. It had been the last time all of them had been together, and even his son, Mickey, whose disposition leaned toward angry and morose, seemed happy in the warm Mediterranean sunshine, running to catch up with Dylan, picking just the right seeds for the project.

He clutched the picture to his chest as if embracing it would bring back those happier days.

Angus shook his head and laid the picture carefully in the storage box. He intended to return to Scotland after he traveled with Mickey, Mickey's wife, Darcie, and Dylan to visit some relatives in the States. First on his list was his niece, Madeleine Boudreau Wilson, whom he had not seen in over thirty years. He remembered her as a bright, happy child with flaming curls and a bouncy nature. Now she was grown, married with twins.

They must be handful. He smiled to himself, wondering if they had the signature red hair that went with being from the family MacAngus. His son didn't, but his grandson did. Angus' own hair was struck through with white now, lightening his youthful carrot top red.

The smile on Angus face faded. He groaned, feeling his age and sank into his favorite overstuffed chair. Suddenly a thought came to him. Why put his grandson's gift to him in storage? It was small enough to fit into his carry-on luggage, and what airport security personnel would deny his bringing into the country his grandson's handmade craft? He got out of the chair and with a spring in his step, he strode into the bedroom where his suitcase lay on the bed. He inserted the picture between a sweater and a pair of dress slacks and closed the case, giving it a reassuring pat on the top. Safe for the trip.

CHAPTER 1

―

I WATCHED NETTY dash across the back yard toward the canal. It seemed my daughter had gone from the crawling stage directly to running with no walking in between. Her energy was boundless and her curiosity without end. I knew she wouldn't be an easy child. After all, she did have me as her mother and, according to my grandmother who raised me, I was a nonstop ball of pure recklessness with no consideration for my own safety or for the rules Grandy tried to impose on me growing up. It was, as Grandy had warned me, pay-back time. It was also exhausting. Now I knew why women had their children earlier in life and not when they were well into their thirties as I was.

"Netty. Stop!" I yelled. She teetered at the water's edge and reached out toward something below.

"Pretty flower," she said, pivoting toward me and losing her balance.

I grabbed her by the waistband on her shorts before she fell into the water.

"Yes. Pretty, but remember what I told you? You don't play

around the canal without me or Daddy with you. You know there are alligators in there."

She wriggled in my arms and twisted her curly head of dark hair around to look at the deep waters.

"Nothing there. Down," she demanded.

"You're being too protective of her. She needs to learn on her own what's dangerous and what's not," said a voice from behind me.

Netty squalled in delight and reached out for her grandfather whom she loved passionately. All my children adored Lionel Egret, and he them. I was happy for my sons and my daughter to be surrounded by relatives. I missed having family when I was growing up. My parents died in a boating accident when I was nine. Grandy was all I had until I met my husband, Sammy, and we adopted his three nephews when they lost their parents. Now, of course, we had this handful, our daughter Netty.

Lionel Egret, Sammy's father, was devoted to his grandchildren. He enjoyed taking them into the swamps for adventures in living wild—good for the boys who were older, but I was not ready for my two-year-old daughter to strike out in a canoe and spend nights camping and hunting even if she had a grandfather who knew more about living in the swamps than most did. He'd spent over thirty years out there until he returned to his family.

"Falling into the canal to be taken by an alligator is not my idea of a learning experience," I said in a snappish voice. Lionel and I often did not see eye to eye. As a Miccosukee, he was suspicious of white people although he had married one, Sammy's mother. The marriage ended when Sammy was little. He had misgivings about my being a good wife for Sammy and more doubts about whether I could raise my Miccosukee children in accordance with the tribal traditions, but we were slowly coming to respect each other. It wasn't easy for either of us.

"Grampie!" said Netty. "Gators?"

"Don't see any. Your mama is just being careful. I'll take you on a ride in the canoe and show you some alligators, some big ones. Maybe this weekend."

"Talk to Sammy. He may have made plans for this weekend."

Lionel took Netty from my arms and swung her into the air exacting a squeal of delight from her.

"Higher. Higher," she insisted.

He gave me a look which said he knew what my daughter liked more than I did.

"She's not some fragile girl from the city, you know. She's half Miccosukee. She's destined to grow into a warrior."

That was what I needed—a daughter, who, like her Indian ancestors, fled into the swamps after doing battle with white folks, probably the boys at school who might tease her or her teachers trying to discipline her. Well, maybe that trait wasn't so bad. I liked women who could stand up for themselves. Like me.

Lionel put his granddaughter down. Netty was off down the canal in a flash.

"I'll get her," he said.

"Is my son giving you trouble again?" asked a voice from behind me. I knew without turning around that it was Grandfather Egret, the patriarch of the Egret clan. The smell of tobacco smoke from his pipe gave him away. Aside from my husband, this was the man I loved most dearly. He was Sammy's grandfather and Lionel's father. Over the years he had become my protector. I touched the amulet I always wore around my neck. He had made it for me out of soft deerskin hide for the bag which hung from a leather thong. Unlike his son and his grandson, Grandfather was a small man, straight in his carriage. He was light of foot so that people were often taken by surprise when he came up behind them. It wasn't as if he was trying to hide his approach. It was a way of walking he'd used all his life.

"Maybe you should make an amulet for Netty," I said, taking

his arm.

He laughed, watching his son catch her and scoop her up. "She'll need it. She's like her mother." He wasn't trying to flatter. It was true. Netty was all me. Except for her black hair from her father, it was if I had cloned this child.

I sighed. So like me. Was that a good or a bad thing? I thought back to all the adventures I'd had in my life. My curiosity had gotten me into more than a few tight spots. My moxie and friends had gotten me out of them. I feared Netty was destined for getting herself into situations that demanded she have a sharp mind and the support of others to help her. And perhaps, I thought Grandfather should make her an amulet.

"And an amulet?" asked Grandfather, finishing my thought by reading my mind as he usually did.

I LEFT CANAL-SIDE to check on the construction progress Sammy and tribal members were making on the house we were building next to Grandfather's. We had decided when Netty was born that we needed more room than Grandfather's one-bedroom cabin afforded us, and even more than my three-bedroom house provided. We were a growing family. Netty would want her own room at some point, and her three brothers were already finding it tight in my spare bedroom.

We were building a house with four bedrooms and an office that could be used as a fifth sleeping area. Grandfather said he would be more comfortable remaining in his tiny canal house. Lionel made clear that he would not live in any "white folks' idea of a house." I was thankful for that. Lionel and I were working on our relationship, but neither of expected it would ever be comfortable or close. He preferred to sleep on a pallet in Grandfather's small cabin. Or on the ground when he took to the swamps, which was often.

It was early summer, already in the nineties here in southern Florida, hot to be working out in the sun to finish shingling the roof. The airboat business, operated by Sammy and his father and located on the other side of Grandfather's small house, had few customers after the winter visitors left. Our new house went up slowly. Summer was the only time Sammy had time to work on the place. On the weekends he had plenty of help from tribal members, many of them skilled craftsmen. Our home would be large, functional and beautiful, the rafters in the ceiling made from cypress trees taken from reservation land. The design would be a blend of traditional Miccosukee architecture and modern touches. It certainly was not a "white folks house."

"Could anyone use a drink of water?" I called up to the workers.

"I'll come down and grab the bottle," said Sammy. He had removed his shirt, and I could see a sheen of sweat on his skin. The muscles of his bronzed chest rippled as he moved down the ladder.

"I'm stinky," he said as I leaned into him.

"I don't care." I didn't. His sweat smelled like hard work, a natural masculine scent. To me Sammy always smelled like love and family. He was my Sammy. No one was quite as attractive with his straight black hair, his nut-brown skin and a face that looked as if it had been chiseled out of stone. His eyes were brown unless he was angry. Then they turned black, and, with his prominent nose, he looked like a bird of prey. In moments of passion his eyes were the color of dark chocolate with flecks of gold in them. I totally adored this man.

"Eve? Is there anyone home? I thought you were going to get us water not stare at me as if I was a juicy rib you were about to consume."

I had gone off there for a while, and it took me a moment to turn my attention to what I had been doing. I heard laughter from the roof and looked up to see the men there starring down at Sammy and me.

"Hey, you two," called one of Sammy's cousins, "we could die of thirst up here while the two of you do your love bird thing."

I ran to grab the water container and handed it to Sammy, who gave me a quick squeeze. He took it and started back up the ladder. "You guys are jealous, that's all."

"You act like you're newlyweds," said another of the men. "How do you manage that?"

"We try to surprise each other." Sammy glanced down at me and winked.

He was right. Our lives were never predictable. When Sammy and I met, I owned a consignment shop with my friend Madeleine. She and I still ran it, but I also had signed on to apprentice with a PI in town. Most of the cases he assigned me were boring, but there were a few big ones involving murder. Crusty said I was coming along…except for my work at the firing range. I hated guns and had a bad relationship with them. I liked to shoot with my eyes closed.

My cell rang. It was Crusty.

"Where are you?" he asked.

"This is my day off, remember? I'm home, where I said I'd be."

"I need you here."

Crusty sounded more excited than he'd been lately.

"You've got a case?"

"Yep. And it's a doozy."

"Murder?" I asked. I hoped he wasn't calling about another insurance fraud case or surveillance on some cheating spouse. Sitting on a house for hours was broadening my butt.

"Better. Sex."

I could almost hear Crusty salivating.

I left Netty with her grandfather and a promise that he wouldn't take her off to the swamps while I was gone. Just in case, I asked Grandfather Egret to keep an eye on the two of them.

With three boys and now Netty, Sammy's truck couldn't

carry all of us together, and my Mustang convertible had the same problem. We decided to buy a small van that could accommodate all the kids, Sammy, Lionel and Grandfather. I couldn't bring myself to give up the convertible. It represented my adventurous side. I still felt like a wild woman when I drove it with the top down. It was fun. To others, I said the convertible was necessary for running errands around town or driving to West Palm to pick up consignment shop donations. I don't think I fooled anyone. I liked speeding down the Beeline Highway with the top down and the wind blowing through my short spikey blond hair. No one questioned me about the car.

I jumped into the convertible, dropped the top and sped off to Crusty's office, which was conveniently located right next to our consignment shop in a small strip mall in the town of Sabal Bay, Florida. For those of you familiar with the coasts of Florida, that's not where you would find us. We're thirty miles inland from the east coast in rural Florida, a land of fields of cattle, cowboys on horses and a whole lot of wildlife like cougars, deer, rabbits, raccoons and especially alligators. Live oaks, cypress and sabal palms along with a lot of scrub palmetto and buffalo grass provide dense vegetation hiding any number of crawly things, spiders, insects and snakes. And did I mention there are swamps, miles of them that can swallow up humans who are unfamiliar with the territory? Even those used to the swamps can become disoriented and lose their way. Taking to them was what saved the Seminoles and Miccosukees from defeat by the US army in the Indian wars during the 1800s.

When I arrived at the office, I noticed a very classy black Mercedes parked out front. Whoever was inquiring about a PI had taste and probably money. I walked into the inner office and found Crusty seated behind his desk, feet on the floor—unusual for him. He was trying to impress someone if he wasn't leaning back in his chair with his boots propped on the desk and an unlit cigar in his mouth. He'd given up smoking a year ago but held on to the props. Seated across from him was a tall, slender woman wearing a dark pin-striped suit, white silk blouse and heels every bit as high as those I favored. She looked at my feet and smiled.

"You must be Eve." She got up and held out her hand, giving me a handshake as firm as any I've ever gotten from a man. Her hair was coiffed into a shoulder length bob and her make-up was perfect, not overdone, simply business professional. This woman knew how to present herself.

"This is Ms. Della Abbot. She's the President of Abbot Aeronautics in Stuart. She's come to us because she has a problem with sexual harassment in her business."

I laughed. "Surely no one is harassing you." What man would take on this woman? She looked as if she would have him arrested on the spot. She probably carried around a lawyer in that sleek black leather briefcase that sat on the floor beside her chair.

"No, of course not."

"I'm guessing it's other women who work for you. Right?"

She nodded. "I have received several phone calls from former employees who complained. They wouldn't give their names. Unfortunately, there's not much I can do. No one will come forth with a credible accusation. I need proof. And here's what I fear: they made accusations against several men. I'm worried I have a work environment hostile to women. I'm a female CEO trying to attract female employees to an industry dominated by men." She ran her hand through her hair. "I've got to take action. Mr. McNabb here thought having a woman undercover as an employee might work. He suggested you."

"A great idea." I was almost salivating at a chance to nab men who took advantage of women in the workplace. Too often in the past I'd been subjected to unwanted sexual attention and knew of other women who had been groped and fondled. Our complaints, if we reported them, had usually been dismissed, but the climate for believing accusations against these guys was changing.

"You won't do," Ms. Abbot said.

"What?"

"Well, look at you. You're almost as tall as most men. You have an athletic build and you present yourself like an Amazon. What guy would take the chance of groping you? You'd probably throw him down and hog tie him before you finished calling the cops. You don't look as if you take guff from anybody."

"Yeah. That's what all my friends say." I hung my head in disappointment. I guess Crusty would put me back on surveillance detail and recommend Ms. Abbot to another firm. Drat.

"No. You won't do for this job," repeated Ms. Abbot. She looked as disappointed as I felt.

There was a soft knock on the door, and Madeleine stuck her head into the office. Ms. Abbot turned toward the door, then smiled.

"I want her," she said, pointing to my friend.

CHAPTER 2

———

Mᴜʏ ᴅᴇᴀʀᴇꜱᴛ ꜰʀɪᴇɴᴅ Madeleine and my partner in the consignment business is the antithesis of me. She's short, has long curly red hair and a heart-shaped face. She is the epitome of a southern lady. She knows what to say to smooth over my usual lack of social grace. Where one would expect this paragon of loveliness to glide across the floor, she can stumble and trip her way into any room. She did that now as she poked her head in the door, stubbed her toe on the threshold, pitched forward and landed at my side. I prevented her from falling on her tush by grabbing her arm. That was our relationship: she rescued me from my social gaffs, and I prevented her from physically hurting herself and others.

"Hi," she said recovering her balance. "Sorry to interrupt, but I saw your car outside, Eve, and I needed to talk to you. I didn't know you were meeting with a client. The "in conference" sign wasn't on the inner door."

"I forgot to put it up when I came in. It's not your fault," I said.

Madeleine started to back out through the door but caught

the sleeve of her dress on the doorknob and knocked the door closed with a bang.

Ms. Abbot eyed Madeleine with interest. "Let me introduce myself," she said. "I'm Della Abbot. You're just the woman I'm looking for."

Madeleine said, "My name is Madeleine Boudreau Wilson. I own the consignment shop next door with Eve. I don't understand why you're looking for me."

"Not you exactly, but someone like you," said Crusty. "Unfortunately, Mizz Wilson is not one of my employees."

"So, hire her," said Della Abbot. It was an order, not a request.

I was right about Ms. Abbot. She was a woman who was used to getting what she wanted.

"Madeleine has the shop to run, and she's the mother of twins. I don't think she needs another job," I said. How absurd. To think of Madeleine as a PI.

"I'm not looking to take on another employee either," added Crusty.

"You'd let me walk out of here and find another agency? That's not very businesslike," said Ms. Abbot.

"This is a small agency, and I'm not looking to grow it. I'm near retirement, and I've got all I can handle having one part-time detective who's often more trouble than she's worth. She's just learning the business, and you're suggesting I teach this little gal?" Crusty gestured at Madeleine.

"What do you mean I'm more trouble than I'm worth?" I asked.

"You can't shoot worth a dang." He rummaged in his desk. I knew he was looking for a cigar to chew on. He may have given up smoking, but he still relied on the props, especially when he wanted the final word.

"Mr. McNabb, I'm not suggesting you shoot these men. I want them caught in the act," said Ms. Abbot.

"Can't do it."

"Aside from not being good with a gun, what do you see as

my shortcomings?" I asked again.

He ignored my question with a wave of his unlit cigar. "Besides, this little mama isn't interested."

"Wait just a minute," said Madeleine.

"We're trying to do detective work here, honey. You don't need to concern yourself with this messy stuff. I can't see you packing," I said, still interested in pursuing why Crusty thought of me as trouble.

"Hey!" Madeleine shouted. "Quit talking as if I'm not here. And, Eve, I'm a whole lot better with a gun than you'll ever be. I keep my eyes open. Now what is this all about?"

Crusty and I were stunned into silence. I had forgotten what a force Madeleine could be when she put her foot down. She had effectively defended herself from a gang of bullies in grade school the year we met. For someone with such tiny hands, she packed a wallop, especially when she took aim at a fella's little boy parts.

Ms. Abbot signaled to me to get up and give Madeleine my chair. Faced with this pair of determined women, I did. Madeleine sat and leaned forward with interest.

"What would your husband say about this?" I whispered in her ear.

"Hush." She turned her back on me and directed her attention to Ms. Abbot.

Crusty raised one eyebrow in skepticism while I shook my head and stared out the office window. I heard Ms. Abbot outline what she needed. Madeleine listened without interrupting.

Madeleine remained silent for several minutes after Ms. Abbot finished, then asked the question guaranteed to get Crusty on board. "How much are you willing to pay this agency for the work?"

Ms. Abbot gave a figure that made Crusty drop the cigar out of his mouth.

Oh, lizard poop. It looked as if I would be gaining a colleague in the detecting business. Maybe she could teach me something about guns.

"Look, I'll leave you three to work out the details. Why don't you call me this afternoon, so we can get on this right away?" She extracted a business card from her briefcase and got out of her chair. She walked toward the door and pulled it open, turning as she did so. "This afternoon," she said firmly, then left.

Madeleine seemed determined to take on the role of a new hire in Ms. Abbot's firm, undercover for Crusty. There were issues Madeleine and I needed to talk about. Crusty cleared his throat and said he was off to get coffee. I glanced over at the full pot of coffee sitting on top of his file cabinet.

"It was made this morning. I should throw it out. Be back in ten." Muttering something under his breath about "Yankee women," he left.

Sometimes I could hug him for being so sensitive. Not often, but sometimes.

I knew better than to open our conversation with the concern about covering the consignment shop. After all, I had left much of the work there in Madeleine and Shelley's hands when I decided to apprentice myself as a detective in the agency. I wasn't going to bring up the question of who would work in Madeleine's place. What I couldn't help mentioning was how concerned I was for Madeleine's safety. She gave me the stink eye when I told her how worried I was.

"You think I can't take care of myself? You think I'm a girlie girl? A little bitty lady with no ability to defend myself?"

That was exactly what I thought but knew better than to tell her that. I lied. "Of course, not. You've got gumption and attitude." I didn't know when I should shut up, so I went on to ask, "What will David think? And what about the twins?"

"Let's see, Eve. You have a husband. You certainly don't ask him for permission to track down killers. And what about your kids?'

I wanted to add something else about how some people had a knack for detective work while others did not, but I stopped myself and just in time.

"I've watched you all these years, and I know you like chasing down criminals. It's not simply exciting for you. It takes brains. I've got a brain that's dying to be used for more than choosing clothing for the shop, selling used items, raising the kids—although that's more challenging than a game of chess—and making certain David is happy. I do all the things you do, Eve, except chase after bad guys. This seems like a fairly tame assignment. It's not like I'm placing myself in danger. I'll be working as an assistant in the HR office, not ducking down alleyways to avoid getting shot."

"I never knew you had a yearning to investigate a crime."

"You never asked. Most of the time I like to watch from the sidelines, but this is something Ms. Abbot thinks I'm right for. I can help take these predators down."

I watched her face as she spoke and saw something there that suggested she knew exactly what the women at Ms. Abbot's firm had encountered. I didn't ask about her own past experiences. She would tell me if she wanted to, and until then, it was her story to keep to herself or share with whomever she liked. Maybe being able to identify these men and exact some kind of justice was what she needed to do for herself and for the women. I admired her resolve. However, I knew David would not like it. She would need someone in her corner when she told David. It was my responsibility as her friend to back her despite any misgivings I might have.

"I apologize for being so wrapped up in my own life that I didn't consider what you might be experiencing. We never have the time to talk like we used to."

"It's my fault, too. Not only do we not talk, but I don't have time to think anymore. I'm almost as surprised at my interest in this case as you are surprised at my attraction to it."

"You know David will go ballistic. He'll tell you not to do it.

He may even forbid you."

"David does not forbid me to do anything."

"He will when he hears about this."

Madeleine sighed and looked at the floor. "I know. Will you help me, Eve?"

I thought about that. I owed it to my best friend to support her, but I knew I wasn't the person to argue her case with David. He loved me, but mostly because Madeleine loved me. I knew he thought me a pushy broad and was secretly happy Madeleine was nothing like me.

"I know of someone who can do a much better job of convincing David than I can."

"Grandy?"

"David knows I got my snoopy, intrusive nature from her. No. He needs to hear it from another man."

"Sammy?"

"Too biased in my favor."

"Not Nappi?"

"Of course not. He likes Nappi, but David thinks he flirts with the edge of the law. It makes him uncomfortable."

"Grandfather!" we both said in unison.

I INTENDED TO talk to Grandfather this evening before everyone arrived at his place for a one of his famous chicken stew and fried catfish dinners, but before I could say anything to him, Madeleine called me.

"Don't say anything about the Abbot case, Eve. I got a call late this afternoon from my Uncle Angus. I don't think you've ever met him. Anyway, he's coming from Scotland to visit the United States, and he thought he'd make one of his stops a visit to see me. He'll be here this weekend, so I don't think this is the time I should tell David my intention to help out on this case."

"Sure. We haven't worked out the strategy yet for how we're going to handle it. We'll meet again with Ms. Abbot next week. There will be plenty of time to prepare David for what you plan to do. Or are you thinking you'll be too busy to take on the assignment?"

"I expect him to be here for only this weekend and leave for Naples, Florida Monday. He's coming with his son, daughter-in-law and grandson. They've booked rooms at the Flamingo Motel in town. I'm dying for you to meet him. I remember him as a big, red-headed man, lots of fun to be around."

"Will he be wearing a kilt?" I asked in a teasing voice.

"Don't be silly, Eve."

"The boys would love it."

"I'll see if he brought one with him. We'll see you later. Are you sure there isn't anything I can bring for dinner tonight?"

"You know how Grandfather is. He wants to do the whole thing himself. Bring a big appetite."

The only person Grandfather ever let help him with his preparations was Grandy, who he said made the best batter for catfish. When I arrived home, she was in the kitchen wearing one of Grandfather's colorful aprons and a whole lot of flour and cornmeal on her face as well as a floury coating in her curls.

"Can I help?" I asked, sweeping my hand through her hair to remove the dusting there. "I thought the flour mixture was to coat the fish, not you."

"Go away, Eve. Everyone knows you cannot cook."

"Maybe you should have taught me."

She guffawed at my comment. "I was too busy trying to keep you out of trouble. Besides you weren't interested."

Netty ran up behind me and tugged at my leg. "Meemie. Up."

Meemie was her name for me, a kind of amalgamation of Eve and Mommy.

I lifted her into my arms and gave her a big kiss. "Who's going to teach my daughter to cook since I don't know how?"

"Nappi can. Now get out of the kitchen, both of you. Go bother Grandfather who's got the stew cooking over the outside fire."

I had smelled the stew when I came in the house. Grandfather still referred to it as an old tribal recipe, but I wondered how many people knew as I did that he substituted chicken for rabbit. He claimed the latter were hard to come by now that the invasive Burmese pythons had taken over the swamps and preyed on all the small mammals. Chicken was fine with me. I'm not into bunny. I like my bunnies delivering Easter eggs, not looking up at me among some stewed vegetables.

Logs for seating had been placed around the firepit. We expected a large gathering to share in the meal: the men who worked with Sammy on the roof, a few other tribal members who were distant relatives of Grandfather's, Madeleine, David and their twins, Sammy, our boys and our daughter, Lionel Egret, Grandy's husband Max and Nappi, our mob boss friend, who had become more like family than simply friend.

When I walked out back with Netty, I noticed everyone was already there including, unfortunately, my ex-husband Jerry who always seemed to wheedle an invitation out of someone in charge. In this case it had to be Grandfather.

I leaned over and whispered in Grandfather's ear as he was stirring his stew, "So you took pity on Jerry and invited him?"

Grandfather looked up at me with a puzzled look on his face. "I thought you invited him."

"More likely he smelled your stew on the wind and invited himself." I smiled at Jerry. "Hi, Jerry. Alone again tonight?"

"Hi, Evie," he said, calling me a name he knew I hated.

We got along well enough, although we liked to take jabs at each other. Everyone knew we played this game of "gotcha," and they didn't take the insults seriously. Neither did we, except sometimes he did annoy me with his bumbling inability to do much of anything right and his intrusion in our lives. You'd think divorce would have severed ties between us, but, since he worked for Nappi, he was around and included in many of our gatherings. I often felt more like a mother to him than an ex-wife. Maybe that's what sometimes got to me. He was so needy.

After dinner, groans of pleasure could be heard from everyone as we settled back with full stomachs. There was nothing so satisfying as country cooking with a Miccosukee twist. David and Nappi volunteered to do cleanup, insisting that everyone else had worked hard either in food prep or on the house. Nappi gave Jerry a pointed look, but he ignored the signal that he should help. Lionel took the boys down to the canal to search for frogs and sticks to use in making 'smores. As darkness set in, Grandfather stoked up the fire. The boys grabbed the sticks Lionel had prepared for them, and Grandy brought the making for the 'smores.

"Something sweet to top off your meal?" asked Sammy, his arm around my shoulders.

"I couldn't eat one morsel more."

Car headlights shone on the side of Grandfather's house as someone pulled into his drive.

"Expecting someone else?" Lionel asked. There was suspicion in his voice, but Lionel was always suspicious. Living alone in the swamps most of his life made him more comfortable with swamp critters and a bit paranoid about humans. When Grandfather said no, Lionel got up to confront whoever was intruding on our party. He touched the knife he always wore at his waist and stepped beyond the light of the fire. A car door slammed, I then heard the car drive off, and I could hear talking. Lionel returned, accompanied by a young woman.

"She says she's your daughter," announced Lionel, directing his words to David.

"Bethany. What are you doing here? Is something wrong?" David rushed over to her and hugged her.

"Here. Have a seat by the fire. We're having "smores," said Grandy.

"I'm on a diet. I don't eat sugar," snapped Bethany.

David's face flushed red with embarrassment and anger for his daughter's rudeness, but he said nothing and directed her to a seat near him.

I'd never met Bethany before, but I knew she had spent some time at David and Madeleine's house on the game reserve David owned. Madeleine said little about her to me except that she was "a bit spoiled" and that "her mother was overprotective" of her. Over ten years ago and a year before the divorce, David's wife had moved to Boca Raton to afford her daughter "a more civilized" upbringing.

"How did you find me here?" asked David.

"Mom talked about how you hung out with some Indians running an airboat business, so when I got off the bus in town, I got directions here and hitched a ride. I want to go home now."

The way she said "Indians" with a note of disgust got my attention, and I felt Sammy's arm tense on my shoulder.

Bethany was slender with shoulder length auburn hair, an oval face and big blue eyes, a young woman only a year or so older than my oldest son Jason. I turned to look at him, wondering what his reaction to another teen, a girl, would be. He stared at her with his mouth open. His marshmallow dropped into the flames without his noticing.

"Tell me what's going on," insisted David.

Bethany shook her head. "I'm thirsty. Got a beer?"

"No," Madeleine said. "Even if we did have beer, you're too young to have one."

"Mom lets me drink."

"Well, goody for Mom," retorted Madeleine.

"I'm calling your mother to find out what's going on if you won't tell me," said David, taking out his cellphone.

"Don't, Dad. It won't do any good. I've made up my mind. I'm not going to live one second more with that witch. I'm moving in with you."

CHAPTER 3

"WELL, THAT WAS interesting," I said, as David and Madeleine packed up the twins and left with Bethany. "What I wouldn't give to be a mouse in the walls of that house."

"She's really cute, isn't she, Mom?" asked Jason. "And it sounds like we might be going to the same school now."

I looked down into his brown eyes, which were sparkling with adolescent love. *Oh, boy.* I couldn't think of a worse choice for a first crush. Of course, I couldn't tell him that. "We'll have to see what her parents think."

"This fall I can show her around school and everything. Make it easier for her to meet people. Learn the ropes." Jason seemed to vibrate with enthusiasm for this girl.

"Jason's got a girlfriend," teased his younger brothers.

"Do not," he said.

"Do too," they insisted. "He's gonna kiss her."

"Mom, tell them to leave me alone."

"Okay, boys," I said to Jerome and Jeremy, "let's not be mean."

"Kiss, Meemie?" asked Netty and made smacking sounds

with her lips.

"You want a kiss, Netty?' I asked and picked her up in my arms.

"No. Brother. Kiss, kiss, kiss." She continued to smack with her mouth and windmill her arms around toward Jason.

Jason threw down his stick with the gooey marshmallow residue left on the end of it and ran off toward the canal.

"I'll go talk to him," said Sammy.

"You hurt your brother," I told the other boys. "He only wanted to be friendly to Bethany." That was another spin on it, but hardly the whole truth. Jason was smitten with a girl I worried might not return his affection or even be a friend to him.

Lionel came up behind me. "That gal will be trouble."

I had to agree. "She'll take a bit of getting used to if she lives with that family."

"She won't be good for Jason either," he said.

I sighed. "I know how you feel about white folks but give her a break."

"It has nothing to do with her being white. She doesn't like us," said Lionel.

"I don't think right now she likes anybody."

"Jason should be working this summer, not hanging around here.," added Lionel.

Lionel had been grumbling about how little exposure all the boys were getting to traditional Miccosukee culture. Seeing how Jason reacted to Bethany must have brought up his fear that Jason would be tempted by her to indulge in what he saw as decadent white teenage pastimes. If what we saw tonight with Bethany's rude behavior was an indication of what she was like, I didn't want Jason spending much time around her either. But it sounded like she'd had a fight with her mother, so I wanted to give her a break. I knew Lionel was too pig-headed to see her as other than a spoiled white gal, and I also knew I wouldn't be able to convince him he should go easy on her for now. I decided it was best to address his statement about Jason's summer and not mention what I suspected was behind it.

"You should talk to Sammy about that. I gather you have something specific in mind?"

"He could work on my cousin's ranch south of the lake. It would be good for him to get away from babysitting his brothers and learn some useful skills."

Maybe Lionel was right. Jason might jump at the chance to get out from under having his younger brothers and his sister tag along wherever he went. Ranching meant riding, herding cattle and working with other tribe members. I would hate not having him around this summer, but emersion in traditional Miccosukee life is something I wanted for all my children. This would be a good way to do that for Jason. I also conceded that the idea would have been better brought up before he met Bethany and his adolescent hormones kicked in.

THE NEXT DAY when Madeleine entered the shop, she looked as if she hadn't slept a wink. There were dark circles under her eyes, and the bounce in her step was missing. It reminded me of the look she had when the twins were newborns but without the grin of motherhood.

"Hi," she said to Grandy and me. Sorry I'm late, but…"

"You don't need to explain. Bethany's appearance wasn't what you needed right now, not with your uncle and his children and grandson visiting this weekend," I said.

"You don't know the half of it. David spent hours on the phone with Bethany's mother to find out what had happened."

"It was over a boy, right?" said Grandy.

"That might have been simpler. Bethany's grades plunged this spring, and her mother thinks it's because she's spending all her time on her phone texting her friends. She also seems to have fallen in with a fast crowd of girls whose favorite pastime is shoplifting. She hasn't been caught doing it, but one of her friends was arrested yesterday. I guess that was the final straw for her mother, who took her phone away and threatened to enroll her in a private school in Jacksonville. So she ran away. Not that David and I were sympathetic to Bethany's behavior. I think she expected her father to back her. Instead we decided she could stay with us for the summer and work on the game reserve."

My jaw dropped at this announcement. Sammy worked part-time as the ranch's manager as well as running the airboat business and building our house. The last thing he needed was a hostile teenager to supervise.

Madeleine caught my expression. "Don't worry, Eve. We wouldn't think of making her part of Sammy's work on the ranch. David is going to take a more hands on approach. She can do some office work, and, with David's supervision, she'll help schedule clients and eventually accompany folks on the expeditions. When she visited earlier this year she showed some interest in the ranch."

"She's enthusiastic about it?" I asked.

"It's difficult to tell what she's enthusiastic about. Her expression never changes from that sour, you're-oppressing-me look. She'll be even less happy when she learns we'll be limiting her phone time." Madeleine smiled. "Actually, you know how bad cell reception is out at the ranch. That'll be a shock to her."

"She can help out taking care of the twins," suggested Grandy.

Madeleine made a harrumphing sound. "I wouldn't let that young woman babysit a gold fish. The twins spend half a day in daycare anyway. David Jr. loves being with other children, and little Eve gets some help sharpening her socialization skills."

"Of which she appears to have none," I added. I loved both the twins, but my namesake was turning out to be a clone of me, pigheaded, overly curious and too clever for her own good. Locks on cabinets were no challenge to her, and items placed beyond her reach piqued her interest enough for her to take up climbing skills by piling things atop one another. The kid was good at it, too. We waited for her to take a spill, but it never happened. Last week she got to a bag of cookies Madeleine had placed on a high shelf and ate all of them. The only price she paid was a scolding from her mother, not even an upset stomach. She apparently had my iron clad constitution also. How did this happen, I'd often asked Madeleine? She merely shrugged and tried another place to hide the sweets, knowing Eve would eventually find them.

"Bethany threw a tantrum this morning when David rousted her out of bed at six and told her they were saddling up to ride the reserve and check out the waterholes to make certain the wild pigs hadn't dug them all up. She said she was going to go back to her mother, and David told her she's made her choice last night and she was here to stay. More yelling, crying, stomping of feet. Everyone was up, and no one was in a good mood. I'm glad to be out of there. I took the twins to their baby sitter. I'm so glad to be here. Is there coffee?"

Grandy poured her a cup and pushed her gently into a chair. "Sit. Eve can go out and get some pastries."

That appealed to me. There's almost nothing that eating can't cure. I stopped by next door to see if Crusty wanted in on the pastries. He did and offered to accompany me to the donut place down the road.

As we drove past where Madeleine had parked her car, I noticed the car took up two slots and the driver's side door was ajar. I stopped my car and jumped out to close the door on hers.

"Hmm," said Crusty, "it looks like Madeleine was in a hurry this morning."

"More like she was in a fog of fatigue," I said and told him what was happening at her place.

"You know I have reservations about letting her do this job for Ms. Abbot. This turn of events won't help her concentrate on what she needs to do."

"Oh, she'll be fine," I said breezily, wondering how he might react if he knew she would be hosting her uncle and his family this weekend. I kept that to myself. Madeleine had enough trouble without my telling Crusty about her company and setting him off more.

Coffee and an infusion of sugar put Madeleine back on her feet. The morning passed happily as the three of us chatted and waited on customers.

"Can you and the family come over on Saturday for dinner? I'm dying for you to meet my uncle," said Madeleine to Grandy and me.

"Won't that be a lot of work for you, cooking for all of us?" I asked.

"I'm going to order ribs and sides from the Burnt Biscuit. That'll be easy for me and give my uncle and his family a taste of American cuisine."

"Everyone? Including Lionel?" I asked.

"Grandfather, Lionel, Nappi and…" she said.

"Don't you dare include Jerry," I said, shaking my finger at her.

"He'll find some way to show up," said Grandy.

Our attention shifted from dinner when the bell on the front door tingled. It was Shelley carrying an armload of clothing.

"Hi, all. I've completed redoing all these orders. That should catch us up for now. Any new tailoring requests come in this morning?"

Shelley worked as our tailor and owned a share of the shop. We were one of the only consignment shops to have a tailor on site. It gave us an edge on the other shops in town and even many of those located on the coast.

"You got your hair cut," I said.

Shelley's usual long brown locks had been shorn into a short curly bob. It fit her bubbly personality just fine and brought out the chocolate of her eyes.

"It looks terrific," said Madeleine. Grandy and I shook our

heads in agreement.

"I got tired of the old look." She seemed particularly happy today, and I wondered if the new hair style meant more than simply a change in her appearance. Was there a love interest in her life? She'd unloaded a horrible boyfriend several years ago, but since then we hadn't heard about her social life. She was dedicated to her studies in fashion design and her work here, so I assumed she didn't have the time for much romance. I was about to say something to her, but Grandy caught my eye and signaled me to keep my mouth shut. She mouthed, "It's none of your business." And it wasn't, but that usually didn't stop me from asking an intrusive question.

"Hey," said Madeleine, "if you're not busy Saturday, I've having a bunch of folks over to my place for dinner. It'll be a chance for everyone to meet my uncle from Scotland. How about it? Bring a date if you like."

"Sure," Shelley said. "I'd love it."

"And you can bring a date, too," I added, as if she hadn't heard Madeleine.

Grandy shot me a warning glare. I tipped my head to one side and tried to look innocent, which, as everyone knows, is something I'm not much good at.

I TOOK THE afternoon off from the shop to check the merchandise in our consignment shop on wheels, an RV converted into a store. We use it to sell merchandise at the flea market in Stuart on the weekends. At one point in our business the RV was the only shop we owned, having been burned out of our strip mall location. Now we had both shops, and it was beginning to be too much to handle. Madeleine had her family, I had mine, and I was doing part-time work for Crusty as a PI. Grandy and Shelley worked some hours each week at the shop here in Sabal Bay, but I knew Grandy and her husband Max wanted to spend more time in Key Largo. They had sold their fishing charter boat there, but they liked to visit their Keys friends as well as take their little whaler boat out to fish the flats. Grandy knew Max would never get salt water out of his soul. He needed the deep blue ocean fix that couldn't be satisfied by fishing the fresh water of the Big Lake. We kept putting off the decision about the RV shop, but soon everyone would be over extended. We were almost at that point now.

Assured that we had enough merchandise to make the run to the coast pay off this weekend, I checked to make certain the rig was gassed up and ready to roll tomorrow morning. I headed for home to see how the new house was coming and to settle in for the evening with my family. I knew Madeleine would be dashing home to tidy up her house and to take on whatever crisis Bethany had manufactured during the day. Hmm.

"C'mon, Sammy," I said to him after he stepped out of the shower. "We have some work to do for a friend."

I let Grandfather Egret know he could let the boys roast hotdogs over the fire tonight. When I told him what Sammy and I were up to, he assured me that there was enough leftovers from last night as well as stewed greens for him and Lionel. If he could, he'd convince the boys to eat some of the stewed greens and sweet corn with their dogs. As with all kids, the boys hated vegetables. We took Netty with us.

"Wait a minute," said Lionel when he heard our plans. "I want to have a talk with Sammy tonight."

"It can hold until tomorrow, Dad," said Sammy. "This is a rescue mission."

It was that. We grabbed two extra-large pizzas and headed out to David's ranch. When Sammy appeared at the door with the food and cold soda, Madeleine almost cried with joy.

"We're not here just to eat. Food first, but then everyone is pitching in with the cleaning," I said.

"Not me," piped up Bethany from the couch where she had been lying. "I worked hard today, and I'm saddle sore."

"We all worked hard today, Bethany, and we're all going to

do this together," I said.

"But I don't even know these people who are coming," she whined.

"Help Eve set the table," said David.

"I'm not hungry. I'll be in my room." She stalked off down the hall.

Madeleine rolled her eyes.

"I'll be right back." I followed Bethany to her room and slammed open her door.

"Here's the deal, little lady. You make nice with your father and Madeleine, or you'll be going to a military school in North Florida. You did hear your mother say she would send you off to school if you couldn't make it here."

Bethany looked shocked as well as frightened for a moment, then she squinted her eyes at me and jumped off her bed, fists clenched. She approached me as if she wanted to fight.

"And don't you try to back me down. It won't work. I was the expert on making trouble when I was a kid. Ask my grandmother and Madeleine, if you don't believe me."

She continued to hold my gaze, then she dropped her head and unclenched her fists.

"That's better. I prefer ribs to pizza myself, but pizza is easier tonight. You'll be having ribs tomorrow night. Let's go."

I held out my hand to her. She ignored it but walked past me into the hallway. Scene averted for now, but I knew I had won only a temporary victory.

In a few short hours, we devoured the pizza and tidied the house. I hustled Madeleine and the twins off to bed and put Netty down on the couch. She fell asleep immediately, not bothered by the adults' conversation. Bethany said "goodnight" and went to her room.

"What did you say to her?" asked David nodding his head toward his daughter's room.

"I told her if she didn't buck up her mother would send her to military school."

"Military school? She said she would send her off to a boarding school, but not military school," said David.

"I must have misunderstood," I said with as much innocence as I could fake.

Sammy and I finished our coffees and decided it was time to get our daughter home to her bed. I also needed to get up early tomorrow to take the RV to the coast.

"We'll see you tomorrow night," I said, giving David a kiss. "Don't worry about Bethany. She'll come around in time." I hoped I was right.

"She's a handful," commented Sammy on the drive home. "Are you certain she'll improve?"

"I honestly don't know, but they're doing the right thing with her." I was quiet for several minutes. "I wonder where she learned her attitude toward Indians. Certainly not from David and Madeleine."

"No. She probably got it from her peer group members who probably have no exposure to minority groups," Sammy said.

"Unfortunately, our oldest son didn't pick up on her negativity last night. He was positively drooling when he saw her."

Sammy nodded.

"You noticed then? Your father noticed too, and he didn't like it. I think he wants to remove Jason from her influence by sending him to the ranch for the summer."

"I would miss him."

"I think that's what Lionel wanted to talk to you about tonight."

Sammy glanced over at me. "Don't worry, Eve. The decision about Jason is ours to make, not my father's. We'll talk about it, the two of us."

Would Sammy really stand up to his father on this issue? He respected the older man and missed his council while growing up. Lionel's attitude toward this might sway Sammy more than anything I might say. I chastised myself for framing the issue that way. Sammy didn't have to choose between his father and me, did he?

CHAPTER 4

I LEFT NETTY in her grandfather and great grandfather's capable hands the next day and reminded Sammy as he climbed the ladder to work on the roof shingles that we were expected at Madeleine and David's that night.

"I'll be back from the coast early. The flea market closes at two in the afternoon."

He waved at me, hammer in hand. I was as anxious as he was to see the house finished, but I didn't want him to work himself to death with the house, the airboat business and the game reserve.

I gave Netty a goodbye hug and whispered in Grandfather's ear, "Don't let Lionel talk you into allowing him to take Netty out in the canoe today. You know he'll paddle into the swamps."

"He won't get lost. Don't worry," Grandfather reassured me.

"That's not what I'm worried about. Once he gets out there, he'll lose track of time, and we're all supposed to have dinner at the ranch this evening. He'll use a swamp exploration as a way of getting out of it."

I heard someone breathing over my shoulder. It was Lionel,

who had appeared, as he often did, out of nowhere.

"Why would I want to meet someone from Scotland? He's not part of our family. You should be more concerned with introducing your children to our relatives, not your business partner's family."

I knew better than to argue with him. "Nappi will be there," I said. He and Nappi had shared a hospital room when they were both recovering from gunshot wounds. And for some inexplicable reason, they bonded. Neither of them would admit to being "friends", but they were. I even suspected that Lionel had talked Nappi into one of his impromptu swamp canoe tours.

"Okay," Lionel said. "We'll be back by then."

I sighed. "That man is so pigheaded," I said to Grandfather.

"Piggies?" asked Netty. "I like piggies."

"Eve, I will make certain everything is fine," said Grandfather. "Go. Go."

I jumped into my convertible, drove to the local flea market where we parked our RV and took off for the coast. If anything could make me forget my troubles, it was the drive down the Canopy Road to Stuart. The palms, live oaks, cypress and other vegetation lined the narrow road; the limbs of the oaks overhung the lanes, creating a tunnel of vegetation. Even on the warmest days, the road was shady and cool, the pavement dappled with intermittent areas of sun and shadow. Narrow, water-filled ditches lined either side of the way, making it necessary to concentrate on keeping the rig on the pavement and on my side of highway. Traffic this morning was heavier than during the week as people from Sabal Bay made their way to the coast to shop for the day.

I settled back into the rhythm of the road. The RV wasn't difficult to drive, and I let my attention wander to thoughts of Lionel and his insistence that all the children be immersed in Miccosukee culture in only the way he defined it. I wanted my children to be able to walk in both worlds and be equally

content and comfortable in each. I sighed. *That man was so
…* Suddenly a dark shape rushed out from the side of the
road and into the path of my rig. I jerked the wheel to the left,
narrowly missing the animal, but then had to jerk it back just
as suddenly to avoid a large pickup truck coming toward me.
The driver of the truck slammed on his brakes and swerved to
his right, running off the pavement and nosing his truck down
into the ditch. I saw a driveway ahead into which I pulled the
RV and jumped out, racing back to the truck.

"Are you okay?" I said to the driver, who hopped out of his
cab.

"Yup. Those damn feral hogs. They're a menace on this road.
There's no shoulder. Only the ditch and the trees." He stepped
toward the ditch to look at how far the front of his truck had
descended into the water. "The nose isn't in the water yet. I
think I can get 'er out of here. I got four-wheel drive."

"Lucky you. A car would have gone right into the canal." I
waited to make certain he could back out. Shifting from drive
to reverse and back again, he rocked the truck out. I waved
and ran back to my rig. The ditches weren't deep, but the front
of a car could have been swallowed by the water, leaving only
the back end to stick out. In the shadows and the roadside
vegetation, it might have been difficult to see there was a car
down there.

Sales were steady throughout the morning until the flea
market closed at two. Although it would be smart to consolidate
our shops, I hated losing the revenue from the rig. When I
arrived back in Sabal Bay, I parked the RV in our assigned slot
at the local flea market and drove back to Grandfather's. It was
almost three. I needed to pick up Netty and take her to my
house so both of us could clean up for tonight. I pulled into the
drive at Grandfather's and noticed Lionel's canoe wasn't there,
but he was. Netty was at his side.

"See. You had nothing to worry about," Lionel said as Netty
ran into my arms.

"Where are the boys?" I asked.

"I let them take out the canoe. They'll be back soon." He glanced up the canal.

"What? They went off without you?"

"They've got to learn their way around the swamps sometime." Along with the defiant look on his face, I also caught a flicker of concern in his eyes. "If they're not back soon, I'll take the airboat out to look for them. Don't worry. They're Miccosukee."

"They're also just kids," I snapped back at him. We did one of our eyes-locked stares.

"Okay. I'll go look for them now," Lionel said, dropping his glare only when he turned away and walked toward the airboat.

Grandfather Egret emerged from the house and watched his son walk off.

"I didn't know he let the boys take the canoe. I was making an afternoon snack for Netty after she returned from a paddle with Lionel. The boys must have nagged him for a ride when they saw him bring her back."

Before Lionel had time to start the airboat, we heard laughter as a canoe headed into the nearby shoreline. Lionel turned back to me with a smirk on his face that said, "I was right."

Sammy wasn't working on the house, so I went into Grandfather's place to find him and tell him I was taking Netty with me. I heard the shower running as I entered. Sammy was in it, so I joined him. If we'd had our own house we could have completed our wet interlude with a romp in the bedroom, but there was no privacy for us in Grandfather's tiny house with its one bedroom.

"Am I too protective of our kids?" I asked Sammy as we toweled off.

"A little, maybe. I'm happy you and dad seem to be getting along better.."

"It would help our relationship if I could change into a Miccosukee dark-haired maiden. I'm too durn white for him."

"But not for me," said Sammy, grabbing my towel away and pushing me up against the wall. I giggled as we tried to maneuver an embrace meant for a bed or a much larger space.

Someone rapped on the door. "Hey. There are others here who need to use the bathroom, you know." Lionel, of course.

I opened the door a crack and tossed a bar of soap through, then shouted, "Take a dip in the canal."

"See. It's not your skin color that's the issue with Dad. It's your attitude," Sammy said. He was right, but only partly.

"And he's so charming." I grabbed my clothes off the bathroom floor where I'd dumped them and left, calling Netty's name.

"She's down at the canal doing what you said," Grandfather said.

"What?" I stepped into the yard and saw Lionel seated on the rim of the canal holding a slippery, soapy Netty who screamed with joy and splashed sudsy water around her.

"I thought you meant you wanted the shower," I said to Lionel. I told myself not to panic. It was unlikely she was in danger with Lionel holding her. She wasn't afraid. She was having fun. I sighed and ran back to the house to grab a towel.

"And be sure you remove that clump of water hyacinth from her hair." I tossed him the towel.

"I WONDER WHAT Madeleine's uncle is like," I said as Sammy, Netty and I headed to the game reserve. Grandy and Max rode with us.

"I'm worried that if he has a thick Scottish brogue none of us may understand a word he says," said Sammy.

"Maybe he won't be able to understand us," said Grandy.

The big man with a full head of red hair streaked with white and a beard to match had no problem making himself understood nor in understanding us. He grabbed everyone in a giant hug when we were introduced. I worried that his booming voice and friendly manner might scare Netty, but she giggled in his arms and said, "Tickles," then reached up and pulled his beard. He gave her a roaring chuckle and swung her around.

"This is me son Mickey, and my grandson Dylan. He's six."

Mickey looked not at all like his father. He was slender where Angus was stocky, and Mickey's hair was fine and brown in color. Dylan's hair was red, like his grandfather's. "And… Where's Darcie?" asked Angus.

"Oh, she went off in the car to pick up more soda at the store," said Madeleine. "I told her David would do it, but she wanted to help."

"She doesn't know the way," said Angus.

"I told her to follow the road that way. She'll be fine. She should be back in a jiff. Meantime let's all have some iced tea and sit out back," Madeleine said.

"You look better today. Did you get some sleep last night?" I asked her.

She nodded. "David let me sleep in this morning while he made breakfast for the twins. I got up before Angus and his family arrived mid-morning. We had time to catch up when the twins and Dylan went out with one of the workers in our mud buggy for a ride."

Several more cars pulled into the drive. Grandfather, Lionel and our boys had been picked up by Nappi in his SUV, and Shelley followed in her car. She had accepted the invitation to bring a date, only her date turned out to be Jerry. I might have known he'd show up somehow. I hoped he'd somehow wrangled an invite out of her and they weren't really dating. But I couldn't keep my thoughts to myself.

"What are you doing here, Jerry? Corrupting the women of Sabal Bay?"

"Shelley asked me. She likes me."

"Everyone likes you, Jerry, for about the first five minutes of their acquaintance with you. A relationship with you ages like lettuce left in the crisper too long."

He looked hurt, as I knew he would, but then he shrugged off the comment and followed Shelley into the house.

"Give him a break, Eve," said Sammy. "He's lonely."

"I gave him a break. I divorced him before I took a cleaver to him."

"Maybe he's changing. People do change, you know." Sammy shifted his gaze from me to his father.

I rolled my eyes, but said, "Okay."

As I turned to enter the house, I saw Angus still stood in the driveway, looking down the road, a worried expression on his face.

"Is there something wrong?" I asked.

"Darcie doesn't know her way around here."

"She won't get lost if she follows Madeleine's directions."

"I know but I'm worried about the rental car's brakes. They seemed spongy to me on the way over here." Angus's gaze continued fixated on the road.

"If she's not back in a few minutes, I'll send Nappi out to look for her. I'm sure she's fine."

Mickey stepped back out the door. "What's going on?" I was again struck by how Mickey looked nothing like his father. He was a short, slightly built man. His face was narrow, saved from looking weasel-like by his sparkling blue eyes, the only feature he seemed to have gotten from his father.

"Darcie's not back," I said.

"Don't worry about her. She's probably off taking a cigarette break. That woman can't seem to give up the habit." He turned and entered the house.

"Have you spent anytime in Florida before this visit?" I asked, trying to take Angus' mind off worry about his daughter-in-law.

"No. this is the first visit. We flew into Miami the day before yesterday and did some shopping yesterday, then headed up here this morning. Of course, after we visit Dylan's grandmother in Naples, we'll be going to Disney."

"I'm sure he'll love Disney. Children usually do."

"I bet I'll love it too. I think I'm still a kid at heart."

I had no doubt of that. If Angus' hair were more white than red, he'd look like Santa Claus. His eyes twinkled with good humor.

Angus joined everyone in the back yard, but he said little. As the sun began to set and his daughter-in-law failed to return from her errand, he paced back and forth and wrung his hands. Mickey, on the other hand, appeared to be enjoying more than his share of beers and gave no evidence of worry, laughing loudly and making bad jokes which included language I did not want my children to hear. When Angus approached him and took him to one side, Mickey shook off his father's arm, and I heard him say, "Leave it, Dad. Darcie needs time to herself."

"Now? In the middle of visiting relatives. That's rude and selfish."

"Yeah, well, maybe you haven't noticed, but she is one self-centered little b…."

I interrupted their conversation. "I'm sure your father is right. I can't imagine her going off this long even if she wanted a little down time." I waved at Nappi who interrupted his conversation with Lionel and approached. When I told him our concerns, he jumped in his black SUV with Lionel in the passenger's seat and sped off down the drive and onto the road.

An hour later Nappi arrived back. "I think it's time we called in your police detective friend. We couldn't find anyone who saw the rental car in town."

"Maybe she took off for the coast instead of heading into town," said Mickey.

"What reason would she have for doing that?" I asked, beginning to feel as if Mickey and Darcie had secrets they preferred others not know, not even Angus.

Mickey hesitated for a moment before speaking. "She has a friend in Stuart. I don't think they've had contact for years."

"Do you think she would have gone there?"

He shrugged.

"You don't seem very concerned about your wife. Is there something you should be telling us?" I asked.

"We don't get along," he replied.

I gave a derisive snort. "I'd say so if you can't even work up a little curiosity about where she is. It's been several hours since she drove off."

Mickey dropped his gaze and muttered, "We're getting a divorce."

Angus gave a strangled sound. "When were you going to tell me this?" he asked. "More importantly, does Dylan know?"

For a family who lived close by one another in Scotland, they seemed to know nothing about one another.

Nappi touched my shoulder. "As I said, it's past time the authorities knew about this. They're the ones who have the resources to mount a search for her."

I nodded and moved away from the others while I contacted my friend on the local police force, Detective Frida Martinez. She was working late at her desk, so I was put through to her immediately.

"What now?" she asked, her tone light, expecting it was me with some annoying matter she knew better than to get her feathers ruffled over.

When I told her about Angus' daughter-in-law, she clucked her tongue at me.

"We're dealing with an adult who left of her own free will. That's not a matter for the police, at least not yet."

"She doesn't know her way around these parts, and it's now dark. Who knows where she's got to?"

"Why did she leave?" asked Frida.

"She was going to the store to pick up soda. That's what she said anyway."

"But that's not the real reason?"

"I don't know. She and her husband seem to be having some

marital troubles."

"So we've got an adult woman running away from a troubled marriage."

"I guess," I admitted, then added, "But she's driving a car she didn't rent. Her father-in-law did."

There was a moment's silence. "Well, you could register a stolen vehicle report. There's not a lot the authorities can do about a woman running off because she's in an unhappy marriage. Unless you suspect foul play. Those are your choices."

"There's more. Angus said he thought there was something wrong with the brakes of the car."

I heard Frida groan in frustration. "Of course, there is. With you involved, Eve, there must be some kind of a twist. It can't be a simple matter of the store being out of soda or the woman driving around letting off steam because she argued with her husband. I'll be right there. I'm doing this as a favor to you, Eve. Save me some food. I haven't eaten yet."

FRIDA AND I had one thing in common: she loved to eat as much as I did and like me, the calories never affected her. She remained slim and trim. She was dark-haired with an olive complexion and a no-nonsense attitude toward her work. I knew she wasn't kidding about her request for food. I handed her a plate of ribs and slaw and a soda when she arrived and introduced her to Angus and Mickey. She polished off the food quickly, listening while Angus told her about his daughter-in-law's absence. When he finished, Frida handed her plate to me, wiped her mouth with a napkin and turned her attention to Mickey.

"What's your take on this?"

I could tell from the deep freeze tone in her voice that she had sized up Mickey as someone she didn't care for. I had known Frida for years and could read her body language well. It said she found him suspicious.

"Nothin' much. I keep telling Dad that she's probably gone

to the coast to tell her friend there all about how awful I am to her," said Mickey.

"And are you?"

"What?" Mickey looked startled by Frida's question.

"How awful are you to her?"

Before Mickey could reply to Frida's question, her cell buzzed. When she answered she shot me a look of concern, then walked away to talk privately. She ended the call, then signaled to me to join her.

"Describe the rental car," she said.

"Angus told me it was a dark blue, four door sedan."

"I just took a call from the state police. They've pulled a car matching that description out of the canal that runs alongside the Canopy Road."

"Was anyone hurt?" I asked.

"I don't have the details, but I do know that the driver was taken to the hospital. I don't want to upset Madeleine's relatives if this isn't his daughter-in-law. I'll go to the scene and let you know what I find. If it appears to be Angus' car with his daughter-in-law driving, I'll call you. You can tell the family what we know."

"Why do I get the job of notifying the family?" I asked.

"Because you called me for help, remember? I'm doing my job, and I'm willing to share it with you."

How could I refuse? Frida is so generous.

CHAPTER 5

———

"WHAT'S GOING ON with your cop friend?" asked Mickey.

"She had a lead on the car," I replied. "She'll give me a call when she knows more."

Angus' expression remained concerned, but there was hope in his eyes. "Soon?"

I nodded. "I'll keep you posted." I walked away from Angus and his son and back toward everyone who gazed at me with anxious looks on their faces.

"Sammy," I called to him, took him aside and told him what I knew about the accident. He cast a glance back at Angus and Madeleine, who was stroking her uncle's arm in a soothing manner. Mickey had opened another beer and was drinking it. I reminded myself that whoever drove the family to the hospital, it wouldn't be Mickey, or we'd have all the relatives in the ER.

After a half hour, Frida called me. "I think it's Angus' rental, but could you put him on the phone?"

I handed my cell to Angus. He and Frida talked for several

minutes, then he gave the cell back to me.

"The car is his rental, and the woman in it was his daughter-in-law. She's at the hospital now. She was sitting chest deep in canal water for a good two hours, and the EMTs say she's suffering from hypothermia. No broken bones that they could see, but she's badly bruised and has cuts and abrasions on her face and arms. She's barely conscious," Frida said. "I told Angus an abbreviated version of what happened, but he sounded pretty shocky to me."

"Don't worry. Madeleine and I will take care of him, and I'll drive him and Mickey to the hospital."

"Maybe you can leave Mickey out of the ride. She told the EMTs she's not interested in seeing him. But she is concerned about her son."

I shouldn't have worried about how to keep Mickey away from the hospital. He was too drunk to stand up and was slumped against a palm tree in Madeleine and David's side yard.

I saw Nappi bend down to check on him. "He'll be fine. He just needs to sober up. I'll handle that, Eve. Sammy can help with the rest of the guests."

I was about to terminate the call with Frida when she stopped me from signing off. "There's something else, Eve. Angus may have been right about the brakes on that car. There are no skid marks on the pavement. She didn't apply the brakes, just drove into the canal. Something is not right here. I'm going to have the car impounded, and we'll look at it."

Frida ended the call. Angus and I got into my car while Sammy let everyone know what was going on.

On the way to the hospital I told Angus about what Frida had told me about the accident.

"I should have called the rental company as soon as we left Miami. I knew there was something not right about the feel of those brakes, but I got carried away with seeing my niece again and forgot about the car."

"It's not your fault, and it looks as if Darcie will be just fine."

By the time we arrived at the hospital, Darcie had been seen in emergency, sent upstairs for X-Rays and an MRI, and she was about to be admitted.

"Can I see her?" asked Angus. "I'm her father-in-law."

"As soon as we get her settled in her room, you can visit." The admitting nurse smiled encouragingly at Angus, then turned to me. "Hi, Eve. How's everyone?"

I had spent some time in the ER because of a few incidents and had also visited friends and relatives who ended up here with their own scrapes, bruises and gunshot wounds. I was a familiar face in ER.

"Aside from tonight, everyone is doing well."

She whispered in my ear. "Is this one a friend or a relative?"

"She's a member of Madeleine's uncle's family here on a visit."

"Well, these narrow roads can be tricky to navigate at night especially if you're unfamiliar with them."

"I always thought the Canopy Road was the most beautiful drive in this part of the state," I said.

"In the daytime, but you never can tell what's going to dash out into the road, and there are no shoulders."

I remembered my close call with the pig earlier today and nodded. That had to be what happened to Darcie. One of those feral hogs ran out in front of her, she tried to stop, swerved and went into the ditch. But if Frida was right about the accident, Darcie hadn't tried to put on her brakes. Or had she, and they didn't work?

"Oh, oh," said the nurse. "Here come the troops."

Almost all the adults from the dinner tonight except for Mickey began to crowd into the emergency room.

Madeleine had her arm around Dylan. "I want my mommy," he cried. Angus took his hand and began to explain about Darcie's accident. "Mommy had a little trouble with the car, and it ran into the water, but the doctors here will fix her up tonight, and she'll be good as new."

"Grandy and Max volunteered to stay with the kids at our place," said Madeleine.

Frida had entered the room and overheard Angus's explanation to his grandson. "How did you know about the car trouble, Mr. MacAngus?" she asked.

He repeated to her what he had told me earlier about the "spongy" brakes.

"We'll be taking a look at those brakes tomorrow," Frida said, her gaze resting on Angus for a long time as if she was taking a measure of the man.

Another nurse (this one wasn't familiar to me), called Angus' name and told him he could see Darcie now. He asked for permission to take Dylan with him, and the two of them left to take the elevator to Darcie's room.

I pulled Frida to one side. "I saw the way you looked at Angus. You don't think he had anything to do with this accident, do you?"

"I won't know anything until we go over that car. Right now, I've got paperwork to fill out back at the office. And then, I have a date."

"Oh gosh. I'm sorry I called and ruined your plans for the evening. Who's the lucky fella?"

"His name is Serta."

It took a while for her joke to sink in.

"Didn't get much sleep last night, I gather," I said.

"I'm doing double duty without a partner."

Frida's partner Linc Tooney had left the department for a job on the coast, and the department had replaced him with a detective from a large, urban department. The guy had turned out to be unsuitable in many ways, but his worst flaw had been his inability to work with female professionals. He had treated Frida like an inferior rather than a partner. He quit before Frida filed sexual harassment charges against him, but we all knew he wouldn't have lasted anyway when he tried to pursue a fugitive into the swamps at night. He was a city boy and had no experience with wildlife. I think he got scared off by one of those large, Buffo frogs. It was rumored that Linc might return to the department. Frida was thrilled at the possibility. Until then, she was working without a partner.

"Did the department at least increase your pay?"

She rolled her eyes at me. "Don't ask."

I watched her leave, her shoulders slumped in fatigue.

"Who's watching over Mickey?" I asked Madeleine.

"He's out in my car. I made him some hot coffee and told him to drink it. Maybe he'll be in good enough shape to visit his wife later tonight," Madeleine said. From the disgust in her tone of voice, it was clear she shared Frida's low opinion of the man. It was hard to put together the warmth and friendly manner of Angus with his son's obnoxious personality. It was as if they weren't related.

At the rate he'd been guzzling the beers earlier, I worried that all Madeleine would get for her efforts at sobering him up would be vomit in her car. I didn't share my fears with her. Instead I told her that Darcie had been clear about not wanting to see him. "And I don't think she meant tonight. I think she meant ever."

"Maybe her accident will scare him into sobriety," said Madeleine.

"But will it scare him into behaving any better toward her than he has in the past? I think Frida has his number. She thinks he's an abuser, if not physical then emotional."

"I'm not sure I'd go that far, but he's unpleasant," Madeleine said.

Angus returned to the ER, carrying his sleeping grandson from their visit with Darcie in her room. Darcie told Angus she was taking a drive to think about her marriage when an animal ran into the road in front of her. When she attempted to avoid it by stomping on the brakes, she found she had no brakes. She said that was all she remembered until the EMTs loaded her into the ambulance. She was able to give Dylan a reassuring hug good night, and then her sedative kicked in.

"The doctor said she could probably be released tomorrow. She was lucky someone came by and saw the car. She could have died from hypothermia. Funny thing, isn't it, how hot it is here, but how exposure to water over a period of time can drop the body temperature?"

The doors to the ER opened and Mickey staggered in. "I wanna see my wife." He managed to stumble it as far as the admitting desk where he stuck his face in that of the admitting nurse. "Now. I wanna see her now." He sounded angry, and I worried he'd make a scene, but Nappi stepped forward and told him to shut up. He looked at my fashionably dressed, suave friend and made a stupid mistake. "You gonna make me?" Mickey asked.

Nappi gave him his oh so cold smile and said, "Yes, I am."

"Oh," said Mickey. He stood swaying in front of Nappi for a moment, then Nappi took his finger and tapped Mickey on the chest. The man slid backwards, fell into a chair and began to sob. "I'm such a jerk. I should never have let her go off like that. I love her. I really do." His chin fell forward onto his chest, and he began to snore.

Angus looked at his son, a mixture of emotions crossing his face—anger along with disappointment and something like deep sorrow. "Let's go back to the motel," he said. Sammy stepped forward and reached out to wake Mickey and help him to his feet.

"I'll do that," Angus said and nodded to Madeleine, who took Dylan from his arms. He then reached down and picked up his son as if he weighed no more than had his grandson. For an eighty-year-old man, Angus was strong. "I'm so sorry to have brought all this on you," he said to Madeleine. Once outside, he stood for a moment, a man who hours before had looked forward to seeing his niece, but now all joy had been erased from his face. I saw him as a man embarrassed and saddened for what the night had brought to his family and to Madeleine's and to her friends. That burden was heavier than the son he supported with his arm.

We all followed at a distance. What now? The MacAngus family had arrived in two rentals. Mickey drove one, intending to take his family to Naples to visit his mother. Angus drove the other, planning to visit with Madeleine and family for a few days and then to join the others in Naples. I was about to offer to drive Angus, Mickey and Dylan back to the motel rooms they'd rented when David stepped forward. "I'll take them to the motel. You drive Madeleine back home. This had been a tough day for her. I know she didn't want to leave the twins at home with their half-sister, and I'm also worried we are piling too much on my daughter's shoulders at this point."

"Madeleine said the kids were in Grandy's care."

"They are, but Bethany will feel alone with no one there she's familiar with," David replied, a note of defensiveness in his voice.

"Well, boo hoo for her. It's not as if we left her alone with no other adult to help, is it?" I snapped, then quickly realized how little help my judgmental comment was. "Sorry. I'm a little strung out myself. I guess we all are."

If I expected Sammy to put a comforting arm around my shoulders, imagine how surprised I was that the arm supporting me out to my car was that of his father who whispered in my ear, "Kind of snarky, Eve, but I agree with you. That little b.., uh, gal couldn't take care of a turtle even if she had a zookeeper helping her out."

I gave him a surprised look. One side of his mouth lifted in a typical Lionel half- smile, half-frown. "I'm agreeing with you on this, but don't think I agree with you on much else," he said.

"I know," I replied. "I won't get uppity about this one shared sentiment."

Sammy, overhearing the exchange, smiled and inserted himself between the two of us, one arm on either of our shoulders, pulling us close to him.

"Is this a good time to talk about Jason?" asked Lionel.

"No!" Sammy and I said together.

Everyone sorted out cars and rides, and we left for our respective homes.

"Oh, shucks," I said, halfway home.

"What?" asked Sammy.

"We left the ranch in such a hurry that we weren't able to clean up after dinner. Madeleine doesn't need all that mess after the day she's had."

"We'll drop off the boys at your place. Grandy and Max are probably there by now. They left ahead of us. We'll go back and clean up. Call Grandy and let her know, then give Madeleine a call and tell her we're on our way."

The voice answering the cell was not Madeleine's, but Nappi's.

"She's not back with David yet, but we're taking care of clean-up."

"'We' who?" I asked.

"Me, Jerry, Shelley and David's daughter."

"David's daughter. What did you do? Duct tape her to the kitchen sink?"

Nappi laughed. "No. Shelley promised she'd take her to the mall shopping tomorrow if she helped."

I OPENED ONE eye and heard thunder and pounding rain on the roof. It was Sunday, and one of the days we usually drove the RV to the coastal flea market. Not today. No one would be out shopping in this downfall. An inside mall, yes, but schlepping from one shop to another through a muddy parking area wasn't something even the most dedicated bargain hunter would do. Sammy rolled over and gave me a kiss on the lips. "Go back to sleep."

"But we're both awake. Why waste the moment?" So we didn't.

Later, much later, we awoke to the smell of bacon and

pancakes. Our earlier bed exercises left us hungry, so we both dressed and went into the kitchen for Grandy's famous sour dough pancakes.

I looked out the kitchen window and saw the rain was continuing and the wind had kicked up. "Nasty day. Isn't it nice that we all get a day off today?" I said. Sunday was the one day we didn't open our shop in town. "We could all stay in bed with a good book." Sammy and I exchanged looks. He winked at me, and I knew he was contemplating something other than a book in bed.

Someone banged on the front door.

"What idiot is out in this weather?" asked Grandy. Max opened the door and let in Madeleine. She closed her umbrella and stood dripping on the floor. Grandy pulled her into the living room and reached for her raincoat.

"Can't stay. I got a call from Frida. She told me she asked Angus to come into the station to talk to her. The crime people got a chance to look at the brakes on the rental this morning, and it appears someone cut the line. I'm going down to the station." She looked through frightened eyes at me. "I thought you might like to come."

"Of course, I'll come. But it's Sunday," I said. "I assumed the police wouldn't examine the car until tomorrow. And why didn't she call me?"

Grandy gave me a pointed look. "Maybe she didn't want you to interfere like you always do."

"I'll be with you in a jiff, Madeleine. Let me slip on some clothes."

"Interfere like you're going to do now," I heard Grandy say as I ran from the room.

I'd never seen Madeleine drive the way she did this morning. She ran through two traffic lights that were technically yellowish-red. "You're going to get us arrested," I warned.

"I don't care," she said. "Frida acted as if she thought my uncle was responsible for cutting the brake lines. That is so, so, so…"

"Why would she think that?" I asked.

"Because I told her he was looking for David's tool box after they arrived yesterday. He wanted to check the brakes. I have such a big mouth." She slid around a corner and pulled into the police station lot.

"And did he find the tools and take a look at the brakes?" I asked as we ran from the car into the station dodging another downpour.

"I don't know. I was too busy prepping for dinner. And David's daughter was being difficult as usual. But Frida wants to fingerprint Angus."

For a day no one was working, Frida certainly had accomplished a whole heck of a lot already, and it was only ten in the morning. I wondered what the rest of the day held. The officer manning the desk told us to wait and pointed to hard wooden benches to either side of the entrance. Madeleine had had the good sense to carry her umbrella, which kept most of the rain off her, but I had run off with only my raincoat, no hood, no umbrella. I felt water trickle down the back of my neck under the collar of my coat.

After several minutes, Frida appeared at the door leading to the offices and interview rooms and signaled to us. We followed her into her office where Angus sat in a chair looking gray and worn out.

Madeleine ran to him. "Are you okay?" Before he could answer she shot Frida an angry look. "You shouldn't be questioning him without a lawyer present."

"I'm not questioning him. It's an interview." The frown on Frida's face showed her annoyance at Madeleine's assertion.

I decided to step between Frida and Madeleine in hopes of defusing the mounting level of anger. "I don't understand what's happening here. Mr. MacAngus' daughter-in-law is still in the hospital from her injuries. Do you believe he's somehow responsible for the accident?"

"It was no accident, Eve. Those brake lines were intentionally cut, and Mr. MacAngus has admitted to having tampered with them."

"Not 'tampered with.' I wanted to see what was wrong with them," said Angus.

"But you admit you used David Wilson's tools on them?" Frida said.

"No. I found the tool box and then realized I didn't have good light." By now Angus was sweating. He reached into his pocket and pulled out a handkerchief and wiped his forehead.

"Was there any time after the car left the rental company and before it sat in the Wilson driveway that it was left unattended?" Frida leaned forward to press for an answer.

"Well, I parked it at the motel and then drove it the next day to breakfast and to the shopping mall. I parked it out back of the ranch house when we arrived here. Oh, and on the way here, Dylan had to use the bathroom once, and we also stopped for a snack."

"And the brakes felt spongy when?" asked Frida.

Before Angus could answered, an officer appeared at Frida office door. "You may want to take a look at this," he said. Frida perused the paper quickly and then turned to us.

"Your uncle gave us his fingerprints early this morning. We took prints off several tools and some of the prints matched yours, Mr. MacAngus. I'm afraid you have a lot of explaining to do, so let's start again at the beginning. Meantime, I want you two out of here." Frida nodded at Madeleine and me and pointed toward the door.

CHAPTER 6

I SENT MADELEINE off to the hospital to see to Darcie's release while I sat watch outside Frida's office. I didn't want to believe they would charge Angus with Darcie's attempted murder. They couldn't, could they?

Several hours later, Madeleine walked back into the police station followed by Sammy. "Anything?" she asked.

I shook my head.

"How is Darcie?"

"She's been released and is doing well. I moved them out of the motel and into the house. David and I agreed that it was a good idea to have them close by, and we have the room. By the way, Mickey seems to have sobered up and is behaving well. He seems like a changed man today."

"I'm happy to hear that. You don't need two difficult people in your house right now," I said.

Madeleine nodded, then paused. "Uh, about that..." she began.

"I know. There's no way you can take on the sexual harassment job for Crusty. You already have too much to do.

Don't worry. We'll work out something."

"How about a raincheck on working as a junior PI?" she asked.

"Good idea." I secretly hoped Madeleine would forget about her desire to do sleuthing.

Madeleine gave me a tiny smile of gratitude.

Frida walked up the hall from her office with Angus behind her.

"I'm not filing charges. There are still too many loose ends we need to investigate. You can go. For now."

As she turned to re-enter her office, I stopped her. "You can't really think Angus is behind this. What reason could he have to want to hurt his daughter-in-law?"

"Maybe she wasn't the intended target."

"Who then?"

"I don't know, Eve. Perhaps his son. Or maybe he wanted to harm himself. Once his family left for Naples, he would be the only one driving that car."

I let out a derisive snort. "Are you saying he's suicidal?"

She shrugged. "I've seen weirder things in my years at this job. He and his wife are separated, but it's obvious he's lonely. I don't think he's a happy man especially with his son and daughter-in-law about to divorce. His family is falling apart. I've told him to stick around here until we figure out what happened."

"Maybe Mickey had something to do with this," I said.

Frida shook her head and turned on her heel to head back to her office.

"I hope you don't mean that, Eve," said Angus who had overheard my remark.

"Sorry. I'm reaching. People around here will tell you that's often what I do."

Angus ran his fingers through his thick hair. "I want to hire you to prove that my family had nothing to do with what happened to my daughter-in-law. I respect that your friend is a homicide detective, but she's hot on my trail. I need someone who will believe me."

Well, shucks. Why not? I'd been in this position several times before, letting the police do their investigation while I was hired by another party to complete my own.

"I've got to run this by my boss first," I told Angus.

"That surprises me. Madeleine says you pretty much do what you want and don't take orders from anyone, much less any man."

"Usually she's right, but we've got another big case pending, and there's been a glitch in it. We've got to figure out how to handle that one before we can take on yours. We're a small agency. There are only Crusty and me."

"Let me know. I'm going to see how Darcie is doing."

"I'll give you a ride, Mr. MacAngus," said Sammy. "I need to be at the ranch today to survey the property. We have a group of quail hunters scheduled this week, and I'll bet my wife would like a chance to talk over her detective work with Crusty. I noticed he was in his office when I drove by earlier."

"How do you know that? Did he have the lights on? We're not open today," I said.

"Naw. He had the front door wedged open, and there was smoke coming out through the crack."

"That numbskull! He told me he quit smoking, the liar. Even so he knows there's no smoking his cigars in the office, but the minute I'm not there he thinks he can get away with it. How does he think he'll cover up the reek of his cheap smokes?"

Sammy chuckled. "Go get 'em, Eve." He steered Angus out the door toward the truck.

I noticed Frida's door was open a crack. Chances are she heard everything including Angus' offer to hire me. I wondered if that would make her happy, knowing I'd be busy with my own case, or would she view it as another attempt by me to interfere in her work? I'd talk to her later when and if I took on the job. Right now there was an office to fumigate and an old detective to convince we could handle both of these cases. I just had to figure out how.

CRUSTY WAS NOT expecting me to stop by on a Sunday so he thought he had the place to himself. Country music was blaring from his radio and clouds of smoke hung in the air. I quietly opened the front door and made my way toward the back office where I found him with his boots up on the desk, chomping happily on his cigar. The remains of a fast food burger take-out decorated the top of his desk. If there was any work being accomplished, it certainly was not by him. He looked up when I cleared my throat and coughed.

"Aw, Eve. I know what you're going to say, but a man has to have his fun."

"I'd prefer if your fun was dangling a line over the side of your bass boat, choking the wildlife on the water with your vile, cheap cigars. Do you realize how long it took me to make this office presentable to clients? We have an appointment with Della Abbot first thing tomorrow."

"I'll leave all the windows open tonight. It'll be fine by tomorrow."

"Good. Then you can sleep here tonight and make certain no one comes in. There's sensitive and confidential material in here. Who knows that better than you?" I waved my hand back and forth in front of my face and coughed again.

"Sure. Fine. I'll do it." He waved his cigar dismissively at me.

"And put out that darn thing!"

"Is it the smell that bothers you or the fact that you think it's a cheap cigar?"

"Both."

He got up and tossed it out the window into the alley.

"Sure, kill some poor unsuspecting homeless person trying to find a meal in the dumpster out there."

"I'll go get it and toss it into the garbage out back." He headed out the back door.

"Don't forget to seal up the trash bag," I called after him.

He re-entered and politely pulled out a chair for me. "Take a load off. You look as if you have something on your mind."

"We have a problem," I said.

"Something other than your attitude?" he asked.

I told him about Angus' daughter-in-law's accident and Frida's information about the brakes on the car. "Angus wants to hire me, uh, us to find out who did it."

"Fine with me," said Angus.

"But, given the situation with her family, Madeleine can't possibly go undercover for the Abbot case, and Ms. Abbot made it clear that I wouldn't work, so I can't step in for Madeleine."

"We have no choice but to find someone else, someone Ms. Abbot approves of, and we've got to do it before tomorrow morning. You might want to get right on that one, Eve." Crusty pulled himself out of his chair and headed toward the door.

"Where are you going?" I asked.

"I'm doing what you suggested. I'm gonna take my little bass boat out on the lake and do a little fishing." With a wry smile on his face, he waved goodbye and left.

I cleaned the food wrappers off the desktop and flopped down in his chair, feet on the desktop. I needed to think. I pushed the chair onto its back legs and reviewed the case. Ms. Abbot had chosen Madeleine because she looked young and vulnerable, a fresh new target for a predator. Who else did I know who had that demeanor? I let my mind wander over the women I knew. Before I drifted off to sleep, images flitted across my brain including the absurd picture of Jerry dressed like a young woman (something he had done on several occasions, encouraged by me). His willingness to don female garb had helped take down some bad guys. It wasn't Jerry, but another likeness that shook me wide awake. Well, I'll be hogtied to a gator tail. It was perfect. Just perfect.

"Look," I said over the phone. "You don't have to say yes now. Show up at Crusty's office tomorrow morning and meet

Ms. Abbot. She may not agree that you're right for the job. So then, it's all over, and you have no decision to make. If she says she wants you, we'll work out an arrangement and pay to compensate you for your time."

It was agreed not to decide yet. I was certain I had solved the agency's problem and was free until tomorrow morning. Until then I had a friend in need of my support and a family who hadn't had my attention since last night at dinner. If I had been the kind of mother who cooked, I would have made them something special for dinner, but I cooked about as well as I roped a steer. I was lucky. I had Grandy who could cook like Martha Stewart and probably could master steer roping in a few short lessons.

Madeleine greeted me at the door. "You shouldn't be here, Eve. You should be with your own family." She looked ashen, her freckles standing out in stark contrast to her pale skin.

"You forget, my dear, "I said as I hugged her, "you are part of my family. How's Darcie and your uncle?"

She plopped down on the couch. "As well as can be expected given what she's been through and his concern for her and his interview by Frida. No one can possibly believe he could have anything to do with tampering with the brakes."

"Of course not." I reached out and patted her hand.

Angus entered the room followed by his son. "Darcie and Dylan are curled up together napping."

"Look," said Mickey, "I owe everyone an apology for getting so drunk last night. And as for Darcie and me, well, we talked today. We have some issues, but almost losing her scared me to death. I realize how much I love her. We're going to get ourselves a counselor and work this out."

Angus fairly beamed with happiness. "Family is important. I always raised Mickey to believe that. I lost his mother to another man. Luckily, Mickey and Darcie have love going for them. They'll be fine." He reached out and hugged Mickey, then wiped his eyes.

"If you want the agency to investigate for you, my boss has given me the go ahead," I said.

Angus blew his nose noisily into his handkerchief. "That's something I need to talk to you about. I'm certain I will need your services. I didn't tell the detective this when she questioned me, but I did tamper with those brakes."

"What?" I said in surprise. "Uh, look Mr. MacAngus. If that's true, you're going to need a lawyer maybe more than you need a detective."

Mickey laughed. "When dad says he 'tampered' with the brakes, I think he means he tried to find out what was wrong with them and fix them. Let me assure you that he has no repair skills whatsoever. Dylan would be better at repairing a brake line than his grandfather. Isn't that so, Dad?"

Angus turned his face away from us for a moment, but I caught a glimpse of worry on it. He was covering up something. Or protecting someone. He dropped his chin to his chest and stared out the living room window. "This is not the vacation I envisioned. At least now Darcie, Mickey and Dylan can leave for Naples to visit Mickey's mother. I'm sure the police and I will sort through everything to do with the accident soon. Once my family is off to visit Dylan's grandmother, I'm going to go back to the motel to stay as I'd originally planned."

"But we have plenty of room here," said Madeleine, "and we've hardly had time to catch up."

"We will. We will." Angus trudged toward the hallway as if he was a man on the way to prison. I hoped that wasn't the case. He was clearly depressed. I thought back to what Frida had said last night. Could he be suicidal? Should I say something to Madeleine about his state of mind so she could insist he remain here where she could keep an eye on him?

I needn't have worried about alarming Madeleine. She knew what she wanted and how to get it. She might have been tiny, but her attitude was as big as some of the alligators in the swamp and when she made up her mind to something, she was more determined than a hungry calf in search of its mama.

"You are absolutely not going anywhere. A motel? Not likely." She hmphed and stomped off to the kitchen. "Anyone interested in lemonade?" she called to us.

When I pulled up to Crusty's office the next morning, Ms. Abbot and Shelley, our tailor and junior partner, were so deep in conversation, they didn't notice me until I slammed my car door closed and approached them.

"Ah, Eve," said Ms. Abbot, "Shelley introduced herself to me, and we've been going over the strategy for taking down the bad boys at my company."

The look on Shelley's face told me all I needed to know. She was thrilled at being asked to be the onsite operative in the scheme, and it appeared Ms. Abbot believed Shelley was the right woman for the job. A car pulled up behind us. I could tell it was Crusty by the smell of cigar smoke emanating from the open window of his car.

"Ladies," he greeted us politely and ushered us into the office. I held my breath. What would the place smell like this morning after Crusty's smoking marathon yesterday? I sniffed. True to his word, Crusty had aired out the place last night.

"You need to quit smoking, this time for good," I whispered to him.

We entered his private office in the back and got right down to determining how we were going to approach the case.

"Before we go any farther I want to make certain you know what you're getting yourself into, Shelley," said Crusty. "This isn't a game, you know. These guys are predators, sexual predators, and according to Ms. Abbot they've hit on several women and terrified them enough that they quit their jobs at her company."

Shelley got that resolute look on her face I'd seen there when she had taken on a man who had tried to sexually assault her.

"I know about sexual predators, Mr. McNabb, from personal experience. I'm not afraid of them, but I do want their butts prosecuted. If I can help in any way, I'm your woman."

"I'll vouch for her. Don't let that innocent face fool you. She's got her mother's toughness. You remember her, don't you?" I asked.

"I do. She was a hard-working woman who could take the measure of any man. She obviously wasn't fooled by outward appearance. I was real sorry about what happened to her." Crusty was referring to the neighboring rancher who had killed Shelley's mother when she tried to protect Shelley and her land from him.

"Good looks and a smooth manner don't fool me either," said Shelley, shooting me a meaningful look.

I was relieved to hear her say that not only for this job, but I worried, given Shelley had invited him to the dinner last night at Madeleine's, that my ex-husband's sophisticated and urbane manner might have taken her in. He was no predator. His come-on was harmless, but in poor taste, a puppy dog who needed training. I had failed at that when we were married and I was young and naïve. Shelley apparently hadn't been conned by Jerry.

Shelley smiled and said, "You were worried, Eve? I needed a date, and he was available. We're just friends."

"He can use as many of those as he can get," I said.

The four of us talked about how Shelley might fit into this case, and we finally decided to bring Shelley into Abbot's firm as an intern from the nearby college. She would work in one of the vice-presidents' offices doing research in product development.

"You can arrange your hours with human resources," said Ms. Abbot. "I'll notify HR you'll be coming in later this week. However, we need a transcript or something official from the college."

"I did some work with the president there a few years

back. I'll let him know what we're up to. I'm sure he'll arrange something that looks official enough to fool your HR people, at least for the short time Shelley will work there," Crusty said.

"You have any names?" asked Shelley.

"The women who have called in to complain are former employees, and they are terrified these guys can retaliate in some way. Nothing I could say would convince them to give their names or name the men who harassed them. They were, however, quite explicit in telling me what the men did to them—inappropriate touching, lewd remarks, and threats they would lose their jobs if they didn't cooperate with the men. I hired these guys. I'm horrified at what they have done to the women and to the company."

"I guess what I'm hearing is that there's more than one guy who's preying on women?" I said to Ms. Abbot.

"I hate saying this, but I'm afraid so. I don't know how this happened, and I want this out of my company. We assemble electronics for the aerospace industry. Our workers are highly trained techs. We're kind of a computer nerd place and most of the employees here are men. I want to attract women, but I can't do that if I seem to be developing a hostile work environment."

"Word gets around, not only in a single company, but it spreads to others," I said.

"I can't have that. Eventually, I will have the state, local and federal authorities down my back if I don't remove these predators and clean up the work environment. It's the right thing to do. I don't want to fire these guys and let them wander off into another company where they behave the same. I want the law to have a say here."

Well, good, I thought. Abbot wasn't simply trying to meet legal guidelines but also saw the moral imperative to find and prosecute those who denigrated others through sexually inappropriate behavior.

My cell rang, and the ID indicated the call was from Frida.

"I've got to take this." I stepped out of the inner office and found Angus and Mickey sitting in the waiting area.

CHAPTER 7

"Uh, can I call you back?" I disconnected and smiled at my unexpected visitors.

"Are you still interested in working for us?" asked Mickey.

I was a little surprised at how quickly they were moving to hire a detective agency. "Of course. I talked it over with Crusty. The agency would be happy to work on this matter, but I can personally reassure you that the police here are fair and competent..."

"You're talking about your friend, that police detective. We aren't comfortable she would work on our behalf. You should know that Dad had nothing to do with those brakes failing. We, well, I think I know who did. Tell her, Dad."

I held up my hand to stop him. "Let's take this one step at a time. First, we need to discuss how we be can be of aid, what you would like us to do for you. Then, we need to draw up a contract. Right now we have clients in the office, so it would be better if you returned in an hour or so. We can talk at length then."

Mickey gave me a skeptical look. "You're not dragging your

feet here?"

"Not at all."

At that moment the door to the inner office opened, and Shelley and Ms. Abbot walked out. We avoided having clients run into each other by scheduling our clients at times that kept appointments separate. We liked to insure client privacy. When the outer door opened, a buzzer connected to the front door rang in Crusty's office to let us know someone had entered. Either Crusty or I usually stepped into the outer office before we let a client leave through the front door. If someone was there, we ushered clients we had met with out the side door. Crusty and I were so involved with Ms. Abbot's account of the harassment in her company that neither of us had heard the buzzer.

I told Shelley we would meet later. Ms. Abbot nodded and left with Shelley.

Crusty went back into his office, and I signaled Mickey and Angus that I would be with them in a minute.

Crusty and I talked for a few minutes about the Abbot case, I briefed him on the MacAngus clients, and I ushered Mickey and Angus into his office.

After several minutes of discussion, Mickey, who seemed most comfortable doing all the talking, informed us that he wanted to hire us to prove his father innocent of tampering with the brakes.

"We can't prove you innocent or guilty of anything. We can investigate for you. The police, as I told you before, will also be doing that," I said.

"We know more than the police do," said Mickey. He leaned forward and placed his elbows on Crusty's desk looking eager to confide something. "You see, it's all about my father's business, which I told him he needed to retire from and sell, but he wouldn't do that. Instead he merged his firm with another import/export business, but this one, we suspect, is not on the up and up. Dad doesn't like their business practices and let them know what he thought, but they told him it wasn't his concern."

This was proving to be more than tampering with car brakes. Crusty and I might be taking on a case too complicated for us to handle.

"Why are you worried about them? Did they threaten him?" asked Crusty.

"Not in so many words, but it was clear they didn't want him nosing around. I think they might try to remove him from the board or worse." Mickey sat back in his chair and crossed his arms over his chest with a look on his face that said he handed us the key to unlocking the question of who tampered with the brakes and why. Maybe he did, but I had a few questions I wanted to ask.

"I don't quite understand," I said. "What business practices are we talking about? If they're doing something illegal, why not take this to the police? In an import/export business, we're talking about an international crime. The authorities are better equipped to handle that than a small local detective agency."

Mickey dropped his gaze to the floor and said nothing.

Angus finally spoke up. "Because Mickey works for the company, so he's implicated."

"As in, he knows who tampered with those brakes?" I asked.

Mickey nodded. "I have a very good idea it was someone from the company, hired to either frighten Dad or kill him. I told Dad not to merge with them. I warned him they weren't to be trusted."

"Why would you ignore a warning from someone from inside the company, especially your own son?" asked Crusty. He arched his eyebrow in disbelief. I thought he looked like he could use a cigar and a stiff drink. What have you handed me, Eve, he seemed to be asking.

"Because he never thought I knew anything, ever. He thought he was the one who knew business. I was his inexperienced son. I wanted to major in biology in college, but Dad insisted

I have a business major, so I could join him in the firm, but then insisted I get some experience under my belt before he took me on." Mickey turned to face his father. "That's why I hired on to this firm and found how shady their business practices were. What do you do? You decided to merge with them despite what I knew. That's always been the way, hasn't it, Dad? You know everything, and now they're after you. Your stubbornness could have gotten my wife killed.

"You couldn't listen to what I had to say? Oh, no. You went to your old buddies from the pub to ask their advice. They told you everything was fine with the firm you wanted to merge with. They lied to you!" Mickey jumped out of his chair and leaned over his father, his face every bit as red as his father's.

Oh, boy, I thought. How are we going to deal with these two? I worried they might come to blows in the office. I pushed Mickey back into his chair. Angus started to arise from his seat, perhaps to leave.

"Sit!" I pointed to the chairs. "Both of you."

I looked at McCrusty to determine if he wanted to intervene, but he gave me a wry smile, sat back in his chair and relaxed.

"Okay, before we proceed here, let me lay out what I see going on. There is the matter of the relationship between the two of you. You'll have to work that out on your own somehow. Then, we have several thorny legal issues. Mickey is involved in something illegal."

Mickey interrupted me. "I haven't done anything illegal!"

"But you have. You say the company you're working for has broken the law, and you fear they may have taken action to get rid of your father." I held up my finger to prevent him from interrupting me again. "And you have failed to reveal any of this to the authorities either here or in Scotland."

Mickey settled back in his chair and sighed. "Right. Go on."

"You're alleging the company may have hired someone or had an employee of that company try to hurt or kill someone by tampering with the brakes in Angus' rental car. Aside from the bad blood between you two, what part of this situation doesn't demand the involvement of the legal authorities?" I stopped short in my speech. I had talked myself out of a case.

"What Eve isn't saying is that we can't take your case unless you tell the authorities what you told us," Crusty said. "Now come back when you've accomplished that." He stood and gestured toward the door. Our would-be clients were stunned into silence. They both got up and left.

"I thought you said Angus was Madeleine's favorite uncle," Crusty said as we heard the outer door close.

"He is, or rather he was. People change, and people behave differently around close family members. You know that."

"Angus isn't so bad. It's his son that concerns me. He has a short fuse." Crusty began to rummage around in his desk drawers.

"Here," I said. "Try this." I threw him a pack of gum.

CRUSTY AND I had agreed that I would supervise Shelley's work with the Abbot firm. Shelley would call me at the end of each day she worked there and any other time if she thought there was something important I should know. I wanted to closely monitor the situation and make certain Shelley wasn't in any trouble. She was to begin the end of this week. If Angus and Mickey didn't contact us this week, it meant a lull in our schedule for the next few days, but it also meant I had more time to spend with Netty and hours I could work in the store.

Crusty closed the office after Angus and Mickey left and rolled the phone over to his cell. He beat a hasty retreat to his car and sped off. It was close to noon, so I decided I would pop next door to the store and see how Madeleine and Grandy were faring. I also wanted to check the store's inventory. It might be fun to take Netty with me on a run to the coast for more items from our wealthy consignors there. I could do that this afternoon and then relieve Madeleine of work in the store for the rest of the week. She could spend time with her relatives, if she thought after the recent events that she wanted to spend time with them. I assumed Mickey, his son and Darcie, when she was able to travel, would be heading for Naples to visit his mother.

When I walked into our shop I knew by a quick glance at Madeleine's face that something was wrong. Her eyes were bloodshot and bugged out like someone had put a fright into her. A woman with hair a shade of blonde that shouted its love affair with a bottle of dye and clothes too tight for her ample figure stood in front of Madeleine, hands on hips, words spewing from her mouth like pellets from a shotgun.

"What do you mean my daughter-in-law was in an automobile accident? I should have been told. You should have told me."

I caught the gist of the attack and intervened because that's what I do and I'm a genius at it.

"No. Mickey should have called you and told you, not Madeleine. Leave her out of this. She's been overwhelmed with concern for her uncle and his family as well as for her own. Cut her some slack, woman. Now, if you want to see your daughter-in-law because you're concerned for her well-being, I'd be happy to drive you out to the ranch. Or Grandy will." I shot Grandy a look to see if she agreed. She did not. She appeared to have an all-consuming interest in rearranging the lingerie on one of the display tables.

The woman, obviously Mickey's mother from what she had shouted at Madeleine, turned her attention to me and asked, "And what's your interest in all of this? And who are you?"

"Eve Appel Egret," I said, sticking out my hand and clasping her ring-covered fingers in my firm grasp.

"Ouch," she said, extracting her hand. "I'm Carolyn MacAngus." Her haughty tone of voice was meant to inform me of how important she thought she was.

"I figured. What are you doing here? I thought you were supposed to be in Naples awaiting Mickey's arrival."

"Madeleine is my niece also, you know. I thought I'd pop on over here and pay her a visit while Angus and my son and family were here."

I found her announcement odd. I didn't think she'd ever met Madeleine. Maybe she saw her visit as an opportunity to get a jump start on making Angus' life miserable. That only made sense if he'd left her, but I heard she had dumped him for his best friend. What was she up to?

I decided I shouldn't keep my confusion to myself. "Really? I didn't know you and Madeleine were close, and I know you and Angus aren't, not any longer. Right?"

"I'll drive there myself. I have my own car." She gestured out the front window. A pearl gray Lexus was parked there next to a rusted red pick-up.

"Are you certain that bucket of rust will be able to make it to the ranch?" I asked, intentionally identifying the truck as her vehicle.

She made a gurgling, strangling sound in her throat followed by a "well, I never." I heard Grandy attempt to suppress a laugh, which came out sounding like a hiccup. Madeleine stepped in with her usual charm.

"It's really simple to get there," she said, leading Mrs. Self-important out the front door of the shop and making hand gestures to indicate the direction of the ranch. Carolyn MacAngus got into her costly car and drove off.

Madeleine came back into the store, relief written on her face. "Thanks for saving me, Eve."

"I think you're the one who did the saving here. How could your uncle marry such a harridan?"

"He's such a nice man," said Grandy.

Madeleine continued to gaze out the window. "She said the weirdest thing to me when I tried to give her directions. She said she knew all of that. Don't you find that strange?" asked Madeleine. "Did she mean she knew how to get to the house? She's never been out there visiting that I know. In fact, she said she found out where the consignment shop was located and stopped by to get directions to the house because she wasn't sure how to get there. I hope she doesn't get lost."

Grandy muttered something to the push-up bra she was placing on the lingerie table. It sounded like, "Wouldn't that be a shame?"

"I've got the afternoon free. I was going to run down to West Palm to replenish our inventory, but I can take over the store if you want to go home and see to things there," I said to Madeleine.

"Good heavens, no. I don't have a 'home.' I live in a lunatic asylum with the MacAngus family there, David's daughter, and now the ex or about-to-be ex-wife. The whole crew has put David in the most awful mood. He's spending more time out of the house and out in the field. Can I move my twins and me in with you, Eve?" She looked as if she was going to get down on her knees and beg.

"I've got an idea. Grandy, if you don't mind staying here for the afternoon, you can take the rest of the week off. I'll come in and mind the shop. Madeleine, why don't you and I and Netty go to the coast this afternoon and pick up merchandise from our clients? We'll grab a bite at Indiantown on the way down. Netty will be so excited and especially if she has her favorite auntie along."

Madeleine grabbed me around the waist and hugged me until I thought she would crush my ribs.

"I love you, Eve," she said.

"Great idea," said Grandy, "but why can't Shelley come in and work at the end of the week as usual?"

Oops. I'd neglected to come up with a good story for why Shelley would be missing for the next several weeks or so. I rightly guessed that Grandy wouldn't much like my pulling Shelley into the private eye business.

Madeleine caught the look on my face. "Did something happen to Shelley that we should know about?"

I started to say, "Absolutely not," but I decided I had to level with Madeleine and Grandy. They both were so good at finding me out.

"Funny thing, that…" I began.

The conversation between Madeleine and me was strained as we drove to West Palm. Following our burger lunch with Netty in Indiantown, Madeleine finally spoke after checking Netty in her car seat and finding her asleep.

"What were you thinking, Eve, having Shelley take on the undercover work at Abbot's business?"

"Don't you start, too. It was bad enough being chewed out by Grandy for drawing Shelley into this. Shelley is her own woman, and she's a lot stronger than anyone gives her credit for." I stopped talking and listened to what I said. "Huh. Isn't that often what I say about a cute, little friend of mine? Unless that friend thinks she's the only tough broad capable of doing this job."

Madeleine shot me an angry look, then dropped her glance. "Point taken, Eve. I guess I'm jealous because I so wanted to do the work. I never get to do anything exciting lately. Please don't tell me raising twins is exciting enough. I love being a mother and working in the shop, but I sometimes crave the kind of life you have."

"You mean chaotic and crazy?"

"I mean you're doing something big with your PI work. I wanted to make a difference too."

I knew I shouldn't dismiss her feelings. "Okay, kiddo. The next time we need someone on a case, you're elected."

"Really?"

"Sure. Next case." I hoped the next case Crusty and I took on was insurance fraud where a member of the firm was assigned to surveillance for someone who had filed a questionable insurance claim. Twelve straight hours of sitting on your butt in a car to take the necessary pictures of a guy skateboarding down his driveway after he filed a claim for a broken leg. Some fun. I'd done it a hundred times.

"I can hardly wait," Madeline said and settled herself back in her seat, a wide grin on her face.

I knew I shouldn't promise Madeleine a role in one of our cases without checking with Crusty first. Just because he had agreed to use her in the Abbot case didn't mean he'd okay her for another case. Crusty wasn't one to leap into change, and taking on a couple of junior PIs such as Shelley and Madeleine was probably more than Crusty could handle. But I was getting ahead of myself. There was no case now for Madeleine and might never be. One step at a time I told myself. At the same time a voice in my head that sounded identical to Grandy's berated me for making promises to Madeleine I probably couldn't or shouldn't deliver. I looked over at Madeleine and the fatigue that had so enveloped her face this morning was gone, replaced by a twinkle in her eyes and a curve to her cupie doll lips. I wanted her to be happy, so I let her believe she could join me in my sleuthing. What was so wrong about that?

OUR RUN TO West Palm was more successful than I anticipated. Madeleine seemed to be her old self, Netty, filled with her favorite food, French fries, was contentedly babbling to herself in her car seat, and the trunk and remainder of the back seat was piled with clothes and household items, used, but designer quality. I pulled into an empty parking space in front of the shop, extracted Netty from the car and took her inside for Grandy to mind while Madeleine and I unloaded our finds.

"You head home, Madeleine. Grandy and I will finish up arranging things here. It'll soon be time to close up anyway."

"Do I have to go home?" Madeleine asked.

"You can't live in the shop. I'm sure things will have settled down by now. If there were any trouble, David would have called you. Don't be such a wimp. Wimps don't make good sleuths."

Grandy overheard what I said. "What do you mean? Did you tell her she could join you in doing PI work? What were you thinking, Eve?"

Trapped. I looked first at Grandy who shook her head at me, then at Madeleine whose look of hopeful anticipation began to slide off her face.

"Uh, well, Crusty and I might need help at some future date."

"Well, I hope that means I'm included," said Grandy. "You wouldn't leave me out, would you?"

Now I'd really done it. Crusty would have to rename the agency "The Snoopy Women's Detective Agency…and Crusty."

"I HOPE YOU'RE not interested in growing up to become a PI," I said to Netty on our way to our new house.

"Blah," she responded. In the rearview mirror I saw her stick her fist in her mouth, then wave it menacingly in the air. Another tough gal.

"Good for you."

When a glanced in the mirror I noticed a car behind me closing in on my bumper. Instead of slowing down when it caught up to me, I watched as it swerved into the left lane to pass, but another car was coming toward us. Horrified, I slammed on my brakes and twisted the wheel hard right. The car approaching accomplished a similar maneuver edging to the shoulder and allowing the passing idiot to race through the space we'd left. I laid on my horn and shook my fist as the car retreated down the road. The other driver and I shook our heads at one another as we carefully pulled back into our lanes.

Everything had happened so fast that I'd only caught a brief glance at the car that passed us. I hadn't paid attention to the driver, only that huge front end as it closed in on us. In the fading afternoon light, it looked like a pearl gray Lexus.

CHAPTER 8

WORK ON THE roof was over for the day. The tribe members were gone, and Sammy, shirt sweaty from an afternoon's hard labors, sat on the front steps of Grandfather's house drinking a beer. Grandfather and Lionel sat next to him, Lionel carving and Grandfather smoking his pipe while he rocked in his cane rocker.

"You all look very pleased with yourselves," I said, setting Netty on her feet. I had no fear she'd run off toward the canal because she would be too curious about what her grandfather was carving.

"Mine?" she inquired, as he put down his knife and pulled her into his lap.

"Not everything is yours, Netty," I said, wanting to teach her something about not assuming she owned the world, although to me she did.

"Yes." He held up his artwork to show her. "It's mocking bird whistle." He didn't let her take the object. "It's not finished yet."

"Mine!" she repeated and grabbed for it. Lionel gave me a look that begged for my intervention.

"Don't look at me. You told her not to mind what I say. She's your problem now." I leaned over and kissed Sammy and gave Grandfather a hug. "What's for dinner?" I asked.

"Don't you remember, Eve? It's your night to cook," Sammy said.

Oops. In all the excitement of this morning and the trip to the coast, I had forgotten.

"It'll have to be bucket of cluck with sides. I'll be right back." I jumped back into my car to get our takeout. If I weren't for Grandfather and Grandy, the only people in my family who cooked with any ability—I only warmed up food items and often burned them in the process—my children would be malnourished. Tonight, I felt intensely guilty, not only about dinner, but I had to admit the possibility that I might not have this thing of juggling motherhood and two jobs down as well as I'd convinced myself I did. There was hope. Until the MacAngus family let the agency know whether they wanted us to work for them and Shelley's undercover work began, I had some time to get my life in order.

I managed to accomplish that for twenty-four hours and then everything went back to swamp normal.

THE SUN WAS setting over the lake with a splendid display of purple and coral colors. I thought sunsets on the Big Lake were well worth braving the swamps, untamed vegetation, numerous alligators and other crawly things. Sammy and I stood arm in arm in the yard inspecting our house. The structure was shingled, and now work could begin on the inside.

"You're not unhappy we didn't put a traditional thatched roof on the house, are you?" I asked Sammy. I hoped his answer had remained the same as when we discussed it at the beginning of construction. I didn't want my husband to feel as if he had to abandon the Miccosukee style house to satisfy the needs of his white wife.

"Of course not. This complex," he waved his hand toward the

chickee that housed the airboat business, Grandfather's cabin on stilts with the thatched roof and our new, larger house, "is a perfect blend of contemporary life with the traditional life of my people."

I gave a silent sigh of relief. I really wanted electricity and in-door plumbing, not that Grandfather didn't have both in his place, but he also had those tiny little lizards crawling through the thatch above our heads. I wanted to be able to select the wildlife that occupied our home, and it didn't include anything which, when you picked it up by its tail to toss it out the door, could detach the tail and leave it behind wriggling as a ploy to turn attention away from its body.

As if reading my mind, which he often seemed to be able to do, Grandfather said, "I rather like those little fellers crawling around above my head. Keeps me company at night."

I shuddered, and Sammy put his arm around me. "Our house will be a wonderful place to raise our family."

I had made up for my having forgotten to cook last night by making a stew tonight. Everyone seemed to be looking forward to it except for Lionel who opined that, "it smelled like mastodon."

Frida's car pulled into the drive, and she stepped out. I could tell by the determination in her step that what she had to say wouldn't be cheery.

"Just in time for dinner," I said.

"You can have my portion," offered Lionel.

I shot him a dirty look and expected one from him in return, but instead he gave me a wink. I could never predict the guy. It would be easier if I could simply count on him to dislike everything I said and did.

"This is a heads-up, Eve. Mickey and Angus MacAngus visited my office yesterday afternoon. They said you and Crusty insisted they speak to me."

I was relieved to hear they'd taken our advice. I hadn't heard from Madeleine today, so I assumed she was either in control of what was happening in her house or had completely given up and run away from home. Regardless, I had decided not to bother her. She was a big girl. I didn't want her to think I didn't believe she had a hold of the situation by calling or dropping by. The was my new Eve-lets-others-run-their-own-lives approach to organizing my own.

"They told you about Angus' business problems and the threats then?"

She scuffed her boot around in the dirt and chose not to look up at me for several seconds. "Yes, but my boss thinks we should look at the problem with the rental's brakes closer to home. We do have Angus' prints on the tools."

"That's it? You're not going to consider that someone else might have gotten to the car? There was plenty of opportunity."

"I know. I know, but for now the captain wants us to tie up loose ends here."

"Are you ready to arrest him? Is that what you're saying?" I asked.

"Close."

"I reassured them yesterday that, if they went to you, you would consider their story."

"You had no right to tell them that, Eve." She sounded angry for a moment, but then her voice changed. "I'm sorry. I know the evidence is slim, and I can't understand why Angus would tamper with his brakes, but we need to go with what we have. This international story is pretty far out."

"Did you talk to Angus, his family and Madeleine and her family about a possible arrest?"

"No. I came here first as a favor to you to be prepared for Angus and Mickey to hire you and Crusty as they intended to do before. If you believe their story about Angus' firm and Mickey's employment there, this will be a headache to handle for any agency. If my boss wanted us to look in that direction, it would be a reach for us to take on a case with leads in another country."

"Are you saying Crusty and I aren't capable of taking on the case?"

"You'll need help. Someone with reach beyond the United States."

I smiled to myself. I knew just the person.

"Thanks for preparing me, Frida."

She nodded, got back in her car without another word and drove off. My cell rang.

It was Madeleine.

"I'll bet someone at your place needs my help," I said.

"We do. And right now. Bethany has disappeared."

I held my tongue and didn't make a bad joke of saying that her family seemed to keep losing people.

"Be right there."

I quickly told Sammy where I was going.

"Do you want me to come along?" he asked.

"No," I said. "I want you to be sure the mastodon stew doesn't burn."

MADELEINE RUSHED OUT to meet me as soon as I pulled into the drive. I put my arms around her and hugged her to me. "It will be okay. I'm sure she ran back to her mother's in Boca."

"No. That's the first place we checked. She's not there, and when her mother found out why we were calling, she was furious. She's driving here now."

That was what Madeleine did not need, Bethany's mother Angela throwing a fit while a cloud of suspicion hung over Angus and his son and concern remained about Darcie's condition after the accident.

"How long has she been gone?" I asked.

David ran his hand through his hair. "We're not certain when she left. She went to bed early last night but wasn't up this morning when I left for the fields. She likes to sleep late, so some mornings I let her do that." He sighed and added, "It's easier that way."

I got what he was saying. Not having Bethany whining around the house about how she hated the place and her life was pleasanter for everyone.

"Could she have been gone all day? Could she have left last night?"

Madeleine wrung her hands. "It's my fault. It's been so busy around here that I forgot about her. I guess I assumed Bethany went out with David today. I only found out she hadn't when he came back in late this afternoon."

"And I assumed she was in the reserve office doing some paperwork I'd assigned her," David said. "I guess we've ignored her because we were too preoccupied with everything else."

Tears filled Madeline's eyes at David's words. "She's a handful, but she deserves better than to run away from her mother to a home where everyone feels better when she's not around."

David put his arms around her and kissed the top of her head. "I'm not a very good father."

I felt bad for both of them, but now was the time for action, not tears. "Enough, both of you. There's blame enough to go around, but it won't help us find her. Let's see if we can get to the bottom of this. You've called her friends?"

David and Madeleine nodded.

"I'll take a look at her room," I said.

I couldn't tell if any or many of her clothes were missing. Her closet seemed to be packed with outfits as were the drawers of her bureau.

"Madeleine, could you come here?" I asked her to look around and see if she found anything missing.

"I don't know. She had so many clothes that… Wait! Her backpack is gone."

"She could have stashed some clothes in it."

"And her cellphone is gone," Madeleine said. "We tried to call her, but it went to voice mail. I left a message, so she might call back."

David stood at the bedroom door. "Could someone have

taken her?" he asked, his face etched with worry.

"Let's not jump to conclusions yet. She wasn't happy here, was she?" I asked David. The most obvious explanation for her absence was that she ran off.

"I don't think she was happy anywhere. Not here and not with her mother. I thought she was showing some interest in working the game reserve. She seemed to like talking with the clients and setting up shooting parties for quail, but she's a teenager. How can you read them?" He looked to me as if my experience with my oldest boy Jason made me an expert on adolescents.

"He's a boy. Girls are almost another species, and Bethany comes from a different background."

"Frida's here," Angus said from the living room.

"Did someone call her?" I asked.

Madeleine nodded. "I did. I know I overreacted, but I worried someone could have taken her, so I thought I'd call in the big guns as well as you, Eve."

I was sure once Madeleine knew Frida was focusing on Angus as the one who cut the brake lines that she'd regret bringing her into this situation. Well, I sure wasn't going to be the one to tell her.

I looked around the living room and the kitchen and realized Carolyn MacAngus wasn't present.

"Did your mother have trouble finding this place yesterday?" I asked.

"My mother?" asked Mickey. "She wasn't here."

Madeleine tapped me on the arm. "Uh, can I talk to you? Privately. "

Mickey repeated his question to me.

"I guess I thought she was coming here to see you," I said, not meeting Mickey's gaze.

"No. We're going to her place in Naples. I thought you knew that." Mickey gave me a suspicious look.

Madeleine pulled me into the kitchen. "Mickey's mother

never showed up here yesterday afternoon. At least no one reported she stopped by. By the time we got back from our trip to West Palm, I was once more so overwhelmed with everything that I forgot all about her stopping at the shop and saying she was going on out here."

"She never showed up?"

Madeleine shook her head. "I guess not. I told you I was concerned she would get lost. I give lousy directions." Her face scrunched up and she gulped back a sob.

"Sorry, sweetie. I know you've had a lot going on around here." I gave her a hug.

"What's wrong?" asked David, entering the kitchen and catching Madeleine wipe away a tear.

"Nothing. She's dragged out from all this."

"I know," said David. "I'm sorry, honey. This is too much. Your family, my family."

"Our family," Madeleine said, squaring her shoulders. "Let's talk to Frida."

"You should go home to your kids, Eve," David said.

I knew he was trying to be thoughtful, but I needed to be here for my friends. My children had all the support they needed in their father, their grandfather and Grandfather Egret. I thought of the beef stew cooking away on the stove, and smiled, content that I had managed to cook them something nutritious and home-made.

My cell rang.

"Did you remember to put a bay leaf and lots of pepper in that stew?" It was Grandy, and like many people who knew me well, she had read my mind.

I told her what was going on at Madeleine's place.

"Oh, my dear. Don't worry about a thing. I'll check on your stew first, then be right over. I made Lasagna for Max and me, and there's tons. We can feed everyone at Madeleine and David's. No worries."

Grandy to the rescue providing comfort food to everyone

and Frida here to investigate Bethany's absence made me feel totally useless until Madeleine grabbed my hand and pulled me onto the couch next to her. I hugged her tightly.

I heard a car pull into the drive. That had to be Frida.

When she entered the house, Mickey stared daggers into her. Angus ignored her arrival and paced back and forth in front of the living room window.

"Madeleine said Bethany was gone. Do you think she left of her own free will or are you afraid someone took her?" asked Frida.

Frida got right to the point, so I did too. I told her what I had found in Bethany's room, that her cell and backpack were missing and that her mother hadn't heard from her and neither had any of her friends.

Frida looked around the house. "If someone took her, do you have any idea who could have?"

David shook his head.

Mickey cleared his throat. "Maybe now you'll believe us about Dad's business connections. They might threaten his family also."

"But Bethany isn't part of his family," Frida pointed out.

Angus stopped his pacing. "She's Madeleine's stepdaughter. That's probably enough of a link," he said.

David and Madeleine looked at Angus and then in turn at Mickey and Frida in confusion. It was clear they knew nothing about the threats to the MacAngus family, but now was not that time to tell them.

Like me, Frida thought it probable Bethany had run away and said so. "That doesn't mean she won't get into trouble. She's a lone female in an area she's not very familiar with."

"She lived here until my wife and I separated," pointed out David.

"I know where she is," came a voice from behind us. Little Eve, David and Madeleine's daughter, almost five-years-old, but going on forty-five, stood at the entrance to the hallway, holding her Paddington bear.

Madeleine rushed over to her. "You do?"

She stuck her thumb in her mouth. "I'm not supposed to tell."

"But we're worried about her, sweetheart. You can tell us," coaxed Madeleine.

Eve seemed hesitant, but then removed her thumb from her mouth and said, "I'm hungry. Can I have a cookie?"

I was willing to promise her a trip to Disney if she told us what she knew. She could have a whole box of cookies as far as I was concerned.

Madeleine rushed to the kitchen, grabbed a package of cookies out of the cupboard and handed one to her daughter.

"That's not the kind I like," said Eve.

"You can have two," I offered. "One for your bear and one for you."

"Bears don't eat cookies," she said, her tone indicating that this bit of knowledge was something I should have known.

I grabbed the package out of Madeleine's hand and shoved it at Eve. "You can have the whole package and teach your bear to eat them. He'll be thrilled."

"Okay." She took the cookies and began walking down the hall toward her bedroom.

"Hey! You said you knew where Bethany was," I said.

"Out there." Eve pointed toward the swamp behind the ranch house.

THERE WAS LITTLE anyone could do to find Bethany at night. It was already dark, and the area behind the house was swampy with only a few islands of palm trees, cypress and live oaks. A search would have to wait until tomorrow. With a mouth full of cookie, Eve told us she saw Bethany climb out the window of her bedroom and head away from the house and the road.

"How did you see her, sweetie?" Frida had asked.

"She waved bye and went 'shh.' Will she be mad at me cuz I

told?"

"No," said Frida. "You did the right thing." Frida turned to us. "It sounds like it was light enough then for little Eve to be able to tell what way she headed. Tomorrow she can point it out to us. We'll begin searching right after dawn. We're at a disadvantage because we don't know when she left. No one noticed her absence today, and it seems obvious she wasn't where she should be, so I'm thinking she left last night or early this morning."

If Frida had the case of the cut brake lines on her mind, she didn't mention it. I was glad. I thought it could wait until another time, until we had located Bethany and knew she was safe. As Frida was leaving, a car pulled into the drive and a tall woman got out.

"Where's my daughter?" she yelled as she rushed toward the house.

Oh, good. Bethany's mother, Angela was here. That would make things all better, wouldn't it? Before she could storm into the house, Frida recognized her and grabbed her by the arm. She walked her away from the door and out of range of our hearing. They talked for several minutes. In the light from the porch I saw Frida give Angela a good shake. Angela quieted, and her hand flew to her mouth. Frida hugged her. Frida was both a good cop and a mother. She knew she had to calm Angela, but she also recognized how frightened she was for her daughter off in the night by herself. By the time Angela entered the door, she was reasonably calm.

"I'm not leaving here until you find my daughter," she said. "And who are all these people?"

"Family," said Madeleine. "Here." She handed Angela a glass with something that looked suspiciously like a stiff shot of bourbon in it. "Sit down. I know you're upset, but we can take care of all this. Together. We'll do it together."

The front door banged open, and I smelled Italian food.

The lasagna had arrived.

CHAPTER 9

GRANDY TOLD ME she had stopped by the house and my stew was not burned, but that Lionel insisted it needed more pepper and salt as well as other spices Grandy said he refused to identify.

"I took a spoonful. It was pretty tasty," Grandy assured me.

"You want to stay here and eat lasagna instead?" Madeleine asked.

I was in the mood for Italian, but it wasn't food I wanted. I left everyone to their dinner. On my way home, I contacted Nappi with a job I knew he couldn't refuse.

"I can put you on the payroll as a consultant. It won't be much money, but it will cover gas."

"Do not insult me," he said. I could hear the hurt in his voice. I *had* insulted him.

"I'm trying to be professional," I said.

"And I'm trying to be a good friend to you and to Madeleine. You're both like family to me."

I wondered if that was family with a small "f" or the other kind.

"Don't be ridiculous, Eve," he said, reading my mind as so many people close to me seemed to be able to do. It sometimes made me think I was simple-minded. "You're too smart, too tall and too Nordic to think I'd ever try to bring you into the fold."

That was good to know. I chuckled. "This might be a stretch for you. I don't know if you have contacts in Scotland."

"And there you go again, insulting me. Of course, I have contacts in Scotland. I'll be in touch." He disconnected.

THE STEW WAS as tasty as Grandy said it would be.

"Maybe I should give up cooking altogether and let the men here do it," I said as I took another helping.

"I didn't know you were cooking," said Lionel, but at least he said it with half a smile on his lips.

Jason, my oldest son, asked to be excused early, saying he wanted to take a walk down the canal to gather more firewood for the bonfires we often had outside after dark.

"That's so nice of you, honey," I said.

As soon as he left, Lionel got up from the table and went to the window.

"What are you looking at, Dad?" asked Sammy.

"I thought someone borrowed my canoe earlier today."

"Well, you certainly can't believe it's Jason. He knows better than to take your canoe without permission," I said.

Lionel sat back down. "You're probably right."

Jason returned an hour later with an armload of wood.

"Our boys are so good," I said to Sammy as we watched him stack the wood. He turned toward the house, saw us watching him and waved, then took off back down the canal, probably for more wood.

Since Lionel had taken responsibility for the stew when I left, I volunteered to clean up from dinner. There was no stew left over. Growing boys made a dent in every meal, and when I checked the pantry, I noticed there was no more peanut butter and our supply of bread was low. I added the food items to our list on the fridge.

"Add more cookies, too, would you, Mom?" called Jason as he came through the back door, tired and sweaty from his wood gathering.

"Cookie, cookie, cookie," chanted Netty from her highchair.

"Let's get you down from there, Netty, and we'll see if there are any cookies left from this morning." There weren't. These kids would, as the expression went, eat us out of house and home. It wasn't just an expression. It was the reality of raising four children, all of whom seemed to have extra-large stomachs. To be fair, all the adults in this family were good eaters, too.

Sammy had the bonfire going by the time I came out back. I held Netty on my lap while she chewed on a cracker I told her was just another cookie with salt on it. She wasn't convinced.

"Let's make 's'mores," suggested Sammy. "That should satisfy everyone's sweet tooth."

I handed a cracker-covered child to Lionel and ran into the house to get the marshmallows, graham crackers and chocolate.

Netty glanced at the square graham crackers with suspicion. "Don't like crackers," she said.

"You'll like these," promised Sammy and handed her the gooey concoction. Most of it went into her mouth with only a few sticky remnants left on her lips and fingers.

"I'll add logs to the fire, then take her off to bed," said Sammy. "Don't worry, Eve. I'll wash her face and hands before I tuck her in."

Now how did he know that was what I was thinking? Was everyone in this family a mind-reader?

"So," said Lionel to Jason, "We're thinking of sending you off to your cousin's ranch for the summer."

Jason's head snapped around, and I could see an expression of horror on his face. "What? Why didn't you tell me this, Mom?"

I wanted to pick up one of the logs by the fire and bop Lionel over the head. "Your father and I haven't even talked about it. And we would consult your feelings on the subject before we decided anything. Your grandfather is getting ahead of himself because he's so eager for you to learn about tribal culture and history, and he thinks you can do it better on the ranch."

"I can't go there now," he said. "I won't. I won't." Jason jumped up and ran off down the canal.

I had never seen him so distraught.

"What's the matter with Jason?" asked Sammy, watching his son run off.

"Ask your father." I sat back in my chair, arms crossed over my chest. This was Lionel's doing. Let him explain.

Grandfather Egret had remained silent throughout the evening, contentedly smoking his pipe, but now he set it to one side. "There's too much discord in this family. The children are suffering because the adults disagree too much."

"And one of them tries to interfere too much," I snapped.

Grandfather Egret sighed deeply. "We are all to blame. We've been thinking of ourselves more than we have the children. That's never a good thing."

Grandfather was echoing what David had said earlier tonight about Bethany: when adults were embroiled with their own problems, kids got lost.

Lionel kicked a spark that had escaped from the fire back into the flames. "We need to honor our ancestors more, our Miccosukee ancestors." He got up from his seat and strode off in the direction of the house.

No one spoke much after he left. The fire died down until it was only embers. We shooed the two boys into the house.

"Eve, you and I better get to bed early tonight if we want to be at the ranch at dawn to help search for Bethany," Sammy said. "It could be a long day."

I hesitated as Sammy and the two boys headed into the house.

"You should go in, too, Eve," said Grandfather. "I'll wait up for Jason. Don't worry about him."

THE NEXT MORNING Sammy and I got up at dawn to leave for the ranch and help in the search for Bethany. Lionel was gone when we drove off, and so was his canoe. I figured he was about to take another of his long sojourns into the swamp. When would he be back I wondered? Would it be days, weeks or would it be for years as he once did? The man was so unpredictable.

Grandfather handed Sammy and me a mug of coffee as we left.

"What's everyone doing today?" I said, gulping the hot liquid.

"The boys are clearing the undergrowth out of your lot next door. Netty and I are supervising," said Grandfather. "Jason got back late. He's not happy."

Sammy and I needed to talk to Jason, the sooner the better. I sighed. Adolescence. This wasn't going to be fun. Jason felt we had betrayed him by deciding his summer without talking it over with him. I didn't know what tried me most, Jason's confusion about growing out of childhood into an adult or Lionel's version of adulthood which was too much like adolescent moodiness.

DAVID GREETED US when we drove up. "I think we got everybody out of bed for nothing."

"She's back?" I asked.

"No, but it's pretty clear what happened. Little Eve was right. There are her footprints outside her bedroom window. We found it difficult to read her trail because we had a shower last night, but her tracks seem to lead toward the road, and then they disappear. I'll wager she hitched a ride. Frida thinks so too. I don't know whether to think that's good news because she didn't wander off into the swamps or be terrified about who picked her up."

"Any idea where she would head?" I asked.

"None. We've called everyone."

Frida dispatched the officers who had accompanied her and ordered them to continue searching the area between the house and the road and along the highway for any signs of Bethany.

"I'll have them cover the area for a mile up the highway east and west of here. I'll put out an Amber Alert. For now, that's all I can do. Her mother said she's run off before and come back in a few days. Those times she stayed with a friend who finally told her parents Bethany was hiding out in the friend's room."

"She's not at a friend's house this time," David said.

"Well, she may be, and the friend is lying for her. Keep calling her friends' houses. Put pressure on their parents to check," Frida said.

I pulled Frida to one side. "Now do you think there's anything to Mickey's story about the company wanting to get rid of Angus?"

"It's a stretch, don't you think? I think that tale is a lot of hooey. What evidence is there the company is engaged in something illegal and that they might want to harm Angus? And why not the same interest in removing Mickey?" Frida kicked the dirt at her feet in frustration. "I'm going to get a search warrant to search David and Madeleine's house."

"Why? I thought you said the tools used on the brakes had Angus' fingerprints on them?"

"The hoses were only partially severed, enough so that the brake lines were weakened, but my tech guys tell me the tools we examined were not the ones used on the lines."

My mouth dropped open in shock. "Then you have no evidence to link Angus to the severed linings. But you're going to search the whole house, Madeleine and David's house? Why?"

"I'm looking for the tool that was used."

"It seems pretty stupid for the guilty party to hide the tool in the house."

Frida shrugged. "It's the next logical step."

"Maybe you should get that search warrant to cover the nearby swamps also. Or the entire county." I knew I was being unfair, but the words fell out of my mouth in my usual thoughtless way.

"Aw, Eve. I'm just doing my job," she said, as I walked away from her.

I went into the house and had coffee with Madeleine, said hello to Darcie, who was recovering well. The color was returning to her freckled cheeks, and her light brown hair fell in waves around her face, covering the bruises and scrapes from the accident. She gave me a weak smile. It would be a few more days before she was fully recovered. I nodded at Angus and Mickey and saw David and Sammy off to the reserve office. They said they were going to do paperwork, but I knew the two of them would be out in the fields and near the watering holes and stands of oaks and palms and up and down the road searching for signs of Bethany.

"Grandy and I will be at the store today, and Max is out on the lake fishing again. I'll take the twins to the babysitter. Get dressed, Madeleine. You're coming with me."

"Oh, sure, Eve. I guess I didn't think you'd need me at the shop today."

"I don't. You're going to spend the day at my house, watching mindless TV, eating junk food and having an in-home pedicure."

Before she could object that she needed to be here taking care of her visitors, I held up my finger for silence. All eyes in the room turned on me. "Does anyone have any objections?" I asked in my commando Eve voice.

I secured the twins in their car seats in Madeleine's SUV and drove them down the road to their babysitter's, then returned to the ranch and hustled Madeleine into the passenger seat of my convertible.

"I don't want to hear a word from you. Your visitors can fend for themselves for one day. It might be relaxing for them without anyone in the house. Maybe Mickey and Angus can work on their relationship. You know about the so-called business issues?" I asked.

She nodded. "I heard. It must be scary working for a company that tries to cover up its illegal business practices by killing off a board member. I don't understand why the business wouldn't want to kill Mickey also. He must know a lot about what's going on inside."

"They probably figure they've got Mickey right where they want him. If he knew about what was happening in the company and warned his father off, then he's implicated in any dirty dealings. Anyway, we won't worry about that. I've got my business consultant working on it."

Madeleine mouthed, "Nappi."

I nodded. "Nice day. We'll take the long way to my place." I dropped the top, and we sped off.

The day was uneventful as were the several days that followed. There was no word of Bethany. It was if she was abducted by aliens who left no sign of their space ship. Madeleine did her best to make everyone feel at home, although Angus and Mickey wanted to leave for Naples. Darcie seemed to be recovering, although she still had debilitating headaches, so Madeleine's offer for all of them to remain with her made sense. She seemed to be in charge and handling the extra work of visitors well. Funny what a day off and a bit of pampering in the way of binge watching old seasons of *Miss Fisher's Mysteries* on Netflix can do for mental health. Call me the world's best therapist.

Ms. Abbot had informed Crusty that she wanted to get moving on the sexual harassment case at her company as soon as possible, so several mornings after Bethany's disappearance,

Shelley, Crusty and I met to finalize the plans for the undercover work.

"Call me if there's any problem," I told Shelley, after Crusty and I went over the operation with her again. "Anything at all."

"I have radar for sexual predators. I fended one off before. Remember?"

How could I forget how strong she was when the man who killed her mother then came for her? She not only refused his advances but stood in his way when he tried to run from the authorities. The gal was tough. A strong woman wrapped up in lovely, innocent-looking package.

I waved her off and hoped nothing would go wrong her first day. Or any day on this case.

As I watched her leave, I connected by cell with Frida to see if the police had any leads on Bethany's disappearance. Of course, I was hoping she'd also let me know about the search warrant.

"No break yet," Frida said. "I have to assume she wouldn't be stupid enough to wander off onto the reserve. She lived here long enough she knows the danger of wandering around the fields and swamps. She had to head for the road. Someone must have picked her up. I've been in constant touch with Madeleine and David and with Bethany's mother. There have been no ransom demands. I can feel it in my bones. She's off somewhere making everyone sweat as her adolescent way of punishing them," said Frida.

I, too, had talked with Madeleine late last night and the night before. She'd called when she couldn't fall asleep. We talked far into the early morning hours until both of us were too sleepy to exchange worries on the phone.

"I hope you're right," I said to Frida. "Madeleine is pinning her hopes on there being no ransom note and believing she ran off."

"I know the family is worried about her, but they do seem to think she was mad enough to take off. We scoured the area thoroughly. No sign of an abduction."

"I know about adolescent anger." I told Frida about Jason running off several nights before. "He came back late, but he's been in a sour mood since Lionel let it drop he wants Jason to work on the ranch this summer. He thinks all of us are against him."

"Thanks for reminding me about what my future holds. My oldest will be thirteen at the end of the summer. I can hardly wait," said Frida.

"I wouldn't worry about him. With you being a cop, he's probably too terrified to do anything out of line. I know I am."

She laughed and disconnected before I could ask about the search warrant, which was none of my business. But I am one snoopy gal.

Grandy pulled her car into the parking slot next to mine. We opened the shop together, chatted while we selected dresses for a summer sale, and checked the remainder of the store to make certain our inventory was adequate. My recent run down to West Palm had filled our blouse rounds and added to the household items. The store looked great.

"What are you bringing to Madeleine's picnic today?" asked Grandy.

"I'm stopping at the creamery for one of their chocolate pecan cheesecakes."

"Better get going. Those cheesecakes sell out early."

Madeleine had asked me to come out to the ranch for lunch, a picnic with Angus and his family. She said she wanted me to get to know her favorite uncle better. That was fine by me. Crusty and I had taken on Angus' case to examine evidence associated with Darcie's accident. It was my responsibility to find out all I could about him, his business contacts as well as his family and friends. It was an odd position to be in, working as a PI for a family, one of whose members was my best friend. I knew Madeleine was torn between wanting me to like Angus as well as she did and making certain she wasn't mistaken in her support of him and the love she had for him. I worried that her feelings were colored by her childhood memories. People changed and circumstances in their lives made many people do things they wouldn't ordinarily do. What could have influenced Angus to tamper with those brakes? A better question was why he would do it? I placed my bets on the company he merged with being the culprit.

Darcie's headaches had subsided in intensity and frequency, and she assured us she felt good enough to picnic. Since David would take his hunting party to the eastern edge of the ranch, he warned us to stay far west in the grove of live oak trees.

"Sammy and I will be working the field with a group of quail hunters. Make certain no one wanders away from the trees, and I'll keep my men walking the field. There should be no problem," David said.

CHAPTER 10

D AVID USUALLY LET Sammy handle clients in the field, and David did the paperwork, but today he set up over ten hunters to hunt, too many for only one man to oversee. Owning the game reserve was an issue for David. He had inherited the ranch from his father and ran it for over a decade before he ran into a problem. He was torn between the money the ranch brought in from clients and his reluctance to continue to run the ranch as a hunting reserve. A dead client coupled with an accidental shooting of an intruder in his house when his daughter was younger made David dislike anything having to do with guns. Neither of the incidents were his fault, but he was arrested for the client's murder, then let go when it was determined he wasn't the killer.

Attempts to sell the reserve met with no success, so he continued to operate it. Most of the day-to-day work went to Sammy who served as manager on a part-time basis. Sammy's heart wasn't in the business. He preferred to run our family's airboat operation. Everyone had hoped Bethany, who had expressed some interest in the ranch last year, would take over sometime in the near future and become manager. But now she had disappeared.

Sammy and David left with the group of ten hunters while Madeleine and I helped her family pile into our two cars, my convertible and her large SUV, with all our picnic food and collapsible chairs and two tables. A breeze blowing from the east made the late morning cool under the trees where we set up for lunch. From time to time the wind blew the sounds of shotguns from where the clients were hunting birds, but they were too far away for us to take much note of the sound.

Keeping two rambunctious twins and young Dylan corralled under the trees wasn't easy. Madeleine and I both suffered from sleep deprivation and were thoroughly exhausted by the time we finished our food and were ready to pack up everything to leave. Darcie was also tired, and Mickey worried that she had overdone the fun too soon after her accident.

"I think I should get her home. Can I take your car?" he asked.

I handed him the keys. "Good idea."

"Take her back to the house. We'll be right behind you. I think she needs rest."

He thanked me and settled her into the passenger's seat. She leaned her head back on the headrest. The color had left her cheeks. "I guess I'm not yet as strong as I thought I was." She closed her eyes.

"See you back home," said Mickey and drove off.

"Where's Dylan?" asked Angus as we stacked the chairs and table into the back of the SUV. Both twins had been fastened into their car seats and were also dozing off.

"He was heading that way," I said, pointing toward a lone live oak standing apart from the ones we picnicked under. Its branches had grown downward and were touching the ground. What boy wouldn't want to climb that tree? "I'll bet he's hiding from us in there."

Angus and I approached the tree whose lush summer foliage

made it impossible to see into the branches, but we heard a giggle.

"Let's not play hide-and-seek now, Dylan. We need to get back home. Everyone is tired," I said.

Another giggle was followed by, "I'm not tired."

"Well, good then. You can eat all the ice cream at home while the other kids sleep."

There was a rustling of branches and soon a small face appeared through the leaves.

"Do you think there are snakes in here?" Dylan asked, his voice tinged with excitement.

"Absolutely not." Although I worried there were, I knew there was nothing like the possibility of a few snakes to fire up a small boy's determination to find them.

Angus shot me a look of gratitude and whispered, "I would have tried to scare him out of there with the threat of snakes."

"Maybe one snake?" Dylan asked.

"Not even one. Just ice cream at home."

"I thought I'd see an alligator, but I haven't."

"Later I'll take you to see lots of alligators," I promised.

Dylan's face disappeared behind the branches. "Okay, I'm coming down now."

I reached up to give him my hand, which he refused to take. Instead, he jumped from one tree limb to another until he located himself at the other side of the tree. He was having too much fun. Even the promise of ice cream wasn't working.

Enough of this. I was as good a climber as any small boy. Or at least I used to be…when I was younger and didn't wear stiletto heels. I grabbed an overhead limb and pulled myself up. Dylan giggled as I pursued him around the tree. Finally, he jumped down and began to run away from our picnic area toward a locale I was familiar with. Oh, no, I thought. *Don't go there.* Cypress and palms overhung a watering hole where I feared he might encounter an alligator or a group of feral pigs. I jumped down and sprinted after him. This was no longer a game. He could get himself into serious trouble.

From behind me I heard a sound that reverberated through the area like a loud bang. A shot! I looked over my shoulder, the direction the shot came from, and saw Angus grab his chest and then sink to his knees.

Dylan had heard the sound, too. I turned toward him and saw him stop and look back for a moment, then continue running toward an opening in the trees ahead. Maybe he was still playing catch me or perhaps the shot frightened him, and he was running from it. I stole a quick glance at Angus who lay on the ground, unmoving.

I didn't want to yell for Madeleine because I didn't want her to run out to us. I thought she was safer in the cluster of trees. If someone was shooting around here, who knew what they could shoot whether on purpose or accidentally. Maybe she hadn't heard the shot or seen Angus drop to the ground. I glanced over my shoulder again, this time at Madeleine who stood by the SUV, a puzzled look on her face. I waved my hand at her to signal her to stay put.

When I turned my head, I could still see Dylan's orange shirt in the distance. If I dashed after him, I could catch him before he reached the watering hole, but what about Angus? Was he dead? Did he need help? Hesitation might mean the difference between life and death for him.

I heard a car behind me and from the corner of my eye saw my blue convertible pull up next to Madeleine's SUV. What was going on?

Mickey jumped out of the car. Madeleine pointed to Angus and to me. Mickey said something to her, then ran toward his father.

"See to your dad," I yelled to him. "I've got to get Dylan."

He nodded and knelt by his father, then yelled, "It's Darcie. She stopped breathing right after we left."

Why did he head back here? Why not continue to the ranch? Now I had three people whose lives I had to try to save. I had only one choice. Another lie to a gullible boy.

"Dylan!" I shouted at the top of my lungs. "There's a really big alligator right here. Come look."

At first, I thought he didn't hear me, but then he stopped and turned.

"Really?" he said.

I nodded. And by golly. I wasn't lying. Not twenty feet away from me in a small mud hole lay an eight-foot gator. I'd exaggerated the size to Dylan, but not the danger. The gator hissed as Dylan turned and began running toward me.

Not meaning to, I'd made everything worse. Dylan was truly in trouble if he rushed up to this gator, and I'd managed to add one more life to my life and death responsibilities. My own. The gator started toward me. She had good reason to see me as a threat. I spied a nest of her babies at the edge of the mud hole. The only way I could assure her I wasn't interested in her offspring was to beat feet out of there. That I couldn't do, not without taking Dylan with me.

I didn't know if this would work, but I held up my hand and signaled to Dylan. "Slow down. You've got to be very quiet or you'll scare her away." And then you won't see the nest of babies she's protecting, I said to myself. That wasn't information I was going to share with Dylan. Hardly daring to breathe, I watched her slow approach. Alligators can be so deceptive when you see them strolling along a mud hole. They look slow and awkward, but a single encounter with a gator exploding into a run is enough to convince you that they are faster than any Olympic runner. I didn't want this gator gal to have reason to make a dash for us.

Dylan put his finger over his lips in a shh gesture and began a slow tiptoe toward me. I took a chance and looked back at Angus. Mickey still knelt at his side, an expression of helplessness on his face.

"He's been shot," called Mickey.

"I know," I said.

"Grampa?" said Dylan. I didn't want him to panic. I didn't want the gator to panic, and most of all, I didn't want me to panic.

"Your grampa fell down. He'll be fine. I'm going to call a friend of mine to come help." Could I pull my cell out of my pocket or would that movement distress the reptile mama? I also didn't want to talk too much because I feared that would arouse her also. She had stopped her approach and seemed to be deciding how much of a threat I posed to her and her little ones. I carefully extracted the phone from my pocket while keeping an eye on Dylan and the mama gator. I could just make out the faint cries of her tiny babies. Kinda cute if you didn't think about who their guardian was. I called Frida. She answered, probably the best thing that had happened to me today since that large piece of cheesecake at lunch.

"Eve? I can barely hear you."

"Listen closely." I briefly explained everything.

"I'll get an ambulance out there and I'm on my way, but I can't do much else until I get there."

"I'll manage somehow." I ended the call. "Okay, Dylan. Stop right there and don't move."

The gator gave another hiss.

"Is it talking to us?" asked Dylan.

"Yes, so be very quiet."

"What's going on with my boy?" Mickey started to rise to his feet.

"Stay right there."

"There's an alligator right here talking to me, Dad."

No, no, Dylan. Don't tell your father that.

I slowly turned my head to see what Madeleine was doing. She had bent down into the passenger's side of my car and appeared to be tending to Darcie. She looked at me and held up her cell, shaking her head to indicate she had no signal. I held mine in the air, nodded and smiled.

"Okay," she yelled at me.

I wanted her to stay where she was. I didn't know how much she could see of what was happening out here, but she appeared to have made the only smart decision. She was taking care of Darcie and the twins. The alligator hissed to let me know I shouldn't be too hopeful about the outcome of this encounter.

I gestured for Dylan to come over to me slowly and quietly. I wanted to place myself between him and the gator, so that if she attacked she would hit me first. One taste of Eve had to be stringy and poorly seasoned, but the gleam in her eye said she expected I would taste like chicken.

"Okay, Dylan. She doesn't seem to be in the mood for company today, so we're going to leave her here and come back another time."

"Maybe we should wait until she feels better."

I inwardly groaned. Is this what a curious, lively toddler like my Netty would grow into? A nosy, independently minded child of six? He had seemed such a charming kid until this moment.

"If you don't come with me, I'll tell her what a bad boy you've been trying to get away from me, and then I'll feed all your ice cream to her and her kids," I said through gritted teeth. He looked up at me and must have seen something in my face that made him change his mind about how harmless I was.

"'Kay," he said, He dropped his head and reached out for my hand. We began to slowly walk toward his father. I kept my eye on the alligator. She kept her eye on us and seemed to sense we were moving away from her with no intention of endangering her and her kiddies.

"I want to talk to Grampa," said Dylan, trying to pull me toward his grandfather and father instead of the direction I wanted us to head, toward Madeleine.

"Not now, buddy," said Mickey. "Grampa's hurt himself and needs a doctor. I'll take care of him until one arrives."

"But I want to tell him about the alligator. Maybe that would make him feel better."

Angus let out a groan, then lifted his head and spoke in a soft, strained voice. "You tell me all about it later. You go with Eve now."

I walked Dylan toward the SUV and my convertible. Madeleine shielded the view of Darcie's limp form from Dylan.

"How is she?" I whispered to Madeleine.

"She's kind of in and out of consciousness. I can't imagine what happened to her. She seemed fine before the picnic."

"Can I tell Mama about the alligator?" asked Dylan.

"Not now. She's taking a nap," said Madeleine. "Let's get into my car, and we'll head home."

Sirens wailed in the distance. "I think that's the ambulance I had Frida call. I'll bet her SUV isn't far behind. Hey," I said to Dylan, "Here comes the ambulance to help your grandfather. We'll let them do their work, while we stay out of their way." I steered him away from my car and toward Madeleine's. Madeleine was quieting the twins in their car seats as the emergency vehicle stopped by the car and two EMTs hopped out.

Madeleine's boy, David Jr., seemed interested in watching everything happening around him, but Eve was screaming to be let out of the seat.

"Dylan, why don't you come here and help me with the twins? You can tell them about seeing that alligator," Madeleine said.

"Thanks, Madeleine. You've got to be better handling Dylan than I've been. I think he's the male equivalent of little Eve, and you've had more experience with her behavior than I have."

"Really, Eve?" she said. "She behaves just like you." But she smiled and held out her hand for Dylan.

He frowned at me and said, "She wouldn't let me see the alligator and her babies."

"Later. Remember?" I said.

Dylan nodded, then yawned. "I'm kinda tired now anyway." Without further fuss he let Madeleine strap him into the seat.

I signaled one of the EMTs toward the convertible. He leaned in for a moment, then straightened up.

"I was told someone was shot here. What's going on?" he said. Another EMT, a woman, stood behind him.

"We've got two patients. According to her husband, she stopped breathing. The gunshot victim is out there." I pointed toward Mickey and Angus.

The female EMT ran toward them.

Madeleine attended to the three children while I explained as much as I knew about Darcie to the EMT at the car.

"She's breathing now, and her vitals seem normal, but we'll transport her," he said.

"Talk to her husband. He can tell you more about what happened to her."

Frida's car with its blue light flashing and siren blaring pulled up near the ambulance. She jumped out and ran over to me.

"There's an EMT with Angus now," I said.

Frida nodded and strode out to where the EMT was examining Angus. I followed.

"I called in another ambulance when I saw we had two patients. We need more medical personnel to carry and transport them," she said to Frida. "Looks like a shotgun wound. He's lucky it came from a distance away. Back that way, I think." The EMT pointed to an area beyond where the cars and ambulance were parked.

"Anyone hunting here today?" asked Frida.

I nodded and told her about the quail hunting group. "But they're beyond the trees and that field. And there's a ridge between them and us."

"How is he?" asked Frida, bending down near Angus.

"Shot in the shoulder. Not too much bleeding. All the shot missed the artery," said the EMT. "He should be fine."

Angus groaned. "It's nothing," he said. "Let me up. I can walk."

"You'll make things worse," said Frida. "Here's the other ambulance."

"Hey, I know I'm a little overweight," said Angus, "but you don't need two wagons to transport me."

Well, he still had his sense of humor. That was good sign. I told him about Darcie and assured him she was being taken care of.

"You take her to the hospital first," said Angus.

Frida put a hand on his unwounded shoulder. "You let the medical folks do their jobs. Yours is to follow their instructions and to get that shoulder looked after. They'll take care of your daughter-in-law."

Frida stood up and scanned the area.

"Gator gone?" she asked me.

"I don't know, and I'm not going to find out. I think the EMT was right. I heard the sound of the shot come from back there beyond the cars."

"Locating a sound out here can be deceptive, but let's go with that theory for now."

She and I walked back toward the cars, then circled and struck out into the brush and trees behind them.

We saw the main road not far from where we had lunched.

"You were lucky you weren't that far off the road, or the ambulances would have had trouble navigating this rutted drive. I'm surprised your convertible made it without bottoming out."

"I'm a good driver. I avoided the potholes." I shielded my eyes from the sun and looked toward the road. "The road is so close. Mickey could have continued on to the road and driven Darcie into the hospital."

"Folks unfamiliar with this place get confused. Everything looks the same here to city people," Frida said.

"I suppose. And he was in a panic if he thought she'd stopped breathing. He wasn't thinking clearly. When he got back to us, he was even more frantic, torn between trying to help his wife and seeing to his father. I had a similar dilemma wondering whether I should go after Dylan or see what was happening with Angus."

Frida paused at the foot of a palm. "There are a number of issues with this shooting. First, I'm wondering if it was an accident or intentional. Then there's the matter of where I look for the shooter. Of course, I'll have to question that company of quail hunters that David and Sammy took out today. It could also have been someone else, someone trespassing on the property."

I looked around, alerted to the possibility that the shooter might still be out there. If the shooting was intentional, the person responsible might be looking for another target.

Frida picked up on my concerns. "I don't think anyone is going to stick around after they made their shot."

"Unless, they shot the wrong person."

CHAPTER 11

—

$\mathbf{F}$RIDA CONTINUED TO explore the area visually. "My crime scene people should be here shortly. Maybe a thorough search here might turn up something."

"I guess Angus's business associates and his background look a lot more interesting today than they did a while back." I knew I shouldn't have said it. I knew I was doing a I-told-you-so to Frida, but my impulse control was turned off, as usual.

Frida gave me a dark look.

"I hear you, Eve. Don't rub it in. We may have missed something with the brake tampering despite Angus's fingerprints on those tools."

"It's certain he didn't shoot himself today. I mean assuming he was the target."

"I don't know if I have an accidental shooting or not. Is all of this a crime scene?" She swept her hand toward the reserve.

We stood together looking into the distance and said nothing for a few minutes. The sound of the ambulances leaving and the arrival of several crime scene vehicles drew our attention back to the immediate moment.

"I'd better get moving. I'm closing the reserve for further hunting until I know what happened here today. Do you think David and Sammy are back with the hunters?" she asked.

"Probably."

"That's where I need to begin, Maybe the group is still at the reserve office. Otherwise David can supply me with a list of names. I need to know everyone who was on the property today."

She headed back the way we came. I followed, not envying her the job ahead.

Madeleine stood by her vehicle waiting for me. All the children seemed to have settled into their seats and were quiet now.

"How did you manage to get them settled down?" I asked.

"I told all of them you would make them a cake to go with their ice cream."

Bake? Me? Madeleine knew me better than that. I hid my disbelief. Today I'd discovered lying to children had its place in the parenting process. They were quiet, none of them showed any upset, and I could easily buy a cake. There were supermarkets close by.

"Mickey went with the ambulance transporting his wife," Madeleine said. "I'll take the kids home. Will I see you back at the house? I can dig up a late afternoon drink."

It sounded temping. "I'll be right behind you." I needed to talk with Frida.

"I'd like to cordon off the scene out there, but I don't like the idea of running into a protective gator. I think I'll call the gator guy to come out here and see what he can do about mama and the kiddies."

I knew the gator guy better than I wanted to. He had removed a pesky alligator from our shop premises when we were renovating the place. He'd wrangled me into holding the rope with the gator on its other end. I didn't want to be a volunteer for the job today.

"I gotta run," I told Frida.

She gave me a tiny smile. "Not interested in corralling a reptile today?"

"Ah, no. But I am wondering about that search warrant you planned to get for the house at the game reserve."

Frida nervously rubbed her nose. At first, I thought she wasn't going to answer me.

"We're having difficulty convincing a judge we have reason enough to justify the warrant. Maybe if Darcie had died in that accident…I know, I know. That's an awful thing to say, but my boss thinks I'm wasting too much time on this case. He wants me to present the evidence we have to the DA, and if it's not enough to go to trial, we leave it for now…" Her voice trailed off.

"And there's more?"

"In general, it appears to him that I spend too much time and too many resources on cases that involve…"

"Yes?"

"That involve you and your friends."

I kicked the nearest palm tree in anger. "Ouch. Will he see this shooting in that light, too?"

"It could be accidental, you know. I haven't talked yet to David and his clients."

"You know it's not an accidental shooting. Angus was the target of the tampered with brakes, and now he's been shot."

"Here's my crime scene team now. I've got to get them working before we know any more. Then I need to contact David. We can talk later, Eve." She turned abruptly and walked over to the CSI van.

She wasn't interested in any more chit chat with me. I had become her main source of aggravation.

I stopped at the house to check on Madeleine. The drink she promised sounded inviting, but it would have to wait.

"You're up to your curly mop in kids here. I'm at your disposal. I can stay with the twins while you take Dylan to the hospital to visit his mother and grandfather or…" I said.

"I do want to see Angus, and Dylan has been crying for his mother and his grandfather, but it's important I talk with David. I've been trying to call him, but there's no answer. I'm worried."

"Don't be. Frida left when I did. I'll bet she's found him in the field or at the office, and he's busy talking with her."

"Oh, right." Madeleine let out the words in one sigh of relief.

I heard someone pull up outside. "Here he is now. Frida's right behind him. Look, I'll take Dylan to the hospital while you talk with David and Frida. You can follow when you've sorted things out here." I would have preferred to hear what David had to say about his clients, but Madeleine's needs came first as did Dylan's.

I told Dylan I would take him to see his mother and grandfather. His crying ceased for a moment.

"Wait," he said, running into the bedroom he and his grandfather shared.

"This will make him feel better," said Dylan, carrying a backpack he liked to carry. He was still in tears, but he had quieted as he hugged the backpack to him.

"A present for your grandfather?" I asked

He nodded. "I have something for Mom, too." He zipped open the pack and extracted a lollipop which looked as if it had been partially eaten, then rewrapped to be saved for later.

"It's cherry. Her favorite flavor."

"Nice," I said, strapping him into the car.

Whatever he had for his grandfather remained in the pack.

"We need to hurry," he said gravely. "Can you drive fast?"

Can I? "Only if you won't tell on me."

That got a snuffle and a small smile from him.

At the hospital I slid into a parking place with a squeal of my tires. I was showing off, and Dylan seemed to approve of the maneuver. I opened the car door for him and held out my hand.

"Thanks for the ride," he said, in a polite almost adult manner. "You don't need to come in with me or wait for me. I can do this myself." He ignored my hand and marched to the emergency entrance and into the building.

I followed. "I'm here in case you don't have cab fare home."

The emergency room staff assured us that both Angus and Darcie had been admitted, and we could see them soon. We went to see Darcie first. She was being kept overnight for observation. The doctor said she was slightly dehydrated and overtired.

"I don't know what got into Mickey. I told him I was tired, but he overreacted. I never stopped breathing. He was being silly." Darcie was sitting up in bed, Dylan by her side. She held the cherry lollipop in one hand and caressed Dylan's red curls with the other. "How is Dad?"

"I haven't been in to see him yet. They've assigned him a room and are getting him settled. I'll take Dylan there in a few minutes."

Mickey appeared in the doorway. "Honey, honey, honey. Are you going to be okay?"

She nodded and held the lollipop hand out to grab his. He leaned over to give her a kiss and then patted his son on the shoulder.

"You scared me. You lost consciousness," Mickey said.

"I fell asleep because I was so tired. That's all. I think I took too many of those pills I was prescribed to help me sleep. I'm still a little groggy."

Mickey turned toward me and shook his head. "How many did you take?" he asked. "I think we'd better monitor your intake closer. They can be habit forming, you know."

Darcie's eyes fluttered in fatigue, then closed, and she dropped the lollipop on the bed.

"I think we should let her get some rest." I held my hand out to Dylan who gave him mom a quick kiss, retrieved the candy and jumped down from the bed. He still held the backpack tight against his chest.

"Let's go see Grampie," said Mickey. He grabbed Dylan and swung him with two hands away from his mother's side and toward the door. Set back down on his feet, Dylan let go and grabbed my hand.

"I want to hold Auntie Eve's hand. She's like a race car driver."

Mickey raised one eyebrow at me in a questioning look.

I smiled. "It's my car. I put the top down. It feels faster that way."

ANGUS' ARM AND shoulder were wrapped in bandages and his usually florid face was pale, but the smile came quickly to his lips when he saw his grandson. Dylan ran to his bedside, but Mickey prevented him from jumping onto the bed.

"Grampie's a little sore right now, so you can't hug him, or you'll hurt him."

Dylan patted the back of his grandfather's hand lightly and blew him a kiss. He placed the backpack on the end of the bed.

"I've got something for you" He unzipped his backpack, and I wondered what flavor candy he would extract from it for his grandfather, but instead he took out a small picture and held it up for his grandfather to see. "I know you like it so much because you brought it with you in your luggage. We could hang it up here, and it would help you get better."

Tears welled up in Angus' eyes. "I like it so much because you made it for me. We'll put it over there so it's the first thing I see when I wake up."

Dylan handed the picture to me.

"It's a kitty cat, right?" I said, examining the picture.

Dylan nodded.

I took the picture and set it on the shelf across the room. "How's that?"

Well, it was one crooked cat, but if looked at through the eyes of a loving grandfather, it had to be the most beautiful kitty in the world.

"Mr. MacAngus," said a voice from the doorway. A tall, slender woman entered the room and introduced herself as Dr. Blake. "I took shot out of that shoulder. You're lucky it didn't hit the artery. You'll be sore, but I'll release you in a couple days."

"You're sure he's okay?" asked Mickey.

"He'll recover and have full use of his arm," Dr. Blake assured him.

"Maybe we should consider going home to Scotland as soon as you can travel," said Mickey.

"No!" said Angus. "I came here for a vacation to visit friends and relatives. I'm not leaving."

I certainly wasn't going to be the one to tell him that choice might not be his if the case against him for tampering with the brakes was brought to trial.

As if I had conjured up bad news with my thoughts, Frida entered the room. No one, not even me, seemed pleased to see her.

"I need to talk with the patient," said Frida, showing her badge.

"Not tonight, you don't," said Dr. Blake. "This can wait until tomorrow. Everybody out of here. Mr. MacAngus needs rest." She and Frida locked eyes for a moment, then Frida spun on her heel and left the room. I waved a goodbye to Angus, told Mickey I'd give him and his son a ride back to the ranch and ran after Frida.

"Wait!" I called to her. She stopped and turned.

"I've got work to do, Eve."

"I'll only take a minute of your time. You talked with David? Does he think it could have been a stray shot from his quail hunting group?'

Frida gave a deep sigh. "I might as well brief you because David and Sammy will tell you anyway. They think not. By the time I spoke with them, the clients had left, but I got a list of their names. I'll talk with each of them tomorrow."

Frida sounded tired, and I didn't blame her if she wanted to keep her comments to me brief. She was being pressured by her boss to tie up loose ends on the brake tampering case and bring it to trial, she was trying to track down Bethany, and now she had this shooting. Angus MacAngus and his family were involved in two of the cases, maybe even that of Bethany's disappearance. Now Frida had to make sense of them as well as find the guilty parties. Maybe I should offer to help.

"You know I've been hired by the MacAngus family…"

"And you know what I'm about to say: Do your job but stay out of the police investigation."

"Of course, I will," I said, putting as much indignation in my voice as I could muster given that I had every intention of meddling as usual. "Yet you've got to admit they may overlap. I've got someone looking into Angus' business interests in Scotland. I'd be willing to share what I find."

She hesitated before saying, "No, I will not share the list of David's clients in return."

"Did I ask for that? But it would mean I wouldn't have to bother David asking for it. Duplication, you know, and so aggravating for him when he already has so much on his mind."

"I don't know why I'm saying this, but I must be really tired. I'll email you the list as soon as I get back to my office."

"You're a pal," I said.

"Right." She flapped her hand dismissively and walked off.

I sent Nappi a text telling him we needed to meet as soon as possible and giving him a heads up on the list of David's clients. I told him I'd fill him in when we got together.

My cell rang. It was Nappi. Such a prompt fella.

"Can you manage an early dinner tonight at the Biscuit? I've got a hankering for ribs and slaw."

"What?" I asked.

"Dinner?" he asked again.

My mouth watered at the thought of a juicy rack of ribs.

"You're on."

Mickey and Dylan lingered just out of earshot, but when Frida left, Mickey approached me.

"I hope you now understand that the story my father and I told you about his business associates was true. They tried to shoot him! What are you going to do about it? Your detective friend still doesn't seem to be convinced." He spat out the words, the anger in his voice barely contained.

I held up my phone. "I'm on it." I looked at Dylan's face which was white with fear. "You're scaring your son."

"Is someone trying to hurt Grampie?" Dylan stammered.

"Don't worry, Dylan. He'll be safe here. The police and I will make sure he stays safe."

Could we do that? I now was certain someone was serious about doing him harm. Was the culprit simply trying to scare him and deliberately missed the shot, or was it an accidental miss? Either way they might try again.

"What do you think these business associates want?" I asked.

"For my father to get out of the company and for me to quietly resign my position and keep my mouth shut."

"And if they're successful and kill him?"

"Then I inherit the company. I'd sell it rather than continue to work with those people."

Dylan continued to look up at his father throughout the conversation. Although he couldn't have understood what we were discussing, the boy heard the seriousness in our voices. He tugged at his father's hand.

"I want Mommy."

Mickey ignored the tug and stared down the hallway.

I knelt beside Dylan and took his free hand in mine. "Mommy is asleep now, and I know she wants you to get some sleep too. How about we go back to Aunt Madeleine's, and we can have cocoa and cookies there. Then you can take a quick nap?"

He swiped at a tear that had escaped and run down his cheek. "'Kay."

"It'll be fine, son," Mickey said, but his voice was uncertain.

"I HAVE TO work the shop tomorrow afternoon, but I'll visit Darcie and Angus before I go in," said Madeleine. We had gotten Dylan off for a nap after his promised treat.

"Don't worry about working tomorrow. Grandy and I can share the day at the store. Considering how much in upheaval everything was in around here, don't come into the shop this week. Grandy and I will cover the hours."

David looked relieved. I couldn't tell what Madeleine was feeling. Her face registered nothing but lines of fatigue.

"I talked with Frida at the hospital, and she said you couldn't see how any of your quail hunters today could have been responsible for a shot wandering off in our direction," I said to David.

He nodded. "There is something I didn't share with her because I only discovered it after she left. I was hoping you'd show up, Eve, so I could run it past you."

I nodded, eager to hear what he had to say.

"After I checked my notes at the office and talked with Frida, I went back in there to lock up. I store several guns we rarely use in a gun safe there. The safe was locked, but I decided to check it to be sure the guns were still there. A shotgun was missing."

"Who has a key?"

"Only me," David said.

"Where do you keep it?"

"On the keyboard inside the kitchen door."

"So anyone could have taken it to get into the safe?"

"The only people who have been in the house are family," said Madeleine.

"How long has it been missing from the safe?" I asked.

David shrugged. "As I said, we never use those guns, so I don't have any reason to go into the safe. I knew I had left it locked. That's why I didn't say anything to Frida. Days. Weeks."

"Or right before Bethany left here," I said.

"You don't think someone threatened her with the gun and made her come with them? An abduction?" asked Madeleine.

Before I could prevent myself from speaking, I said, "Actually, I was thinking maybe Bethany took it with her when she left." I knew it was too late to take back the words. David and Madeleine shot angry looks at me.

"I'd better leave now. I have a dinner engagement tonight, and I need to hit the shower. I'll show myself out." I gave them a weak apologetic smile and said goodbye. but they didn't reply. I heard the door slam behind me. Nice going, Eve, I said to myself. This family is suffering multiple losses, and you point the finger at one of the people gone and blame her? I kicked the tire of my car in frustration. There was no satisfaction in that. I did, however, bruise my toe, hardly much of a punishment for my thoughtlessness. And it did not terminate my thoughts about Bethany's possible involvement in the missing shotgun. Could she have taken it and shot Angus? Why would she do that? I was relieved I hadn't shared that with Madeleine and David. It was the kind of speculation I was certain Frida had already entertained and, if not, I could always share it with her.

CHAPTER 12

I STOPPED AT the consignment shop to see how the day's sales had gone as well as to catch Grandy up on what had happened at the ranch.

"I hope Darcie and Angus continue to improve. Now Frida has to believe Angus and Mickey's story about threats from their business associates. Whether her boss likes it or not, the police will have to look into the business."

"I've got a head start there. I put my consultant to work on it, and we're meeting tonight at the Biscuit for ribs."

Grandy knew what I meant by "consultant." "Good old Nappi to the rescue. He has contacts all over the world, it seems."

"This time it appears he decided to work the scene in person. I think he flew in from Scotland today."

Grandy sighed and got a faraway look in her eyes. "All this intrigue going on around me, and I sit here selling used clothes and furnishings. I miss the action."

"Sorry, Grandy. I brought Shelley in on one case. I don't think Crusty would like another amateur PI working the MacAngus shooting. In fact, I haven't had a chance to call him and tell him about Angus getting shot."

Before I could extract my phone from my purse, Grandy had hers up to her ear.

"Don't you dare call Crusty. That's my job."

She shot me a puckish look. "Hi, Max. Do you think you can manage dinner for yourself tonight? Something came up." She nodded once and disconnected, raising both eyebrows in a try-and-stop-me look. "I haven't seen Nappi for a while, and if the two of you think I shouldn't hear your business, I'll go to the ladies' room and primp for a while."

"I was hoping you'd take care of Netty while I met Nappi."

"You've got a whole passel of Miccosukee relatives for that and a Grandy who's dying for want of some snooping, even if it's only vicarious snooping."

How could I deny her a dinner out with her favorite mafia boss? "Remember: you are not part of this investigation." I warned, shaking my finger at her, a gesture that did nothing to dim the spark of enthusiasm in her blue eyes.

I called Crusty to let him know about the shooting on the game reserve and informed him I was meeting with Nappi who had returned from Scotland with information about the MacAngus business dealings there.

"Do you want me there tonight?" he asked me, "or can you handle this on your own?"

"You stay put. I'll be fine," I assured him, not letting him know Grandy would be joining me at dinner.

Before I ended the conversation, Crusty asked me if I'd heard from Shelley yet.

"She should be checking with me after she leaves work today. Don't worry about her. She'll do a great job."

"She'd better. I took her on because you convinced me she was up to this. If something happens to blow this case, I'm holding you responsible."

I wasn't the least concerned about Crusty's threat. He liked to bark a lot, especially at me. "It wasn't all my doing that she's working this case. Ms. Abbot didn't want me to do the undercover work," I reminded him.

He muttered something under his breath about my unusual hairdo and attire.

"Yeah, I know. If I looked average, I could have gone undercover instead of Shelley, but if I looked and acted like every other woman around here, you wouldn't have hired me."

I heard more muttering and grumping from him, followed by an admonition that I might go to the gun range and work on my aim, and then he ended the call.

"Problems?" asked Grandy.

"No, just the usual grousing from Crusty."

Grandy and I handled a few last-minute sales, then closed for the night and headed off in our separate cars to a feast of ribs, fries and slaw. I salivated at the thought. I don't know which had me hungrier, the ribs or what Nappi might have to tell me.

Nappi's black SUV was already in the parking lot when we pulled in, and he had arranged a table in the far corner of the dining room. Few diners had yet arrived. Most of the patrons had taken seats in the bar area, having stopped for a cold one on their way home from work.

"I took the liberty of ordering for us," said Nappi, who expressed his delight that Grandy was joining us. He stood and reached out for her hand, kissing her fingertips in his usually suave greeting. Grandy blushed and giggled. He pulled our chairs for each of us, then leaned over and gave me a peck on the cheek. "You didn't think I'd forget you, did you, Eve?"

He signaled to the waitress, who nodded and brought me a Scotch, Grandy a white wine and a Crown and seven for himself. Our dinners soon followed. We engaged in little conversation while we ate, then we sat back in our chairs and sighed in unison our satisfaction with the meal. As usual, I seemed to be covered in sauce up to my elbows, and Grandy, despite the pile of used napkins next to her plate, looked little better. We both excused ourselves to use the ladies' room. Nappi's hands and face looked as if he hadn't eaten anything. How did that man remain so clean after indulging in ribs? I was certain, despite my using several napkins, that my face remained covered in sauce. On my way to the restroom, I stuck out my tongue and licked my lips. Yup. The reflection of my face in the bathroom mirror confirmed it. Saucy.

There was only one wash bowl. Grandy let me go first. "You clean up, and I'll be out soon. You and Nappi can have your talk while I wash."

When I returned to the table, Nappi had ordered coffee and cheesecake for all of us.

"Really. I couldn't eat another bite."

Nappi raised an eyebrow in skepticism.

"Well, maybe a little bite, and I'll take the rest home with me." I ate the whole thing and half of Grandy's.

"Should we wait until Grandy returns before we talk about the MacAngus situation?" Nappi asked, looking toward the ladies' room.

"I told her I couldn't get her involved in the case, and she promised me she would not interfere. She's primping and will be out as soon as she's finished making herself as gorgeous as she was when she came in."

"I'm sure that's what she told you, but she'll be disappointed if she's left out."

"No, really. She's fine. She'll probably find someone in the bar to chat with," I assured him.

He nodded toward the restroom. Peeking around the corner, Grandy tried to remain out of sight, but there was no mistaking that mop of short curly white hair and those twinkling eyes.

Why did I bother? She'd wheedle the specifics of the conversation out of me anyway. I signaled to her, and she walked over to the table. "You might as well hear this. You look absurd standing around the door to the restroom that way."

"No, I don't. Maybe I'm simply waiting for a stall to open up."

"You're waiting outside the gents' room," I pointed out.

"What's up, Nappi?" she asked. "And if this is a long tale, I'll need another glass of wine."

Nappi leaned forward in his chair. "I traveled to Scotland and posed as an American businessman looking for a business to invest money in. As they told you, Angus' company and the one Mickey work for have merged. The executives I spoke with seemed eager to do business with Americans. I told them I wasn't yet willing to move on an offer, that I was looking at other companies. That didn't stop them from opening their books to me. Here's what I found odd. As nearly as I can tell, and I'm pretty good at books, there was no money missing, no improprieties in expenditures or in business practices. The company seemed sound to me, although I didn't get a chance to see the actual merchandise, so they could look good on paper and the inventory that goes in and out could be suspect. I'm having one of my associates peek into their warehouses, and another is asking questions among the employees. I haven't heard back from the person investigating the warehouses, but employees had some interesting things to say about the MacAnguses."

"Like what?" I asked.

"It seems that Angus can't give up the reins of the company. He attends board meetings but does more than that. I was told he's always in one of the vice-president's offices suggesting how they run the business. He's—according to my sources—intrusive."

"How intrusive is he?"

"Most of the executives try to avoid him aside from when the board has a meeting. If they could keep him off the premises, they would."

"Would they do something physical to remove him?"

"I think they'd like to. Mickey wasn't supposed to have any vacation time coming to him, but the CEO called him into his office and, according my sources, recommended he take some time off and accompany his father to the States. I gather the CEO hoped Mickey could talk his father into keeping his nose out of the business."

"Did Mickey agree to talk with him?"

Nappi shook his head. "Mickey supposedly told the CEO to handle his own problems."

"That's really not what I meant by doing something physical to get rid of him. Do you think the company would go so far as to kill Angus to get him out of their hair? That sounds absurd, doesn't it?"

Nappi gave me a thoughtful look. "It's been known to happen."

I was about to say, "well, yes, in your line of work," but I thought better of it.

"I know what you're thinking, Eve. You expect the Scots to be more gentlemanly in their business dealings than us Americans. You may be right. You might find this interesting. Some of the executives in the firm, friends of Mickey's, are here in the States on a kind of working vacation."

"Here? As in rural Florida?"

"I don't know what their itinerary was once in the States. If I can locate them, it would be good to have a conversation."

"What did your sources tell you about Mickey?" I asked.

"I got the sense Mickey was a bit of a disappointment, not the brilliant man his father was or is, for that matter."

"Did you get the sense that Mickey would make up lies about the company? Do you think he knows the company is somewhat disappointed in him? He's been with them for a number of years, so I gather he does his job, but maybe not as competently as his father might have."

"A good guess, but I'm not certain if that's true. I apologize for not being able to ferret out more. It's a funny thing, a paradox almost—a feeling the company was exactly what Angus thought it was, open, honest, ethical. I'm not picking up anything odd, yet Mickey seems to have a quite different take on the business, and he's been with them for years." Angus tapped his spoon against his cup.

I sat back in my chair. I can't say I wasn't disappointed in what he found, but I knew if he finally worked through what was bothering him, I'd be the first he'd tell.

"I assume you're concerned about the shooting at the ranch. Angus is fine and will recover?" he asked.

I nodded. "But the incident confirms what Mickey and Angus told me. Paired with the information that the brakes were tampered with causing the accident to Angus' rental, the shooting strongly suggests someone is after Angus. Even Frida is convinced Angus' life is in jeopardy."

"There's no idea who was responsible?"

"Frida will be interviewing the clients who were at the ranch today. I managed to get a list of their names." I handed it to Nappi.

He perused the list, then said, "This is interesting."

"What is?"

"I recognize two of the names on the list. They're the executives I mentioned, here in the States on a company project."

"A project as in carrying out some threats? Or is this simply a coincidence that they appear at the hunting ranch owned by Angus' niece and her husband? I guess Mickey could have told them about the ranch and suggested they visit."

"Why wouldn't they get in touch with Angus to let him know they were coming?"

"I don't believe in coincidence," I said.

"Either do I," said Frida, taking the empty chair at our table. "I need to have a little chat with Angus when he's better. For now, I'm off duty, and I hear the Karaoke getting started in the bar. If you order me a beer, Eve and I will get up and do a rendition of some country song. Let's go see what the songbook has to offer. How about it, Eve?"

How interesting, I thought, so I followed Frida into the bar area. She was in a good mood. In fact, a great mood.

"What's with you?" I asked.

"I got a break in the MacAngus case, and I'll bet for once I know more than you do about it. Want to trade info?"

I looked over my shoulder at Nappi and winked. He raised his glass to me in a salute.

Frida and I launched into a country classic by Patsy Cline and were booed off the stage midway through it.

"Wow, we must have been really bad. Usually, the Karaoke crowd is kinder than that," Frida said, hurrying back to our table.

"Maybe we need to drink more before we try this again." I suggested. "Can we talk about the case in front of Grandy and Nappi?"

"Sure." Frida plopped herself down in the empty chair and grabbed her beer, taking a long sip and uttering a deep sigh of satisfaction. "You want to go first?"

"No, you."

"The hunters at the ranch today?" Frida said.

Nappi and I smiled at her.

"Two of them are with Angus' company, the one Mickey works for. I talked with them by phone late this afternoon. They're staying in West Palm. They had some interesting information for me."

Oh, toad's breath! She knew what I knew and a lot more.

I waited.

"Mickey was the one who alerted them to David's hunting ranch and told him it might be a good place to hunt quail. They tried to call him on his cell to see if he was around today before they came out to the ranch, but they couldn't make contact."

"Do you think one of them…?"

"Wait. Wait. There's more. In the chat we had on the phone, they said when they couldn't get in touch with him they called the number they had for his mother in Naples, thinking they might get in touch that way."

"And?" I was fairly vibrating with impatience, something I have little of most days, but when there are criminals to track down and clues to investigate, I'm like a firecracker about to go off.

Frida smiled and took another sip of her beer.

"You're killing me, here, lady. Get on with it."

"No answer at her place, but they left a message letting her know they'd be at the ranch."

"And she told who?"

Frida shrugged. "I don't know because I haven't talked with her yet."

"It appears you have a lot of leads that you need to follow up."

She nodded. "That's more than I usually have. I'm going to finish this beer, go home and get a good night's sleep and get started early in the morning. Before I leave, Eve. What have you got?"

My cell rang. I held up my finger to let her know I'd be right back and left the noisy restaurant so I could hear. The caller ID said the call was from Madeleine. I listened to what she had to say, then told her I would be on my way to her place in a few minutes. "I'm at the Biscuit and need to say goodnight to Nappi and Frida. It's okay if I bring Grandy along, isn't it?"

"Sure. You can even bring Nappi, but I think Frida might be one too many right now. I think we've had our share of police authorities today."

"Grandy and I have to run," I said back at the table. "I'll get back to you soon, Nappi. I know you're anxious to get home to your bed, Frida, so I'll say goodnight."

"Wait a minute," Frida said, standing up and placing her hands on her hips. "You said you had some information. Is this your way of saying you don't have anything?"

"Yeah. I got nothing. I was bluffing." I helped Grandy up from her chair, and we headed out to the parking lot. Nappi followed us to my car while Frida got into her cruiser and pulled out of the lot.

"Who was the call from, if you don't mind my asking? You look like the proverbial cat who swallowed the canary," Nappi said.

"Madeleine told me that Mickey's mother is at the house."

"Isn't that something Frida should know?"

"She will. Tomorrow. After I chat with the woman. Want to come along? Madeleine said to invite you."

"Sure. I've got nothing to do tonight." Nappi waved and headed for his car.

"You're not dropping me off at home, are you?" asked Grandy.

"You wanted to be in on the action, didn't you? This is it." I dropped the top on the convertible, stepped on the accelerator, and we sped out of the parking lot. My headlights pierced the dark, deserted highway ahead, the stars hanging in a velvety black sky our only companions. I knew how Frida felt earlier: she had clues to follow up on, and she was elated at what her work that day had produced. I was glad I hadn't ruined her good mood by doing a one up on her, telling her Mrs. MacAngus was at the ranch. Tomorrow was soon enough for me to let her know I had talked with the woman before she got a shot at her. Well, maybe it wasn't about being generous and letting her get a good night's sleep. Maybe I was feeling a little haughty about what I was sure would crack this case.

"Nice night," Grandy said, a big smile on her face.

"Close your mouth or you'll get bugs in your teeth," I warned her.

She smiled wider.

Behind me I could see the headlights of Nappi's car. Ahead was Mickey's mother and some answers to who might be after Angus.

I RECOGNIZED THE woman sitting on the couch as the one who had come to the consignment shop several days before, furious that someone hadn't told her about the accident with Angus' rental. She held a drink in her hand and seemed comfortable enough that I wondered if she intended to stay the night. She certainly sounded drunk enough to need a bed more than a drive in her car.

"I was here earlier today, and no one was around. This seems like a pretty sloppy way to run a business," she remarked, holding her glass out to Madeleine. "Not bad bourbon."

"Uh, Mrs. MacAngus, I don't think you should have another drink. It's a long drive to Naples from here, the roads are poorly lit, and you never can tell when some animal might dash out in front of you," Madeleine said.

"I'll have to stay for the night. If you had been here earlier, I could have talked with Mickey and Angus then. Instead I had to drive all the way to the hospital in town to see them and then back here to find out what happened. Another accident."

"I don't think anyone believes it was an accident, certainly not the authorities," I told her, taking a seat across from her. Grandy joined me.

"You're Madeleine's partner in the consignment business. I remember seeing you when I was in the shop."

"You mean the day you said you were heading out here, but never showed up?"

"Well, uh, see…"

"The day you told Madeleine you didn't need directions to the ranch because you had alrcady been here?" Grandy asked her.

"And, you," she said directing her remarks to Grandy, "were also in the shop. Should I know you or are you just some clerk there?"

"Could you have been sneaking around here the day your ex-husband and family arrived?" I added.

"I don't have to answer your questions," she said, set her glass down on the coffee table and got up. "I think I'll be going now."

"If you get into your car, I'll have to arrest you," said Frida, standing in the open doorway. "You're too impaired to drive."

Grandy let out a laugh. She liked Mrs. MacAngus no better than I did. "I'll bet she's always too impaired to drive," Grandy said under her breath to me.

"Sorry for barging in without knocking," Frida said to Madeleine.

"You are supposed to be in bed. Asleep. Resting so you can be fresh for the job tomorrow. You lied to me about going home," I said.

"Yeah, well, you lied to me about knowing nothing about the shooting."

We locked eyes for a moment, then turned our attention to Mrs. MacAngus.

"I think the biggest liar here might be you," I said.

Mrs. MacAngus fell back into the couch. Either the accusation or the booze had caught up with her.

CHAPTER 13

———

"**I** THINK SHE passed out," said Madeleine.

"How many drinks did she have?" Grandy asked.

Madeleine shook her head. "I didn't realize it before I offered her a drink, but I think she'd had a few before she got here."

"What's all the ruckus?" asked David who had entered the house by the kitchen door. For a moment his face lit up. "News about my daughter?" he asked Frida. She shook her head, and David's face darkened when he caught sight of Mrs. MacAngus on the couch. "I was at the ranch office, but I kept seeing cars turn off the road and down our lane. What's going on?" He tossed his hat onto the kitchen island. "And who's the woman lying on the couch?"

As tired as I knew Madeleine was—and she looked it with the dark circles under her eyes and her dull, unfocused gaze—David looked worse. The attacks upon Angus along with his daughter's disappearance were taking a toll on him. He looked as if he had dropped ten pounds in the past few days.

Madeleine explained about Mrs. MacAngus and asked David to carry her to their bedroom.

"I'm not putting a drunk woman up in my bedroom. This had been a long day, and we all need sleep." He looked as if he wanted to say more but didn't. Who would blame him if he exploded? His family was in a state of upheaval, his house filled to the rafters with visitors and now his business had experienced a shooting, something no hunting ranch wanted.

"There's no room anywhere else. Every bedroom is taken. Angus, Mickey and Darcie will be back tomorrow. Dylan is bunked with our kids," Madeleine said.

David scratched his head. "I can put her out in the ranch office. There's a set of bunkbeds in the back room there."

"Someone needs to keep an eye on her. She has important information about the clients who hunted here today," I said. "Frida and I need to talk to her, don't we, Frida?"

Frida looked a bit confused for a moment, then seemed to regain her composure. "Sure. Good idea, Eve. You can bunk in there with her, and we'll all meet back at the office early tomorrow morning."

"Can't you arrest her and put her in a cell overnight?" I asked.

"No. I cannot. She hasn't broken the law."

"She was going to drive her car intoxicated." I pointed out.

"I don't think she can even find her car right now. I'm off to bed." Frida turned and left. Before she could close the outside door, Nappi entered.

"I apologize for being late. I got behind a slow-moving truck and couldn't pass. Did I miss all the fun?"

"You're just in time. You can help Eve and me carry Mrs. MacAngus here to the office," David said.

"Your new secretary?" joked Nappi.

Everyone gave him a dirty look.

"Hey. Aren't all of you forgetting something? I've got a family to think about. I can't stay here and babysit a drunk and especially one I don't particularly like," I said.

"Well, I guess we could take her home with us," Grandy said.

"You like her less than I do," I replied.

"I'll explain everything to Sammy if you don't want to tell him you're babysitting," Grandy offered.

"No, it's…" I began.

"Okay then, Eve. You and David should be able to carry Mrs. MacAngus between the two of you. Nappi can give me a ride home." Grandy grabbed his arm, and the two of them headed out the door. "Don't worry, Eve. I'll fill Nappi in on what happened here. But don't forget to call Sammy."

David and I settled Mrs. MacAngus on the bottom bunk in the ranch office's bedroom, turning her on her side in case she was sick during the night.

When David left, I called Sammy. Lionel answered the land line at Grandfather Egret's place. He was the last person I wanted to inform that I wouldn't be home tonight, so I got out my message to Sammy as quickly as I could and then ended the call. I'm such a coward when it comes to confronting someone when I know what I'm doing is exactly what I shouldn't be doing.

I climbed into the top bunk and despite the thoughts racing around in my mind and my bunkmate's snoring, I fell asleep immediately. I was drifting off into a dream about Sammy and me at our favorite hideaway in the swamps, when my cell awakened me. Caller ID told me it was Sammy. My watch said it was after two in the morning. Something was wrong.

"What?" I asked, the possibilities of what might have happened to the boys, Netty, Grandfather or even Lionel making my hand shake as I held the phone.

"What?" yelled Mrs. MacAngus from the lower bunk.

"Shut up!" I shouted. "Not you, Sammy."

I heard her give a snort then roll over and continue her snoring.

"There's been some trouble here tonight. I don't want to explain everything on the phone, but is there any chance you can find someone to spell you on your babysitting duties? I think we need you at home. Now."

Sammy didn't need to say anything more. If they needed me, that's where I belonged. Mrs. MacAngus' breathing was regular and deep. She was out for the night and wasn't going anywhere. I rummaged in her purse and took her car keys, then left a note on David's desk in the office to tell him where I had gone.

As I dashed for my car, I stopped and gave a groan. I hadn't put up the top on the convertible last night and heavy dew had settled on the seats. They were leather, so I wiped the driver's seat off with my hand and tossed away a clump of Spanish moss that had fallen on the seat from the overhead trees. Yuck! Chiggers! There were always chiggers in the moss. I decided to leave the top down and let the night air dry everything and blow away what other debris might have fallen onto the seats and floor.

If it hadn't been for my concern about what was happening to my family, I might have enjoyed the warm, damp night air blowing through my hair. I scratched a place on my arm that itched and stomped on the accelerator, hoping there would be no cops out at this time of night to give me a speeding ticket. I needed to get to Sammy fast. I scratched another itch, this one on my leg.

All the lights were on in Grandfather Egret's house. The two youngest boys were up as was Netty who was running around the room, waving her favorite doll in the air and yelling, "Hide and seek."

Grandfather and Lionel sat on the rockers in front of the fireplace while Sammy leaned back on the kitchen counter, a cup in his hand. Aside from Netty who was enjoying herself, the adults had scowls on their faces, and the boys looked frightened.

"Where's Jason?" I asked.

"He's gone," said Sammy.

"And so is my canoe," Lionel said through tight lips. "He's been using my canoe without my permission, so I confronted him earlier tonight and told him he was being disrespectful of my me by taking my property."

I couldn't disagree with Lionel, but I knew there was something more going on, so I let him say what he wanted.

"I told him he needed to learn to show consideration for his elders, and I knew the only way he could do that was to spend time with the tribe."

I knew what was coming.

"I told him he would be spending the remainder of the summer at my cousin's ranch south of the lake. He didn't like that, so he ran off down the canal. We waited for him to return, but when he did not, I went looking for him. When I got back from my search, he was here."

"Did you talk with him then?" I asked Sammy.

Sammy shook his head. "Only Lionel spoke with him tonight. I woke up a half hour ago and heard someone leave the house. When I checked the boys, Jason had left again."

"I might have known." I put my hand to my forehead, then ran it through my spiky hair in a gesture of frustration. "I've about had it with you, Lionel. You forget that Sammy and I are his parents. We haven't yet discussed his summer."

"That's because you never have time for the family. You're either off to the coast to buy merchandise or sell it, or you're in the store or chasing down criminals."

I started across the room toward Lionel. I wasn't sure what I had in mind, but I curled my hands into fists. I knew words were not enough to express my anger. I wanted to physically hurt him. Something made me stop. Perhaps it was the look of disappointment Grandfather gave me, disappointment that I would resort to violence against his son or disappointment that I hadn't heard the truth in Lionel's words.

I stopped and let my hands relax. I gave Sammy a questioning look. "Sammy?"

Would he confirm what Lionel had said?

"You speak honestly, Father, but you forget that these children have two parents. As busy as Eve has been, I have two jobs and the house to finish. I've been as much to blame as Eve for not talking with Jason. We knew he took your canoe without permission. You told us that. We should have grounded him, but the decision to send him off is not yours. It's Eve's and mine. You don't take care of a problem by sending the child away."

I'd never heard Sammy stand up to his father that way. I think he usually deferred to his father's judgment because he grew up without Lionel in his life. I knew Sammy worried that any discord might chase him back out into the swamps. But now we were talking about Sammy's sons, and he felt a responsibility to be the best father to them he could, to be there for them, so they knew they always could count on him and come to him to discuss problems they might encounter. I felt as Sammy did. These boys were precious to us because they had come to us when their father was killed. We chose them to be our children, and we wanted them to know that. The responsibility we felt as parents to Netty was as strong, but the foundation of biological parents to their children was different, not less, not more, just different.

Lionel gave a grunt and got up from his chair. Was I hearing things? That sounded like a grunt of agreement.

Sammy and I gazed across the room at Grandfather who appeared to have fallen asleep.

His eyes opened. "Leave me out of this. They're your children as Sammy said." He paused for a moment, looking down at his feet searching for his pipe. Finding it, he tapped it against the stone hearth and gazed into the bowl as if the tarred depths there held the answers to our troubles. We waited for him to light the pipe and continue.

"But, I think there's more going on with Jason than reluctance to live the summer with his relatives and learn tribal ways."

It suddenly hit me. "You mean…?"

"Girl trouble," Grandfather said.

Sammy's mouth dropped open. "He's just a kid."

"He's a teenager. Why didn't I see this sooner?" I had noticed his behavior when he met David's daughter. Since then he hadn't been the same open, fun-loving boy we knew. I had an idea.

"Sammy, go fire up the airboat. We need to take a ride."

By the time we had gathered our supplies together, talked with the boys, failed to locate Lionel and readied the airboat for a trip to our favorite swamp shack, it was close to four in the morning. Soon the sun would be coming up. Sammy and I weren't off for a romantic adventure. We were focused on finding our son.

"Because we don't have the canoe, we can't get in as close to the shack. We'll have to do some swamp walking," Sammy said. "Have you got your hiking shoes on?"

I looked down at my ostrich skin, four-inch stiletto boots. Well, of course I was ready for a stroll in the swamp.

I held up my foot to show Sammy.

"I thought so. I brought some rubber boots. They're Jason's. They should fit you fine."

We beached the air boat at the entrance to the small canal that led to the swamp shack. The shack held memories both terrifying and wonderful for Sammy and me. The first time we did an overnight, we had been stranded there by some bad boys who were human traffickers. They thought we'd never find our way out, but we did. On another occasion Grandfather and I held off some Russian mobsters intent upon killing us and, more recently, Lionel and I took on one of Nappi's old enemies. Despite these bad times, Sammy and I had used the shack for our romantic get-togethers and brought our children here for overnights. We'd made it our "special" place and made the best memories the strongest ones.

We also had a guard for the place, a mama gator who liked to build her nests nearby. We left her alone, and she returned the favor. She only threatened the bad guys, never the family.

"Do you think mama gator will be around?" I asked Sammy.

It's been so long since we've visited the place."

Sammy laughed. "Let's make plenty of noise to let her know we're coming."

"That will warn anybody else who might be here, and they might run off," I said.

"You think I can't track anybody through these swamps? I'm half Miccosukee."

He needn't have reminded me. His Indian heritage was what made him so uniquely Sammy Egret and was one of the many reasons I loved him.

"If you could lead us out of the swamps the first time we came here, I have no doubt you inherited your tribe's sense of this wilderness."

We had trekked for about an hour. The sun peeked over the horizon. As we neared the shack, a man stepped out onto the path. He was hidden in the shadows of the cypress trees.

"You made enough noise that you scared them away," said Lionel.

"How did you get here? No canoe, no boat of any kind?" I said.

"I walked here. I checked out the shack. You might want to look at it. It's been trashed," Lionel said. He waved us on up the path until we came to the timbers that were once a swamp home for someone. Now they were the ruins of Sammy and my trysting place.

Empty peanut butter jars, bread wrappers, chip bags and soda cans littered the place.

"Jason's been here," said Lionel.

"Lionel, I know Jason did not do this. Why would he be eating all this food out here when he was also enjoying dinners at home? Do you think he had a tapeworm?"

Lionel said nothing.

"He was supplying food to someone out here," I said.

"A friend? Someone on the run?" asked Lionel.

"Someone who doesn't want to be found. Someone who's

into punishing others for personal unhappiness. A girl. And I think I know what girl."

"Let's call David and tell him we found his daughter," said Sammy.

"But we haven't," I pointed out. "Now we've lost both of them, David's daughter and our son."

"I'll find them," said Lionel. He started off into the brush.

Sammy reached out and grabbed his father's arm. "I can do it."

"Let your father do it, Sammy. He needs to have a talk with his grandson, don't you, Lionel?"

Lionel shot me a challenging look which then faded into one of understanding.

"I think Jason and I could use some time together. To talk, not argue," Lionel admitted.

"They've got a head start on you. They have the canoe," said Sammy.

"I have the swamp knowledge. I'll find them."

"Promise us you won't scare the stuffing out of Bethany. She's really a city girl and not used to the country," I said.

"I'll make nice. They're sure to be hungry, so I'll do a barbecue for them." He smiled his feral, wild man smile.

"He'll cook them up some swamp toad, won't he?" I asked Sammy.

Sammy shook his head. "Toads aren't edible. If the pythons hadn't taken all the rabbits, squirrels and other small mammals in these swamps, he could do small game, but the only thing left around here are…"

"Gators and snakes. Great. I hope he'll keep that to himself."

"Since we're here anyway…" Sammy said.

"We should clean up, right?"

"Oh, I was thinking of something requiring a bit more intimate contact."

"Sammy! We need to get back to talk to the boys, Grandfather, Netty and…"

I couldn't get the rest of my sentence out because Sammy pulled me to him and placed his full lips on mine.

"Don't worry, Eve. We can have what you white folks call "a quickie.""

That was foolish. Sammy and I had never had a "quickie" in our lives together, and I was certain we weren't going to start now. But we did have important family issues, so we got right to it, the clean-up, I mean. Then I used my cell to call everyone necessary, and then we did other friendlier things.

After an hour-long hike back to the airboat and the trip down the canal to Grandfather's house, we were starved and exhausted. Grandfather cooked eggs and toast for us, we sat out back and watched the boys and Netty play by the canal, and then, with Grandy minding the store and Grandfather watching the kids, we drove back to my house and fell onto my king-sized bed for much needed rest. Since it seemed a shame to waste the bed, we decided on another get together and, I assure you, this one was no "quickie" either.

I tuned off my cell before we began our, uh, activities.

Later, I said, "I think we could use a hot shower."

"Good," Sammy replied. "I was worried you'd want to take a cold shower." He gave me a funny look.

"Why are you looking at me that way?"

"I was trying to leer at you."

"Your leer looks like you're in pain."

We were giggling like school kids, when I heard someone in the house.

"There's someone here," I said to Sammy.

"Grandy or Max?" he asked.

"No. Grandy is at the shop, and Max is on the lake."

I slid the glass shower door back an inch and looked out. The steam made it impossible to see if anyone was there. Sammy was behind me, the soap-on-a-rope in his hand like a bola. He pushed me to one side and swung the soap at the figure looming in the mist.

CHAPTER 14

— ⚊ —

"JERRY!" I SAID, recognizing the person who lay sprawled on the bathroom floor. "I hope you haven't killed him." I grabbed a towel off the rack and wrapped it around me, then kneeled to check out my ex-husband. "Are you okay?" A better question would have been: what are you doing in my bathroom?

Sammy turned off the shower and toweled dry. "He's fine. No one is killed by a bar of soap flung at him." Sammy scowled at Jerry who reached up with his hand and massaged his head.

"Why aren't you answering your phone?" he asked. "I called and called, but it kept going to voice mail, so I decided to check on you."

"In my shower?"

He got slowly up and leaned against the wall, continuing to rub his head. "This was really important."

"Is it about Jason?" I asked hopefully.

"Huh? No. It's about Shelley."

Sammy had dressed in the bedroom and stood at the door, the scowl still on his face. "I think we should all go to the living room. Eve, you need to put on something more."

I looked down at myself and realized I had nothing on but a towel. I was sure the look on Jerry's face was a leer, a genuine one. I tugged the towel tighter around me.

"Go with Sammy, Jerry. We usually do our entertaining of guests in the living room." I slipped into my jeans and shirt and joined Sammy and Jerry.

"What about Shelley?" I perched on the end of the couch and toweled my hair dry.

"She told me what she's doing for you, and I think it's irresponsible for you to assign her this job. It could be dangerous. In fact, I know it's dangerous."

"Let's get something straight. First, I did not assign her the job. She volunteered for the detective agency. Second, she never should have told you about the job. And finally, and most important, Jerry, never, never enter someone's house simply because the door is unlocked, or it could be something more lethal than bar of soap that's thrown at you."

"Aw, Evie…" Jerry began, but Sammy, knowing how I hated the name "Evie" gripped his shoulder and shook his head at him. "That's not her name, is it?"

"Uh no. I meant Eve."

"You've got about two seconds to explain yourself before we both toss you out. Aside from poking your nose into what's not your business, is there something specific you're worried about?" Sammy's tone of voice said he wanted Jerry to get on with his story and then get out of the house.

With Jerry, one never could tell whether his sudden and unwelcome appearance was substantive or simply a whim on his part to bother people with one of his hare-brained ideas.

"She hasn't been herself lately, so…"

"How would you know that? Have you been seeing her? I mean, has she been seeing you, I mean, voluntarily on her part?" I asked.

Jerry pursed his lower lip in a hurt look. "Some people like me, Eve."

I rolled my eyes.

As we had arranged, Shelley called me every night after she got home from her assignment on the coast. We'd had brief conversations during which she said nothing was happening. Because she wasn't working the shop during the day, I hadn't seen her in person, and I'd heard nothing to worry me in her voice, but perhaps I should arrange to meet with her soon.

"We talked yesterday on the phone, and she sounded fine."

"That might have changed today." Jerry looked at the floor.

Oh, oh. "Why do you think that would have changed.? Did you do something to change it?

"I only wanted to help."

I gave a deep sigh. Whenever Jerry developed a plan to help someone, it was always a disaster. He could even manage to mess up plans developed by others. A simple trip to the bank to pick up money for a ransom payment had resulted in Jerry shooting himself. He's more of a klutz with guns than I am, but he always seems to find an excuse to carry one and shoot someone he never intended to while the bad guys are left unscathed. He's kind of like a protective Teddy bear. He means well, but nothing he attempts turns out quite as he planned it. That's Jerry.

"Tell me, and make it quick." I pointed to the chair. He fell into it and covered his face . "I think I made it worse."

I held my breath and waited. Maybe it wouldn't be so bad, I thought. Oh, it would be bad, I realized, but I had no idea how bad.

"I followed Shelley this morning when she left for the company. I hung around outside, then I got a great idea. Why sit here doing nothing, I thought. I should take action."

I put my head in my hands. It was never a good thing when Jerry got one of his "great ideas."

Jerry hesitated, then continued. "I posed as someone looking for a position. I went to HR to apply for a job. I was hoping someone would show me around the place, so I could get some idea of what she was in for. I used her name as a reference. I don't know anything about the aerospace industry, so I told the head of HR I was a salesman and I could sell anything, even space stuff."

"Did you use the term 'space stuff?'" I asked.

I could almost not hear his reply. He'd dropped his gaze to the floor. "Yeah. I guess so."

When he looked up, his blue eyes gazed into mine, trying for innocent. I must admit he's better at that look than I am, but knowing him for years taught me Jerry might not intend to do bad things, but he was anything but an innocent.

"You seemed to be in a hurry to locate me and tell me this, so get on with your story."

"Okay. I think the head of HR didn't believe I was serious about a job, so as he was ushering me out of his office, we ran into Shelley. Boy, was she surprised to see me."

"I'll bet," I said.

"I think he saw her face and then mine, too. He said, 'Here's the guy you sent to me for a job, Shelley, but I don't think we can use him.' Shelley looked confused and then said, 'I don't know what you mean.' I couldn't think of what to say to cover for her, so I beat feet out of there and came back here. But, see, I've been thinking for a while, so I thought I should talk to you. Tell me I didn't make it worse, Eve."

I ignored his question and ran to the bedroom where I'd left my cellphone on the night table. I had to know she was okay. Her cell went to voice mail. Oh, no, just like mine did because I'd turned it off this morning. If she had tried to connect with me, she couldn't have. I checked my voice mail messages, but there were none from her, only several from Frida.

Maybe everything was fine with Shelley. She was a smart gal. She might have made up a reasonable story for why Jerry, someone she denied knowing would have used her name. I crossed my fingers and left a message for her to get in touch with me.

"Time for Jerry to leave?" asked Sammy. I nodded. Sammy walked him to the door.

I called after Jerry on his way to his car, "And, Jerr, keep your nose out of what Shelley's doing."

"Are you saying I can't see her anymore?"

"That's up to her, not me. No more prying, no more following her, no more playing undercover detective. That's my job, not yours. Remind her she should be talking to me if there's any trouble."

"But I can…"

"You can do nothing helpful, Jerry. Believe me."

He nodded and continued to his car, his hands in his pockets, head down, the picture of failure and dejection. Would this teach him a lesson? Probably not.

Sammy and I exchanged glances, then both of us broke into laughter.

"Typical Jerry," said Sammy. "The man is so clueless and still so hung up on you, Eve."

I quickly stopped laughing. "I hope he didn't mess up this case, but I'm more worried he might have put Shelley in jeopardy."

On the way back to the ranch, Sammy said, "Grandfather was right, you know. Both of us have been ignoring the boys and Netty."

"I took Netty to West Palm with me a few days ago. Or was it over a week ago? You're right. We're too distracted with our jobs."

"I'm going to hire more tribe members so we can get the house finished faster. We need someplace that is physically home where we sleep and eat together, where the boys have their own rooms and Netty has hers." He then gave me that funny look he labeled a "leer". He was getting better at it. He lowered his voice and put his arm around my shoulder. "A place where we sleep together. Home, where I can defend our privacy with more than a bar of soap."

"What are you thinking of using? Knife, gun, hatchet?"

"Maybe a guard dog," he said.

"You mean we'll have your father wandering around our front yard chained to a stake with a sign out there that says, "Beware of Dog." I thought it was funny. Sammy didn't laugh.

"I'm going to make some changes, too. Madeleine is overburdened right now with her family, and I have my responsibilities in the store and with the MacAngus case," I said.

"You can't very well shirk those duties."

"But I can hire someone to work in the store part-time."

"My dad needs a job," Sammy said.

"I want to maintain business, not chase away customers with a surly, defensive, always suspicious Indian who carries a Bowie knife in his belt."

"You've got nothing against hiring a tribe member, do you?"

"No, but not Lionel."

Sammy was silent for several minutes. "I know someone who would be great for the job."

"It would probably only be temporary For now, that is."

"I think that would work well," said Sammy. He gave me another look. This time it wasn't a leer. This time he appeared pleased with himself, and there was a bit of the sly fox in the grin he gave me. What was he up to? Usually I was the one in the family who kept things to myself.

"Okay," I said to Sammy, "Let's see what today on the ranch will bring."

Darcie and Angus were out of the hospital, released this morning as Sammy and I slept and played. When we arrived, Madeleine drew me to one side.

"Thanks for helping with Mrs. MacAngus."

"How did she like sleeping on a bunkbed?"

"She was too hung over to have noticed, but she did scream

bloody murder when she woke this morning and couldn't figure out where she was."

"She's still around?"

"Yes. I remained here with the kids while David went to the hospital earlier to pick up Darcie and Angus. Mickey stayed with them all night. Everyone is back now, and Angus and his wife are having a talk in the bedroom."

There was a tug on my arm. "When are you going to show me some alligators like you promised?" asked Dylan.

"How about tomorrow? I'll bet Grandfather Egret would be happy to take you out with Sammy's father in the air boat," I said.

He grinned and nodded.

"The twins are out in the back yard. Why don't you join them? I'll be out with lemonade and cookies soon." Madeleine steered him out the door, then turned back to me. "He's terribly worried about his mother and would like to be at her side constantly, but she needs rest. And he's a little boy. He should be playing, not babysitting his mother."

"That's his dad's job if she needs taking care off." I tried to stifle a yawn.

"You look as if you could use sleep too. What's up?" she asked.

"Family stuff," I said and told her about Jason's disappearance. "So now we have two kids on the lamb."

"But you're not going to tell Frida about Jason, are you?" she asked.

"Lionel has a better chance of finding him than Frida does. And it's his responsibility. I worry about Jason out there in the swamps, but he's a whole lot safer there than David's daughter is where there are people." I gave Frida a concerned look, realizing I might have added to her worries. "I probably shouldn't have said that."

"David and I both know the danger she's in. She'd be better off in a canoe in the swamps."

I thought about that. I assumed that was where she was, but I didn't want to get Madeleine's hopes up. Not until Jason was found, hopefully with her.

Our conversation was interrupted by shouting coming from the back bedroom.

Mrs. MacAngus burst out the door. "You are such a pig-headed man. Don't you understand? You are not safe here. You should come with me, all of you. This place isn't civilized. Someone is trying to kill you!"

"Oh dear," said Madeleine. Mrs. MacAngus pushed past her and plopped herself on the couch. Madeleine turned as if to join her.

"You go see to your uncle," I said to Madeleine. "I'm going to have a long overdue chat with the Missus."

I sat beside her on the couch. "How are you feeling this morning? Better?"

"What do you care?" she said. "You abandoned me and locked me in that awful place."

"Well, now. You're right. I really don't care. I'm simply worried about several things. If you continue to create the scenes you did last night and now, Madeleine will feel obligated to take care of you, and she has more than enough to do."

She twisted around toward me and opened her mouth to speak.

"I'm not finished. When I am, it will be your turn. The other issue here is your presence. I don't get why you keep coming back here. My understanding is that Angus, Mickey, Darcie and Dylan will be joining you in Naples as soon as they can. Considering the friction I've picked up in this family among all of you, I don't get your pretense at the helpful, loving wife and mother. What's up?"

She leaned toward me, fire in her eyes, then it seemed to fade away, replaced by tears. Oh, boy. I waited for the manipulation I expected her to pull on me, but instead she sank back into the couch, deflating like a leftover party balloon.

"I had to head them off. I've lost my condo on the beach, and I'm living in a trailer park."

Huh? What was this?

"But you told Angus you wanted him to leave here."

She nodded. "I do. It isn't safe here. Look at what's happened. I'll put everyone up in a nice motel, tell them I'm having the condo painted."

"Wouldn't it be easier to tell everyone the truth?"

She shook her head. "No. It's so humiliating. You'll think badly of me."

She was already at the bottom of the list of people I liked, and I was thinking of moving her to the very top of those to be poked in the eye with something pointy. But I wanted to make things better for Madeleine, and I also needed to talk to Mrs. MacAngus about Angus and his company. I especially wanted to ask her about the phone call she received from the company employees who appeared at the ranch yesterday to hunt.

"Try me. I can be quite open." I can also lie a bit.

"Angus' best friend, Bruce? The man I left Angus and our marriage for? We had a disagreement over some stuff, and he tossed me out on my ear."

"I need to know about the 'stuff' you fought over."

"Oh, it was family issues."

"Your family or his?"

"Both really." She dabbed at her eyes with a tissue and then looked at me. I knew the look. It was feigned innocence, a look I had tried to master and failed. She was even worse at it than I was.

Madeleine entered the room and dashed over to Mrs. MacAngus. Madeleine would coddle her, offer her breakfast and ruin the progress I had made with her using my tough love approach. Instead I was surprised when Madeleine leaned over and shook her.

"Why would you try to chase Angus out of my house? He's recovering from a gunshot would. How insensitive can you be? He's welcome here, but you're not. Leave. Now." Madeleine straightened up to her imposing five feet nothing and pointed dramatically at the door.

Wow! My tiny friend had found her groove.

Mrs. Angus leaned back as if she wanted to burrow into the couch to get away from Madeleine's angry outburst.

"You don't understand. I still love him," she whispered.

"You're right. I don't understand your kind of love. You're making him and everybody miserable." Madeleine continued to point toward the door.

I was so hypnotized by the two women, one cowering into the couch cushions, the other doing miniature Amazon that it took me a few moments before I realized someone was knocking on the front door. Madeleine and Mrs. MacAngus didn't move from their positions. I don't think either of them blinked. I popped off the couch and answered the door. It was Frida.

"Morning all." The chipper look slid from her face when she saw the frozen tableau before her. "I thought I might have a word with Mrs. MacAngus about that telephone…"

Frida never got the remainder of the inquiry out because Madeleine, without moving from her combative stance or softening her, look said, "She was just leaving."

"This won't take long, and it may help figure out who shot Angus," said Frida.

Madeleine slowly leveled her gaze at Frida. "This is not a police interview room. This woman is not welcome in my house, so take her someplace else and ask your questions."

With Madeleine's attention on Frida, Mrs. MacAngus made a break for it. She grabbed her purse off the couch and ran for the door. Once out on the driveway, she dashed for her car and got in. She sat there for a minute, then buzzed down her window.

"Where are my keys?" she yelled.

I grinned and dangled them from my fingers.

Chapter 15

RIDA OPENED THE passenger side door, and I slid into the back seat. Frida turned around and wrinkled her forehead in an annoyed look, but she then seemed to think better of it. I guess she figured two imposing women might have better luck getting Mrs. MacAngus to tell the truth than one cop. I tried on my new, fierce PI look.

"I understand two of the employees from your husband's firm called you the other day looking for your son," said Frida.

"So?" she said. It sounded like she had gotten back her attitude and felt she had nothing to fear from a cop and a PI.

"I'd like to know what they had to say."

"Why?"

This was like trying to pull an impacted wisdom tooth.

What was Frida thinking? Being reasonable wasn't going to move this woman.

I jumped in to move things along. "Because if you don't tell the nice detective about the call, she'll arrest you."

"She can't do that." Mrs. MacAngus rummaged around in her purse and took out a lipstick. "I look a fright. I could use a long, hot bath and clean clothes."

"Okay. How about this then? No keys for you, and I tell everyone your little secret. I'll start with Angus." I opened the back door as if I was going to go into the house to speak with Angus.

It took her only a few moments to make her decision. "Fine. A message was left on my cell. I don't know why this is so important to you, but someone who identified himself as Charles Mitchell, one of Mickey's fellow employees, said he and a buddy were in Florida and wanted to do some hunting. He told me Mickey had recommended the Wilson ranch, that David Wilson was married to Angus' niece. He also knew that the MacAngus family would be visiting the ranch, so he wondered if they were there now and maybe they could meet up with Mickey at the hunting reserve. By the time I got the message it was too late to get in touch with Mickey and tell him about his buddies, but I was planning to visit here anyway. And it's a good thing I came. Someone is trying to kill Angus, and I need to get him to safety. It's obvious the cops around here are of no use." She pounded on the steering wheel in frustration.

Frida turned around to look at me. I returned her gaze.

"Okay, Mrs. MacAngus. You can leave now if you want to," Frida said.

"If you make any progress on this case, you can reach me in town. I'll be staying at your finest motel."

Frida and I got out of the car and watched her drive off.

"Boy, is she going to be surprised," Frida said.

"How so?"

"There are no 'fine' motels in town. I assume she's thinking of a Hilton."

"Maybe not." I shared with Frida Mrs. MacAngus' confession about living in a trailer in Naples. "She might find the accommodations around here a step up from the trailer park."

"I think I need to keep an eye on that lady. She might be making moves to get back in her husband's good graces or..."

"She might be wondering how she can get rid of him and cash in on his estate."

"You want to check on his will, or should I?' asked Frida.

"I already checked. Everything is split between her and Mickey."

"Thanks for the info. I should have checked that already." Frida threw her arm around my shoulder. "Friends?"

"Sure."

"Still competitors?"

"Sure."

Before we opened the door to the house, I asked, "Was Mrs. MacAngus' summary of the phone call what those guys told you yesterday?"

"Yup. I think, given what David said and what they told me, the possibility of their being involved in the shooting isn't possible, but I've arranged an interview with them this afternoon. I like to see people's faces when I ask them questions in a case."

"I thought I'd let you know a couple of things. I don't think they'll come to anything, but this is a heads up to a friend."

She nodded.

"Jason took off for the swamps in Lionel's canoe."

"That must have ticked off Lionel."

"It did, but it's really his fault. Lionel is out now looking for him."

"Okay, then I shouldn't worry?"

"He'll find Jason, but there is something else. Shelley had been working a case for Crusty."

Frida slapped her forehead and moaned. "Oh, man. Is everyone becoming a PI? Did you infect the girl with your PI thing? How about Grandy? Is she after her license too?"

"No. Grandy wants to maintain her amateur status." I gave Frida no details, but I did say I was concerned about Shelley because I couldn't get in touch with her, and I also informed Frida that Jerry had intervened in the case. "I'm going to stop by Shelley's apartment today. She hasn't checked in with me yet, and I'm getting worried."

"I don't think there's much I can do unless I have evidence she's in danger. Maybe I'm not the one you should be talking to about this."

"I already talked with Jerry and warned him off bothering her again."

"I didn't mean Jerry. I meant someone who could help you out, not make things worse." Frida knew Jerry almost as well as I did.

I couldn't think who that could be.

"Nappi, you idiot," she said.

I must be exhausted if I couldn't figure out that one.

FRIDA ASKED TO walk the hunting area again with David. I decided I should visit Angus and see how he was doing. Before I could enter his room, Mickey stopped me in the hallway.

"I know Mom gave everyone a bad time, but you know, she's worried. I'm more than worried. I'm furious. The shooting was the second attempt on my father's life, and your detective friend and you, the person we hired to find out who is after him, neither of you have a clue who's behind all of this., I'll give you until we leave here in a few days to deliver, or we'll hire another firm, not some old swamp boy and his clothes happy sidekick." He spun on his heel and stomped off to his wife's bedroom.

His word stung, and they were beyond insulting, but part of what he said was correct. I was certainly doing a bang-up job on these cases, wasn't I? No leads on who was gunning for Angus plus I'd lost contact with Shelley whom I was supposed to supervise for the sexual harassment case. I knew I should have notified Crusty because he is my boss, but I wanted to keep it from him. I was certain I could sort out everything. He might forgive my not being able to find out who was after Angus, but Shelley? That was bad management on my part. I was supposed to keep an eye on her. He could fire me, a thought that upset me more than I wanted to admit. This PI thing was growing on me. The consignment shop business would always be in my blood, but the PI work satisfied that snoopy itch I'd never been able to scratch properly. Then there was my family. I had to put them first. Had I taken on more than I was capable of handling? I thought about that question. Naw. I just needed to get organized. I yawned so wide that I thought I'd crack my jaw. Sleep would help.

Family first, I reminded myself as I started down the hall to Angus' room. I connected to Grandfather on my cell.

"Any news?" I said.

"None," he replied.

"Do you need us at home?"

"No. there's nothing either you or Sammy can do. This is on Lionel. But once Jason is home…"

"I know. Sammy and I need to spend time with the family. How's Netty?"

"She misses her grandfather."

Wasn't that the way. Sammy and I has acknowledged that we should focus on family more, and my daughter missed not me or Sammy, but Lionel.

"She wants time with you, too," Grandfather said, reading my troubled thoughts.

"Sammy will be home in a few minutes. He's on his way now to round up more help on the house. We want to get it finished and move in as soon as possible."

"I was wondering when he'd think of that."

"And I'm hiring someone from the tribe to help in the consignment shop." I paused, then said, "Don't tell me you wondered when *I'd* think of that."

When I walked in Angus' room, Dylan was leaning against him on the bed as Angus read to him. Although I knew Angus needed the sleep, it was Dylan whose eyes were closing. At the sound of my footsteps, Dylan was wide awake.

"Did you arrange for the alligators?" he asked.

I nodded. "I thought you were in the backyard with the twins having lemonade and cookies."

"I was, but I wanted to be with grandpa."

Angus and I exchanged worried looks. This boy was too concerned with the well-being of others when he should just be a boy, enjoying the things boys do at age six.

"Why don't you check to see if Madeleine might have a few cookies left?" Angus said.

Dylan scooted off the bed and left.

"He's such a serious little guy," said Angus.

"He loves you and is worried about you and his mom. It's a lot for a small boy to deal with."

"I see you remembered to bring it home from the hospital with you," I said, gesturing to the Dylan's cat picture which sat propped on the bedside table.

"It's always with me."

"Tell me, Angus. Who do you think is trying to kill you?"

He ran his freckled hand over his beard, smoothing it. "I have no idea," he replied, but his gaze did not meet mine. He was keeping something to himself.

"Your son thinks Crusty and I are the wrong detectives to have hired to find out."

"Mickey is impatient."

"Don't you think he has a right to be? It's your life we're talking about here."

"It could have been a hunting accident." Angus said.

"No one believes that, and neither do you. What are you hiding, Angus?"

"I'm tired. I think I should rest now, so I can heal. We'll want to be leaving here soon." He rolled onto his good shoulder and closed his eyes.

I couldn't do anymore here, so it was time I drove to Shelley's place. If she wasn't there and she wasn't at the company, I'd have work to do. Sleep would have to wait until later. I told

Madeleine I was leaving.

"You look beat," she said.

"We both do."

We hugged, and I stepped out onto the porch to find Nappi's black SUV idling there.

"How about a lift?" he asked.

"Who called you?" I asked.

"I don't have to be summoned when a friend needs a helping hand. Hop in."

I did and slid down into the soft leather seat. "Sammy…"

"I told him I'd give you a ride. So, where to?"

"Shelley's place."

"Ah," he said, "repairing the damage Jerry might have caused?"

I didn't ask how he knew all this. I had come to accept that many of my dearest friends and closest family members somehow could read my mind. Originally, I thought it was a tribal thing because Grandfather was accomplished at doing it, but Grandy did it also, as did Nappi. It saved my having to explain a lot of things.

I caught a few moments of a catnap. We pulled up to Shelley's house and saw her car wasn't in the drive. I checked the mailbox by the door and noticed it was empty. The shades were drawn in the front of the house, so we walked around to the back. I stepped onto the small porch there and looked in the kitchen windows, but it was difficult to see much in the dimly lit room.

"She might be inside and need our help," said Nappi.

I nodded. "Did I hear someone inside call for help?" Of course, I hadn't, but it was a good excuse to enter and one the police might believe if they caught us. Unless the cop that caught us was Frida. She'd know better.

I'd seen Nappi break into a house before. He was skilled at the B and E act, but I had a better idea. I looked around in the landscaped bed in the front of the house until I found a broken flower pot. Beneath one of the shards was a key.

Nappi and I let ourselves into the living room.

"Very interesting. There's mail on the table on top of the afternoon newspaper. Someone was here today picking it up. If it was Shelley, then we must have missed her."

"I'll take a closer look in the kitchen," he said.

I went to the single bedroom off the living room. Clothes hung neatly in the closet. I couldn't tell if anything was missing. Her bureau drawers contained pajamas and underwear plus a few tee shirts. Her sewing machine was set up on a small table overlooking the front yard. Yard goods were piled in a cabinet next to the machine.

I opened the medicine cabinet in the nearby bathroom and found a few over-the-counter drugs such as aspirin and an antihistamine. A lone tooth brush stood in a holder on the sink.

"I didn't find anything odd," I said to Nappi, joining him in the kitchen.

I tried her cell again. No answer and the voice mail said her mailbox was full. I didn't like the feeling I was getting from the situation.

"You know what you have to do," said Nappi. "You're going to have to bring Crusty in on this now."

"You're wrong. I need to handle this one myself. I hate to do this, but I'm going to call Ms. Abbot. It's late, but I'll bet she's still in her office."

"And say what?"

"I'll figure out something."

Before I could connect, we heard a car pull up out front.

"Cops?" I asked. Nappi peaked out the front blinds.

"You're not going to like this, but it's Jerry's car."

I threw myself into the living room chair and groaned. I was too tired and too overwhelmed to deal with Jerry right now.

Nappi opened the front door. Jerry's expression changed from sadness to one of alarm.

"Shelley's here?"

Nappi shook his head. "Eve's inside. We used Shelley's key to get in. Eve was worried about her after what you pulled at the company this morning."

I pushed past Nappi and grabbed Jerry by his shoulders and shook him. "What do you know about Shelley?"

"Nothing. You told me to butt out, so I did."

I gave Jerry a look through squinted eyes. I did not entirely believe him.

"Well, I mostly butted out. I came here late this afternoon, thinking I'd wait until she got home."

"You were the one who brought in the paper and the mail?" Nappi said.

Jerry nodded. "Usually she's home around three, but I waited an hour and she didn't show up, so I drove back to the coast, to the company. Her car is still in the lot, but I was afraid to go in and ask about her since you warned me off."

Okay. Now I knew I had to get in touch with Ms. Abbot. I connected with her cell and found her still in her office working.

"I don't want to alarm you, Ms. Abbot, but I haven't been able to get in touch with Shelley. She isn't still there, is she?"

"I wouldn't worry about her if I were you. She's been fitting in well here. In fact, she went off with some members of my staff after work. They decided to have a few beers at one of the local watering holes. My secretary was the designated driver. She usually is. When I acted concerned about our new hire, she told me Shelley could stay the night at her place."

"Shelley usually checks in with me after work. She didn't today. Do you know where the group was going?"

"Sure. To Shrimpy's. It right off US 1 near the county highway."

"I know the place."

Ms. Abbot's voice took on a note of concern. "Do you think there's any reason to be worried?"

"Part of her responsibilities include checking in with me. I want to make certain she's doing her job." I did not tell Ms. Abbot about Jerry's stupid intervention earlier in the day.

"Thanks, Eve," said Jerry, when I disconnected. "Now what?"

"Now you stay here while Nappi and I go to the coast and drop in on happy hour's at Shrimpy's"

"I want to come, too," said Jerry.

Nappi put his hand on Jerry's shoulder and squeezed. It looked like a friendly enough gesture, but Jerry's eyes filled with tears.

"Ouch," Jerry whispered.

We left Jerry washing dishes. I told him I thought bringing in the paper and the mail was a nice gesture, but he could do more. I pointed to the kitchen.

This was one time I did not notice the beauty of the Canopy Road to the coast. Nappi drove it so fast the scenery blew past us. Most of the late afternoon traffic was light, so we made good time taking the right onto US1 and then a left onto Salerno. Shrimpy's lot was still full of happy hours folks when we got there, but there was no Shelley.

I called Ms. Abbot again.

"Did you find her?" she asked when we connected.

"No. Tell me what your secretary looks like and her name."

Ms. Abbot described her as a very tall woman with brown hair. "Her name is Sally Wall."

I scanned the crowd. "When you say very tall, you mean over six feet?"

Ms. Abbot said yes. I spotted a woman who fit the description. She was in the outside bar area. When I approached her and asked if she was Ms. Wall, she nodded.

"I was told Shelley came here with you."

"Yes. We were just leaving. I'm settling the bill. She headed to the car. There she is." Sally Wall pointed toward the parking area. There was barely enough light to make out Shelley's figure.

I yelled at her "Hey, Shelley, wait. It's Eve."

Shelley turned and flashed me a smile. "Eve. What are you doing here? As she raised her arm to wave, a car screeched to a halt next to her, and a man jumped out. He grabbed her, and threw her in the back seat. The car sped off.

CHAPTER 16

"NAPPI," I YELLED, "Did you see that? Someone grabbed Shelley and threw her into that car."

Nappi and I raced to his car and jumped in. He revved the engine, shifted into gear, and we flew after the car, which made an abrupt right turn. It raced ahead for a few blocks, then careened around a corner. Nappi gained on it, then a car from behind us pulled into the left lane and passed us swerving back into the right lane and narrowly missing an oncoming vehicle.

I gritted my teeth. "That was close. What was that guy thinking?"

"He's crazy, but now he's between us and the car Shelley's in, and there's too much traffic for me to pull the same maneuver," said Nappi.

I watched both cars make a sudden turn at the next corner. We followed tight behind. We picked up speed for several blocks. Ahead I could see a busy cross street and a traffic signal. It was the main north and south artery down the coast, US 1. Nappi and I stayed with both cars, but the one between us and the car we were pursuing put us in a difficult position.

Once we were on US 1, we could lose them.

"The traffic signal ahead is turning red," I said, gripping my seat.

"I've got to stay with them." Nappi stepped on the gas, and we shot ahead, almost riding the bumper of the second car. The signal turned to red, but the two cars ahead turned onto the busy highway, narrowing avoiding the cross traffic now streaming into the intersection.

"I can't make it." Nappi slammed on his brakes.

We were stuck. The car we were pursuing disappeared into the distance, a stream of traffic behind it.

"We've lost her," I said.

"I don't think so," said Nappi.

"What?"

"I got a glimpse of that crazy driver who passed us back there. It was the man who can't follow orders."

"Jerry?"

"Yep. I thought someone was behind us when we drove over here, but I decided to ignore it because getting here and finding Shelley was most important. I figured I could take care of anyone on our tail later."

"What do we do now?"

"Coffee. And we wait."

"How long? Maybe I should contact Frida."

"Let's give it an hour."

We found a small neighborhood diner and went in. The sandwiches looked great, especially the pastrami. I yawned my way through the sandwich while Nappi sipped his coffee and tried to rouse Jerry on his cell but got no answer. I finally gave up and put my head down on the table to grab a nap. Nappi's cell woke me.

"Jerry? Where are you? Did you find Shelley?" Nappi paused for a minute to listen, then said, "Okay. We'll meet you there."

Nappi tapped me on the hand. "We're going back home. Jerry and Shelley are at her place. She's a little shook up, but fine otherwise."

The trip back down the Canopy Road was almost as fast as the one earlier. By now I was wide awake, thinking of what I was going to say to Jerry. I would be using words I wouldn't want my kids to hear.

"I can hear you swearing in your head," said Nappi. "Try to remember that Jerry saved our bacon."

"I'm trying, but Jerry was also the one who tossed the bacon in the frying pan." Angry as I was, my words reminded me I hadn't eaten all my sandwich. I should have asked for a to go box. My stomach growled.

When I stepped into Shelley's house, she ran into my arms, and I hugged her tight, aware that I had failed her. I was overwhelmed with relief that she was okay.

"I am so, so sorry, Shelley. I should have realized I was putting you in danger with this undercover work. What was I thinking?"

"I'm fine. They didn't so a thing to me. I think they were desperate and knew something was up at the company, so they decided to warn me off."

"But they could have harmed you."

"I don't think so. If anything had happened to me, they knew there would be an investigation, big time."

"How many of them were there? What did they say to you once they had you in the car?"

"There were two of them, two dumb guys. They said they wanted to have an informal talk with me, something friendly, unofficial. The one in the passenger's seat said he and some of his buddies suspected something funny was going on with me after Jerry appeared this morning applying for a job and claiming I recommended him. He asked me what I was doing at the company. 'Are you some kind of a company spy?' is what he asked me."

"What did you say?"

"I kept quiet."

"Did you recognize them?"

Shelley laughed. "They bound my hands in front of me and tied this over my eyes." She held out a terry towel, smaller than a bath towel but larger than a hand towel. On it the words, "Abbot Golf League" were embroidered.

"I don't get it," I said.

"Ms. Abbot told me they have a golf league at the company with teams and all. At the end of the season there's a golf banquet. Last year these golf towels were given as second or third places for the teams."

"I guess there's not much doubt where your nabbers came from," I said. "How did Jerry find you?"

"They tossed her out of the car at the corner of Indiantown Road. She was standing in the drugstore parking lot when I pulled in behind them. I decided it was more important to see if Shelley was okay than to pursue them."

"Finally, you made an intelligent choice," I said.

Jerry started to say something in reply to my sarcasm, but Nappi shook his head and asked, "Did you get their license plate number?"

"No," Jerry said, sheepishly.

"Eve?"

"No, I didn't think of that." I didn't want to confess to him that I was so terrified during the car chase I wasn't thinking clearly. That didn't sound like something a professional detective would do.

"Can you identify them?" Nappi asked Shelley.

"I'm not certain, but I think one of them works in the advertising area. I think they knew someone had seen them grab me and they were being followed, so they cut their losses and unloaded me." Shelley leaned back into the couch. "I think the event is catching up with me. I'm exhausted."

I shot Jerry an angry look.

"Jerry and I will make tea," said Nappi. I think he had guessed I was about to let Jerry have what I'd been storing up all day.

"Tea with a lot of sugar," said Shelley leaning further back into the couch.

Several fingers of Scotch sounded good to me, but I knew Shelley wasn't much of a drinker and didn't keep anything stronger than white wine in her house. Besides, I admitted to myself, liquor would put me out for the night.

"Well, that's that. I'm going to call Crusty in the morning and we are going to shut down this operation."

Shelley sat up. "What do you mean? We've got them on the run. They're scared. I'm going to go in there tomorrow and make fun of the "two jerks who kidnapped me.""

"No, you are not," I said.

"I can't identify who they were, so we need some way to make they reveal themselves. They think they've frightened me. Let's push them and see what their next move will be. They certainly won't expect me to return to work." Shelley, tired and frightened as she was, also sounded determined. Who was it that had asked me if I had infected Shelley with my PI bug? I had, and right now it wasn't something I was proud of.

"You said they sounded desperate, but desperation can lead to an ugly outcome. This is something we need to run by Crusty and Ms. Abbot."

"I'm with Eve," said Jerry carrying a tray with tea and toast on it.

"I don't think you get a vote," I snapped.

"Let's sleep on this until tomorrow when we'll all be thinking more clearly," said Nappi.

No one seemed interested in the toast, so I ate all of it and drank two cups of tea. Jerry wanted to stay with Shelley for a while.

"She needs sleep," I told Jerry and pushed him toward the door.

"Thanks for rescuing me," Shelley said to Jerry. "We can talk some other time."

"Sure. I'll call you," Jerry replied.

I walked Shelley into her bedroom and settled her into bed. "I can stay here if you like, or you could come back to my house with me for the night in case you're worried about those guys paying you a visit."

"I'm fine. I don't think they know where I live, but I've got my cell phone right here." She reached out and tapped the phone on the bedside table.

"We'll meet at Crusty's office in the morning. Okay?"

"Yup." She turned on her side and was out.

Nappi and I made certain her doors and windows were closed and locked. We let ourselves out and stood on the front porch for a moment. The damp night air hung like a blanket around our shoulders. Despite the warmth, I shivered. Shelley had had a close call. I would not put her in that position again.

There was only one street light on her block. It shone yellow through the dense air, a corona around it. I sniffed and caught the smell of the swamps, heavy, dense, primitive. My son was out there somewhere, and so was David's daughter. If they were together, and right now I hoped they were, I had faith that Lionel would find them. I checked in again with Sammy as I had been doing all day and night long, but he had no word from his father about Jason.

"Would you mind driving me back out to the ranch so I can pick up my car?" I asked Nappi. "I can also check on Madeleine and family."

"Are you certain you don't want to go to your house and join Sammy there? You can pick up your car tomorrow. I'll stop by and drive you out to the ranch."

"I'm good." I sank back into the soft leather seats. I so wanted to sleep on the way out to the ranch, but instead I called Crusty and caught him up on the Abbot situation. He said he would call Ms. Abbot, let her know what happened tonight and make certain she was free to drive over from her office for a meeting tomorrow. Crusty must have heard the fatigue and worry in my voice, because he made no comments about how bad this looked for the agency. I had convinced him Shelley could do the work, and my persuasive arguments had put an inexperienced young woman in jeopardy. I had to make it right somehow.

"You're muttering, Eve," said Nappi. "And from what I can hear, you're being too hard on yourself. None of this would have happened if Jerry hadn't interfered."

"Maybe not, but I think I misjudged the possible danger in the situation. I saw it as sexual harassment, lewd sexual verbal behavior, maybe a little paw and grab, not kidnapping and threats."

"Power. It's all about the abuse of power," said Nappi.

If anyone knew about power, it was my friend Nappi. He'd wielded it many times in his position. I wondered how far he had gone in his role as Family head.

"To answer your question, Eve...."

Question? I hadn't asked anything. Not out loud anyway. Oh, right. It was that mind reading thing again.

"I know how to use power when necessary, but I never have abused it."

I believed him.

I stuck my head in the door at the ranch. David sat on the couch nursing a drink. He held it up and asked," Everyone else is in bed. Join me?"

"If I have a drop of alcohol, I'll fall asleep on your couch and I don't think you need any more company. I'll talk to all of you tomorrow."

I drove home at a conservative speed, well, conservative for me—only five miles over the speed limit. In my rear-view mirror, I saw headlights and knew they were from Nappi's SUV, following me to make certain I got home safely.

Grandy, Max and Sammy had waited up for me. Grandy handed me a Scotch as I walked in the door.

"Let me warn you. If I drink this, my story about tonight will be short."

"You don't have to say a thing. Tomorrow is soon enough," said Grandy.

I took her at her word and slugged the drink down in one gulp, then grabbed Sammy by the arm, and we went to the bedroom. I fell into bed after I removed my outer clothing, leaving my undies and bra on. Sammy kissed me softly on my lips.

"I hope you don't expect a repeat of this morning," I murmured.

"As Grandy said, tomorrow is soon enough."

"Good." I kissed him back and fell asleep with his arms around me and his sweet breath in my hair.

AFTER FILLING IN the details of the day before with Grandy, Max and Sammy, Sammy and I drove in our separate vehicles to our new homesite. Our two boys were up and playing in the yard while Grandfather fed Netty in his kitchen.

"Before you begin work on the house, can you give me the name and contact information for the tribal member you said might be interested in helping out at the store." I caught him before he headed up the ladder to do a final check of the roof.

"Sure. Are you going to spend some time with Netty today?" he asked.

In our discussion yesterday, we had promised each other we would do better as parents, spending more time with the boys and Netty.

"I'm taking her with me and dropping her off at the shop until after my meeting with Crusty, Shelley and Ms. Abbot. Then we're going to visit Madeleine at the ranch for lunch. Takeout, and I'm responsible for the burgers."

"Great. Here come the extra crew needed to complete the house in a hurry," said Sammy.

"The name," I reminded him.

"Later," he replied.

I looked toward the road but saw no vehicles approaching

the house. Someone tugged at my hand. It was Jeremy and Jerome. They were dressed in jeans and old tees.

I got it. "You're going to help Daddy with the house today?"

They both nodded with enthusiasm.

"They can help organize and run errands. Don't worry, Eve. Neither of them will be on ladders."

"Do I look worried?"

"Yes." Sammy smiled down at me from the ladder. "Here come the rest of the crew."

This time I saw a dust cloud on the dirt drive from the boat location.

"Have a good day," I said, "Let's hope Lionel gets back to us with some news."

Sammy nodded.

Grandfather carried Netty out of the house and put her in my arms.

"What do you think, Grandfather? Is the swamp sending you any messages today?"

"My son Lionel lived in the swamp for over twenty years and nothing ever moved in the waters or on the wind to let me know where he was. It's the same now. I know he's out there looking for Jason because he told us he would go, but that's all I sense today from the swamps."

Netty reached out for me and gave me a hug. Her breath smelled like coffee.

"Did you give Netty coffee with her breakfast?" I asked him.

"All Miccosukee children like coffee with their meals, and it was only a sip from my cup," he replied.

I put Netty in her car seat, and we left for the shop where Grandy was about to open for the day.

"I'm going to get us some help around here. Things are getting out of hand with everyone being so busy lately. And you need time to be with Max."

"What would I do with him? He's out on the lake every morning, and I don't fancy sitting out there in the hot sun waiting for a fish to bite."

"The two of you deserve some time in Key Largo with your old friends, fishing the blue waters of the ocean for a change," I said. "Netty, you listen to your grandmother, and when I get back, we'll go see the twins and Dylan. Would you like that?"

Netty's face grew solemn. "Dylan is not happy."

"No, but you can help him have fun. Grandfather will take all of you out in the airboat this afternoon to look for alligators."

"Don't' like alligators," she said.

"I know, honey, but I promised Dylan he could see one up close."

"They eat people."

"Only if you get too close and aggravate them. You know that."

"Okay, then ice cream?"

What a little negotiator she was.

Shelley and Ms. Abbot were already in the office with Crusty when I arrived.

"I think we'll have to end this operation. It's not this agency's fault. Like you, I underestimated how ruthless these guys can be. I'm going to have to reconsider how I handle this." Ms. Abbot chewed on one of her well-manicured nails.

"You could get in touch with the women who quit because they were harassed and see if they're willing to identify the men and file a complaint," Crusty said.

"I want to go back to work this morning and call their bluff, whoever they are," Shelley said.

An idea began to take shape in my head.

"Actually, we could do both," I suggested.

Ms. Abbot said, "Both? The women were clear before that they wouldn't go public."

"But things are different now. Tell them what happened to Shelley when two male employees thought she was in league with the company trying to dig dirt some dirt, and they didn't even know about what, yet they kidnapped and threatened her. The women might see how serious the situation is, and better yet," I said, "if Shelley showed up today and told folks at work what happened to her and added that she thought she recognized one of the men by his voice, that might shake up the guys."

Ms. Abbot and Crusty shook their heads.

"Wait. If, in addition to what Shelley says at work this morning, suppose a rumor went around the place that women who left their jobs because they were sexually harassed were now willing to name names and that the company talked to the authorities this morning and was told there was a good case of sexual harassment as well as kidnapping that could be made against these guys? Suppose the rumor also included the information that the authorities are open to dropping the kidnaping charges if the men came forward and admitted to sexual harassment? I know we're assuming the men who took Shelley are the same ones who sexually harassed your female employees, but we all know it's likely. Why else would they nab Shelley and try to find out what she was doing for the company?"

"You mean even if I talk to the women and they refuse to come forth?" asked Ms. Abbot.

"It's a bluff worth running," I said. "What else have we got? Shelley can go to work this morning. Jerry put her in this situation by showing up there yesterday, so he'll be happy to drive her in today. You can keep an eye on her while she's there, Ms. Abbot. She can work the morning and leave with Jerry at noon. She'll be perfectly protected."

"Jerry," said Crusty.

"Yeah, I know, but now he can be helpful for once," I said. Could he? Or was I making a mistake in assuming Jerry wouldn't mess up again?

CHAPTER 17

———

IT WAS AGREED; Shelley would spread the appropriate rumors while Ms. Abbot again contacted the women who had been harassed. If this didn't work, there was no Plan B. Shelley would no longer be a private eye in training, the agency wouldn't have Ms. Abbot as a client, and I might be out of the job of almost PI. My snoopy nature would have to find another outlet, maybe back to intruding into Frida's cases. She wouldn't like that.

I called Jerry to see if he would agree to help. Need I say he was more than eager and pledged not to mess this one up? He was almost weeping when he promised to do it right, so I had some hope it might succeed. Jerry might then avoid a tongue lashing of gargantuan proportions from me (and no more do-overs).

I walked out of the agency and into the door of our shop. It looked crowded, but when I took a closer look I could see everyone in the shop was either related to me or was my best friend or a member of her family. Madeleine had all the kids, her twins and Dylan, and when I added my little gal to the mix, it seemed like an awful lot of kids to shuffle around for the day. I felt sorry for Madeleine, and then I remembered that I would be the other adult doing the herding. Lunch wasn't an issue, they all loved burgers, but getting all the littluns on the air boat for a ride to find alligators wasn't an easy task. We were to meet Grandfather Egret at the airboat business, and he would shepherd us into the swamps on our tour. Could we keep all these kids in the boat, hands out of the water, fannies firmly planted in the seats, and airboat ride nausea held at bay until we got back to the landing? Four squirming kids.

Madeleine and I finished wiping ketchup and mustard off faces and hands, loaded all the kiddos in our cars and were headed out to the Egret airboat business. When we got there, my two sons were waiting with Grandfather at the landing.

"Dad said he didn't have any jobs for us this afternoon, so he thought you and Madeleine might want us to help you out on the ride," said Jerome, my middle son.

I wanted to throw my arms around him and squeeze him, but I knew he was getting to that age where it's embarrassing to have mothers hugging and kissing boys who want to see themselves as almost teens and, therefore, too old for kissy stuff.

"We're going to see a lot of alligators, birds, fish and other swamp creatures, but we must be careful not to upset them by getting too close," said Grandfather.

"Eve said I would see an alligator real close," said Dylan.

"I said you'd see big alligators, and you will. Be patient," I said.

With a roar of the powerful engine, off we went, flying down the main canal, then swerving into smaller channels. The boat skimmed across the water's surface, as smooth as an iceboat on a frozen lake. Only an occasional shift of the boat right and left gave hint of the deep water beneath. We spent more than an hour looking at wildlife and to Dylan's delight, Grandfather spotted a ten-foot alligator on the far shore. He pointed the nose of the boat toward the animal, shut off the engine and let us drift in until we were within fifteen feet of the large reptile.

"Don't make noise or move around a lot," Grandfather warned.

Soundlessly, we glided closer. I had one hand on Dylan's shoulder and the other around Netty. I could feel the tension inside Dylan and saw his eyes grow large as the alligator sat placidly with the front half of its body in the water, his tail on land. Netty slumped against my side, and I realized she was half asleep. Swamp tours were a common event for her. She'd seen it all before.

The wind began to pick up, and the skies to the north darkened.

"Time for us to get back," said Grandfather. "There's a storm coming. Hang on." He guided us back into the middle of the canal, gunned the boat, and we flew across the water, down the small canals and toward the turn that would take us into the main canal. Grandfather suddenly throttled down. Ahead we could see something adrift in the water. As we approached it, the waves slapping and pounding our boat, the object dipping and bobbing as the wind tossed it around, I could see it was a canoe. Grandfather maneuvered us closer.

"It's pretty beat up," he said.

I shaded my eyes against the wind and the rain which began to pelt us with big droplets. "Do you think the storm pushed it out here?" I asked.

He nodded. "I hope no one was in that craft in this wind. I'd like to beach it somewhere so we could find it again. Then we should come back here when the storm lets up and see if we can find anyone. There's nothing else we can do right now. We need to get back to the dock and safely out of this storm."

The wind came at us in gusts. Water blew into the air boat and made it impossible to see ahead and to breathe. I grasped Netty and Dylan tightly and saw the others hold onto their seats and each other.

"It's too rough to grab the canoe," said Grandfather. "We'll have to leave it."

I watched the canoe shoot into the canal and disappear behind curtains of water rushing up to shake the airboat.

As the wind grew stronger, our boat rocked and dipped into the waves. A large swell came across the side of the boat and almost tipped it. It righted itself for a moment, but then yawed to the other side.

Another big wave would toss us into the water, but as suddenly as the storm came up, it passed. The canal water again calmed and flattened. I turned back toward Grandfather to ask him if he wanted to chase down the canoe, but when I looked up to the pilot's seat, he was gone.

"Grandfather!" I yelled.

The storm had left everything as still as if the world was holding its breath for another onslaught of wind and water. It didn't come. The storm clouds continued their path south, and the sun came from behind them bathing us in its welcome warmth.

I continued to call but got no answer. I was worried for Grandfather, but I also was concerned about us: two women and six children caught in the middle of the swamps.

"That was fun," said Netty.

"Like a roller coaster," Dylan added.

Well, the kids weren't scared, but I was, and Madeleine's face had lost all its color.

The boys continued to scan the surface of the water and both shores, looking for any sign of Grandfather.

"Mom," said little Eve, "You're holding me too tight. I can't breathe."

"Sorry, honey."

Madeleine looked to me for reassurance. "How do we get out of this pickle, Eve? You must know how to run an air boat, right?"

"Must I? Well, no. I've no idea. Sammy and I usually took to the water in a canoe."

"So call him," said Madeleine.

I held my cell aloft, but there was no signal out here. Madeleine took hers out and did the same as I, moving her arm around to see if she could pull in a signal. She shook her head, and looked at me, her forehead wrinkled in desperation.

Canoe, I thought. Now there was an idea. Maybe now that the rain wasn't obscuring visibility, we could see where that canoe had gone.

"Look for the canoe. One of us could use it to get back to the air boat landing and get Sammy out here," I said.

"Why don't we start the engine and take the airboat back home?" asked Jeremy, my youngest.

"I don't know how to start the engine or how to run the boat," I said. Neither did Madeleine.

"I do," said Jerome. He climbed into the pilot's seat and started the engine. I wanted to climb up there with him and hug him until he squealed.

"Should we look for Grandfather?" he asked.

"I think we should go home. I'm sure your father saw the storm, and he'll be worried about us. Grandfather knows these swamps better than anyone. He'll take care of himself," I said. "Your dad and some of the men can come back here to look for Grandfather. I'm sure he's holed up somewhere on one of these canals, trying to dry out." I hoped I sounded reassuring. I didn't want my children to worry their great grandfather had drowned.

"You're right, Mom," said Jerome. "Grandfather will be fine, but we need to get all of you home."

How grownup he sounded for a boy who recently had fallen from a tree, scraped his knee and shed tears over having it bandaged.

The canoe seemed to have been forgotten by everyone but me. I wanted to find Grandfather to make certain he was safe, but I also wanted another look at that canoe because I thought it might be Lionel's, the canoe my oldest son had taken and paddled off into the night. Now the swamps had taken three members of my family and maybe one of Madeleine's also.

The wind from the speeding air boat made all of us shiver, so that by the time we pulled up at the landing, I was concerned about the onset of hypothermia for all of us. We needed to get warm and fast.

Sammy was at the landing waiting for us. "I was about to borrow the neighbor's bass boat to find out what happened. Where's Grandfather?" he asked, taking Netty from my arms and holding out his hand to help Madeleine and the twins out of the boat. Dylan jumped onto the landing. Jerome tied up the boat, then he and Jeremy joined us on the dock.

"Grandfather is still out there," I said, as if it was a choice he had made. Sammy gave a moment's hesitation, then nodded, knowing I didn't want the children to be upset about Grandfather. "I'll tell you all about it when we get everyone into the house and warm."

Once we were wrapped in blankets, and I had put a kettle on the stove to make us something warm, I took Sammy to one side and gave him the details about our trip including the finding of the canoe and our attempt to beach it.

"I'm going to take my canoe out and look for Grandfather. It will allow me access to small canals that the air boat couldn't get into."

"Don't you get lost, too," I warned as I walked with him out to the canal.

He kissed me on the cheek. "I'm an Egret. The swamps are part of me."

I watched him run to canoe, push it into the canal and jump in. With a wave of his hand, he paddled swiftly and powerfully down the water.

The men I loved most in this world were out there, among the snakes, alligators and deep, black waters. Despite the cup of hot tea I held in my hand, I still shivered, not from the cold, but from bone deep fear for their lives.

My cell rang as I kept an eye on the canal. The caller ID said it was Crusty.

"Is everything okay?" I asked. "Did the plan work?"

"Not yet, but we need to give it a little time."

"We're not going to send Shelley back in there tomorrow, are we?"

"Nope. Her detecting days are over. Yours are not. Angus and his son called me this afternoon. I tried to get you, but your cell went to voice mail. Where were you?"

"Out having fun by getting swallowed up by the swamp." I told him of our trip and how we lost Grandfather.

"That old codger owns those swamps. Don't worry about him. He'll show up. And so will your son. There's a map of the swamps on the Egret DNA."

"I'll be in after I make certain Madeleine is recovered enough to drive back to the ranch."

She assured me she was fine and didn't mind taking Netty with her to the ranch for several hours.

I gave her a hug and Netty a big, ole wet kiss, told the boys to await their father's return at Grandfather's house and warned them not to go out into the swamps to help in the search.

"You stay here, do you understand? Your father will return soon, and I'll be back after I take care of a few things in town," I said, expecting not to be gone long. I jumped in my car and tossed gravel as I sped out of the drive and onto the main road.

My cell rang once more. It was Grandy. I got a bad feeling I wasn't going to like what she said. I should have called her sooner.

"Why didn't you tell me Grandfather Egret fell overboard and is out there…somewhere where the gators can get him."

"Sorry Grandy. But how did you find out?"

"Word gets around. I called Nappi as soon as I heard, and he's rounding up some of his friends to help out with a search."

I chuckled.

"What's so funny?" she asked a note of aggravation in her voice.

"I don't think Nappi's family connections will do much good out there. They can't drive their SUVs into the swamps, and the usual GPS will not do them a bit of good."

"You really are something. Nappi probably has more connections around here than you do. I can't believe you don't know that."

I was still wondering how Grandy found out about Grandfather when I saw a silver car almost run up my rear bumper. I took a closer look in the rear-view mirror and groaned. Not again. The driver was Mrs. Angus, her face twisted in frustration. She honked and shook her fist at me.

I pulled over. What did she want to say to me?

I was mistaken. She roared past me and raced on down the road.

Oh my. That was what Madeleine needed right now. MacAngus overload.

I had not gone another mile when I spotted another car in the rearview mirror, this one an SUV. It came up fast and, like Mrs. MacAngus car, it also almost kissed the back of my car. The driver honked, and this time I was certain the driver wanted me to pull over. Lights and a siren came on.

Okay, Okay. It wasn't necessary to make such a public announcement. It was Frida.

I remained in my car, hands on the steering wheel. Frida didn't get out of her car. My cell rang.

"I need to talk to you, Eve."

"I'm right here."

"Let's talk in my car."

"Look, I've had one horrible day, and it's not over yet. Either we talk on our cells or you join me in my car."

I guess Frida could hear the fatigue and irritation in my voice. I heard her door slam, and she slid into the seat next to me.

"Sorry, Eve. I heard about what happened to Grandfather. I'm sure he'll be just fine."

"How does everybody already know about this?"

"Crusty told Grandy who called Nappi and me. I guess there were some customers in the shop when she talked to us, and they overheard. I think the entire town knows by now. Why shouldn't I know? Think about it. It's easier on you. You won't have to explain your bad mood." She smiled.

"Very funny. I'm guessing my mood will only get worse. MacAngus father and son want a meeting with Crusty and me. I'm on my way to the office."

"I wouldn't say this to Madeleine, but since her relatives arrived on the scene there's been nothing but trouble. Two attempts on Angus' life and Bethany disappearing."

"Don't blame Madeleine. Now Jason, Lionel, Grandfather and Sammy are out there somewhere in the swamps. Also, there's Shelley…" Oops, that was something Frida didn't know and shouldn't. It was a private matter for now.

"Shelley? How does she figure into this?"

"It's not something you need to know right now. It's a case Crusty and I are working on."

"I thought you might like to know that I talked to the two hunters who were at the ranch the other day, the ones from the MacAngus company. Their story is the same as the one David told me. I can't see how they could be involved in the shooting. However, I need to know more about them before I dismiss them as possible suspects."

I waited knowing that she had more to say, knowing it involved a favor.

She hesitated before she added, "I'm wondering if you could do me a favor?" She dropped her glance and wouldn't look me in the eye.

"Oh, for heaven's sake, say it."

"I know Nappi did some work for you on this case. I know it would be unethical for me to ask him what he discovered when he went to Scotland. I don't want to know what he found out about the MacAngus company per se. I want to talk with him about his impressions of the place. Would you allow that?"

"That's a slippery slope. Impressions are usually based on information. The information he gathered was done as a consultant to us."

"I know, but could the three of us sit down over a beer? You'd be there to make certain I didn't cross any lines."

"Only his impressions, no hard data?"

"Right."

"I'll run it by Crusty. I'm on my way there now. I'll get back to you."

"Thanks, Eve. I'll owe you one." She hopped out of the car and went back to her SUV.

I watched her pull back onto the road, and I followed. As I sped up to highway speed, I felt the car pull to the left. Something wasn't right. I slowed and pulled back onto the shoulder, stopped the car and got out.

Oh, turtle doodoo. My left front tire was flat.

Frida saw I was in trouble, made a U-turn and came back.

She rolled down her window and asked, "What's going on?"

"Flat."

She hopped out of her car. "Do you know how to fix a flat?" she asked.

I gave her an irritated look. "Of course, I do. Kinda."

I went around to the back of the car and pushed the trunk release on my key fob.

"The spare and the jack are in here somewhere," I said, looking into the trunk.

"Well, that's certainly not it," said Frida. "And I'll bet it's not a consignment item from your trips to West Palm, is it?"

She pointed to the shotgun which lay on top of the spare tire well.

CHAPTER 18

"**Y**OURS?" SHE ASKED.

"You know better than that. I don't own a shotgun. The only gun I've handled is the one I borrow from Crusty, a hand gun that I use at the range."

"When was the last time you opened the trunk?" she asked.

I thought back to the trip I had made to West Palm over a week ago.

"Not recently."

"Before Mr. MacAngus was shot?"

I nodded.

"Don't touch it." She pulled a pair of latex gloves from her pocket, lifted the gun out of the trunk and carried it to her car.

"Do you think it was the one used to shoot Mr. MacAngus?"

"I'd bet on it. Someone put it there, someone at the ranch."

"My car has been parked at the ranch numerous times. Anyone could have put it in. You don't need the key fob to get in there. There's a button on the center console. Push it, and the trunk opens."

"I don't suppose you lock your car when you park it at the

ranch?" asked Frida.

"Why would I? I parked it right outside the house and assumed no one would try to take it or vandalize it, certainly not any of the family."

"It wasn't a stranger who put the gun there," said Frida.

I began to go through the list of people who had been at the ranch recently. The list included Madeleine's relatives as well as any hunters there the day Angus was shot. As Frida and I worked on the tire, I knew she was compiling her own list. I assumed the lists might be overlapping.

The tire changed, I headed for the strip mall where our shop and the detective agency were located. Frida gave me a wave and continued up the street toward the police station.

"Sorry I'm late. I had a flat." I said when I got in the office. I grabbed a folding chair and opened it, setting it next to Crusty. Shelley and Ms. Abbot sat in the client chairs across from his desk.

"Maybe this will turn out fine, but I'm the one who hired the agency to put someone undercover to flush out the sexual harassers in my company. I take full responsibility for what happened to Shelley," Ms. Abbot said.

"You're wrong," said Crusty. "The agency is responsible for our employees."

"Yes, and the responsible party or parties are those horrible guys," I added.

"I wish they were behind bars," said Shelley.

"Let's hold tight and see what happens by the end of the day. Maybe someone will come forward.," said Ms. Abbot.

"If you don't hear anything, then we need access to personnel records. I'd like to look at the files of the men who could have overheard the exchange among Jerry, the head of HR and Shelley. No one else would have reason to suspect Shelley of not being who she claimed to be."

"I can tell you the names of the employees who work in that area, but their personnel files are private. I can't allow you into those," Ms. Abbot said.

"No, of course not," I said, quickly, "but don't you think it's time you had someone take an undercover look at your security system, you know, try to break in to detect its weak points?"

I knew the person for the job.

Ms. Abbot looked confused for a moment. "My security system?" Then she got my drift and smiled. She didn't say no or act horrified that I was suggesting something not quite legal, but she did say, "What if you, I mean, they get caught?" she asked.

"Don't worry. They won't."

"I'll call you tonight after work to let you know if there's news," she said, getting out of her chair and grabbing her briefcase. "I can't have such people working in my company." She left, her usually firm and determined steps more hesitant now.

"Let's not despair yet," I said. "I think those guys have to be mighty scared. Let's give them today to realize they have no options."

Shelley and Crusty nodded. I didn't believe those creeps would do the right thing, but someone in the company might come forward today with information. Meantime I needed to get in touch with my B and E guy.

"Nappi?" I said when he answered my call, "You busy tonight?" I also asked him if he was willing to talk to Frida about MacAngus' company. "I'll be there, of course, so don't worry about violating the terms of your contract as the agency's consultant."

"We have a contract?" he asked, a smile in his voice.

"There must be one somewhere in Crusty's file cabinet. We'll all meet at his office tonight before we go to the coast to do our reconnaissance work."

"You're not telling Frida what we're about to do, are you?"

"I haven't even told you the specifics of the job yet, and

you're assuming it's something she wouldn't like?"

"How long have we been friends, Eve?"

"Long enough for you to read my mind like everyone who knows me well."

"Later then," he said and disconnected.

Shelley caught up with me on the sidewalk. She looked dejected, her brown eyes filled with sadness.

"You did fine," I said, grabbing her around the shoulders and squeezing. "Those are the breaks in detective work. You can't always predict how things will turn out or where information you uncover might take you. Most times it leads to nothing, and you spend your time sitting in a car, eating bad take-out, drinking too much coffee and wondering where the nearest restroom is. Or you're up to your elbows going through death or marriage records or trying to track down wills."

"I know, but I really wanted to make a difference with this case because it reminded me of what almost happened to me."

"I know, honey, but your time is wasted on PI work. You are one of the most creative people I've ever met. We know you could go to New York and do design work, and I worry that someday you'll leave us and do that. Until then, you do what you do best and leave the surveillance work to Crusty and me."

She gave me a tiny smile, "Okay."

"I need to ask you something. I know it may be none of my business, but is there anything going on between you and Jerry?"

"Oh, my gosh! No. Absolutely no. He's kind of sweet, but he can't seem to find a direction in his life. I'm still young and struggling with my own issues of what I want to do. I don't need a man who hasn't found himself and is looking to me to fulfill him."

"Good for you. You do have the people savvy to be a good PI, but, like I said, I'd focus on the design work."

"I overheard you talking to Nappi. Do you need any more help with whatever you're going to do tonight?"

I wanted to say yes to her, but I couldn't do that both for her sake and because if we did need another posse member, someone else had dibs on that position. Grandy would never speak to me again if I didn't include her.

When we entered the shop, it appeared Grandy and Netty were playing a game of catch me, and Grandy had cornered Netty behind the counter.

"What's going on here?" I asked.

"She took one of the dresses off the mannequin and has put it on. I'm trying to get it back from her. I've been chasing her around the store for about fifteen minutes."

"Netty Egret," I said in my sternest voice. "You come out here right now and give that dress back to the lady you stole it from."

"The lady didn't seem to mind," said Netty.

"She's naked. She needs clothes."

"Okay." Netty came out from behind the counter and walked over to the mannequin. She refused to meet my look, and she dragged her feet. I had ruined her game.

"Good girl," I said. The store's phone rang. "I'll get it," I told Grandy. "Sit down and catch your breath. I've got something to ask you."

"Eve? It's Lionel," said the voice.

"Did you find them?" I asked.

"I did."

"Let me talk to my son."

"I can't do that."

"Why not?"

"He's busy right now."

"Busy? Doing what?"

"He's with that girl. They're looking for my canoe."

He was making sense, I supposed, but it wasn't anything I wanted to hear. I wanted to scream at him, but I worried he might hang up on me. I took a deep breath.

"Okay. Let me see if I understand. You found Jason?"

"Yes."

"He was with someone?"

"Yes."

"Was it Bethany?"

"That could be her name."

"And Grandfather?" Now I was speaking through clenched teeth worried I'd crack one if I gritted them any harder.

"I sent him home."

"And he's fine, healthy, not hurt?"

"He's old, but he's not stupid. He knows the swamps almost as well as I do. I hate to admit this, but he found me, and then we located the kids after that. I think he expects everyone for dinner tonight."

"Lionel, have you called David, Bethany's father yet?"

"Yes, I did. And he felt the same way I did: those two kids needed to learn a lesson."

"What lesson?" Sometimes Lionel's view of lessons wasn't the same as that of most other folks

"They took my canoe and lost it, so I told them they had to find it and repair it."

"They're still lost somewhere in the swamp?"

"I know exactly where they are, and I know where the canoe is too. It shouldn't take them more than a few days to find it and bring it back."

"I'm calling Sammy."

"No need. He must already know about everything because Grandfather would have told him." He disconnected.

"Am I the last person to know about my own son?" I asked.

Grandy looked at me, her brow wrinkled in confusion, but before I could tell her about Jason, she said, "Look at what Netty did." She pointed at the mannequin which now had Netty's clothing draped on it. Netty still wore the mannequin's dress.

"I gave her my clothes. Are you mad?"

"No, darling. That was very generous of you." I dashed across the room and enveloped her in a giant hug. If I didn't have Jason here, at least I could squeeze one of my children close to me.

"Too tight," Natty said and wiggled, "All wet."

Tears flowed down my cheeks, my feelings a combination of frustration at Lionel, but also relief and joy that he had assured me in his own way that he found Jason and Bethany, and Grandfather was home. I shared the news with Grandy and Netty.

"That man," said Grandy.

I knew what she meant. Lionel was a trial for everyone, but I also knew that no one else could have located Grandfather, Jason and Bethany. The questions about how Bethany and Jason hooked up would come later.

"I'm going to take Netty home and check on Grandfather. I'm sure he's fine. But I want to see him in the flesh. And I need to talk with Sammy. Before I go, I was wondering if you're free this evening to do a little late-night work where your dark blue velvet warm-up suit might be the perfect outfit."

Grandy's blue eyes lit up. "Is Nappi coming along?"

I nodded.

"Do you mind if I close the shop a little early? I'll need to get my hair done."

WHEN NETTY AND I pulled up in the car, Grandfather was sitting on his porch in the old rocker, puffing contentedly at his pipe. Lionel sat on the steps sharpening that huge Bowie knife of his. Netty wriggled out of my arms and ran to both, first hugging Lionel and then jumping into Grandfather's lap.

I told Lionel it was good to have him back—a stretch of the truth—and leaned over to give Grandfather a peck on the cheek.

"I was so worried about you. We all were," I said.

"I know how to swim."

"I know, but you could have hit your head when you went in

or gotten snagged or something."

"I didn't. I was swept down the canal by the strong current, but I got to shore and found my way to a fallen tree where I took cover. I knew you'd never find me, and I couldn't work my way back to you, but I was certain one of the boys would take the airboat home, that all of you would be safe. Once the rain let up, I smelled a fire, followed the smell of wood smoke and found Lionel and the two kids."

"And do you approve of letting those kids wander around out there looking for Lionel's old ratty canoe?"

He leaned close to my ear so that Lionel couldn't hear. "I told them the best place to look, down the canal in an inlet where I knew the canoe would get snagged. They will be back here before the sun goes down." He winked at me.

Sammy had heard me pull into the drive and came out of our house to give me a hug.

"How's the house going?" I asked.

"Come inside and see for yourself. We're working on the plumbing now, and the painters will be here tomorrow. We'll be able to move in soon."

We walked through the house, Sammy pointing out that the sink was in place and hooked into the water and sewage lines. "Cabinets will be in in a few days. Same with the two bathrooms. It's a large house, but not a palace by any means."

"No, but it's what we wanted, and it will be a cozy home for us. We can all be together here and right next door to Grandfather," I said.

"And to me," added Lionel, walking up behind us. "Nice work, Sammy. That's how to put family first."

"That reminds me, Sammy. I need to talk to you about tonight," I said.

AFTER A TASTY chicken stew prepared by Grandfather, I said goodbye to the family and left for the office and my meeting with Nappi and Frida. Crusty had called earlier to say Ms.

Abbot hadn't heard anything from the men who took Shelley.

"Go ahead and do what you have in mind, Eve, but I don't want to hear about it," Crusty told me on the phone. "And remember, you're doing this work tonight as a private citizen, not as a representative of this agency."

I assured him I understood. I disconnected and stepped onto the porch. I had hoped that I would see Jason and Bethany appear, but there was no sign of them.

"It's early yet," said Grandfather.

"Days early," added Lionel with a chuckle.

I ignored him and focused on the evening ahead.

On the way to the office, I called Madeleine to see how she was coping with the family.

"They want to leave soon. The doctor said both Angus and Darcie were fine to travel, so I think they will be heading to Naples to see Mickey's mother, unless she appears here again to stop them. They're going to stay in a motel while her condo is being painted."

I wondered if I should tell Madeleine about Mrs. MacAngus' change of circumstances and her new home in a trailer park, but I decided it was one more thing she didn't need to worry about.

"I had so wanted this visit to be a good one but look what happened."

"None of it was your fault, honey. That family seems to have a load of troubles of their own. Someone appears to be after Angus. I'm going to be talking with Frida tonight. Maybe we can figure out what's going on." I decided telling Madeleine about the shotgun in my car also wasn't information she needed right now. "I'll see you tomorrow." I disconnected and wondered if I was right to keep so much from her.

Frida was waiting for me when I pulled up in front of the office. I unlocked the door to let us in.

"I thought you'd like to know, Eve. The shotgun in your trunk? David identified it as the one missing from the hunting ranch." She smiled and held up her finger. "And it has been fired recently, but there were no prints on it. I'm betting it was the gun used to shoot Angus. I asked some of my men to continue looking for spent casings. So far we've found nothing out there, but that's a difficult area to search. Maybe the casing will turn up yet."

"Could the shooter have taken the shell casing?"

Frida nodded.

"I guess you'll need to get back to the hunters for another talk?"

"Don't I wish. They checked out of their motel and left no forwarding address. I'm checking the airports to see if they flew out or left the country entirely."

"That seems fishy, doesn't it?"

"Maybe they have something to hide."

"Like attempted murder?" I said.

The door to the office opened and Nappi came in.

"Ladies," he said. He was dressed for the evening's events: black cotton sweater, black silk trousers and dark leather boots.

Frida gave him the once over. "You look like a second story man. Should I be worried?" Her glance shifted to me. I also was in black from head to toe.

"I like black. It's very slimming," I said.

"Oh, like you of all people, Eve, need to look slimmer."

We were about to begin talking when there was a tap at the door and Grandy stuck her head in.

"I know you said you'd pick me up, but Max and I ate out and were on the way home when we passed and saw your car here, Eve." Her glance took in Frida. "Oh, am I interrupting?"

"C'mon in," said Frida. Grandy waved back out the door to signal Max and came in wearing her dark B and E warm up suit. "I thought I had the Bobbsey twins in here with Eve and Nappi, but now that you've appeared, I see I have the three musketeers. What's up, guys?"

CHAPTER 19

——

"WE'RE ALL GOING out to the Burnt Biscuit for Karaoke. We thought we could do the hits from *Mama Mia*," said Grandy. Her newly coiffed hair shone bluish-white in the light.

Wow, she was quick. I couldn't have thought up a story that outlandish in a lifetime.

Frida lifted one eyebrow in a look of disbelief and appeared about to say something, but she sighed and waved her hand dismissively. "Whatever."

"You don't mind if Grandy sits in on this discussion, do you?" I asked Frida.

"Not if you don't."

I shook my head.

"Okay, so tell me, Nappi, what your impressions were of the MacAngus company. Eve said you didn't find anything that sent up red flags, but I want to know what your gut might have told you about the company and the people you talked with there."

Nappi reviewed what he had told me, that the company

appeared to be on the up and up with no financial or operating issues.

"They seemed to like Mr. MacAngus, maybe better than they liked his son, but you've witnessed what a short fuse he has at times. They didn't come right out and say that. It's just an impression. However, I got a strong sense that as much as they appreciated what Angus had done in the past to build up the company, they now wished he could rest on his laurels and not interfere in the company's day-to-day operations. He was beginning to get on everyone's nerves, a micromanager, it appears."

"You don't think they would hire someone to get rid of him, do you?"

"I couldn't say. They certainly were sick of having the old guy around very minute, but…"

"Do you think Mickey knew they felt this way?" Frida asked.

"Maybe. Probably."

"I'm certain Mickey himself felt that way. Given the tension in the father-son relationship, I'll be Mickey would have loved it if his father stayed out of the office," I said.

"Enough to kill him?" asked Frida.

We were all silent, thinking about that possibility. I thought about how I sometimes would have loved it if Lionel would disappear for another long stretch into the swamps and leave our family alone. That didn't mean I would attempt to kill him to make it happen.

"I doubt it," I said.

There was really nothing else Nappi could add about his visit to Scotland, so we broke up the meeting.

"You three have a great time entertaining the folks at the Biscuit," said Frida as we stepped out to our cars.

We nodded and smiled.

"Even though tonight is not a karaoke night," Frida added as she got into her cruiser, smiled back at us and waved.

"She's onto us," Nappi said.

"Yep. That was such a dumb story," I told Grandy.

"Well, I didn't hear a better one out of your mouth," she said. "Let's get out of here and have some fun."

We piled into Nappi's black SUV and headed for the coast.

"Ms. Abbot emailed me a list of people who might have overheard Jerry when he showed up at the Abbot corporation. I also have information about their security system. This will test your skills, Nappi."

He pulled over less than a block from the business and perused the specifications of the system. "Electronic security is a piece of cake. The other may be a problem."

"What other?" I asked.

"The dog." He nodded at the canine patrolling the fence at Abbot's and pulled a U-turn.

"We're giving up?" I asked.

"No. We're going food shopping for doggie delights," Nappi said.

"You're going to put some drugs in the food so the dog goes to sleep?" I asked.

"You don't think I carry around drugs to make dogs sleepy, do you?" asked Nappi. "We are going to use food to distract the dog. We'll need someone who is fast on their feet." He pulled into the parking lot of a super market and parked. The two of them looked at me.

"I'm not going to act as dog food. Forget it," I said.

"I'll do it," said a voice from the third row of the car. It was Jerry, hiding there.

"Jerry, why are you always following us around?" I asked.

"I'm not. I was riding with you back here, under this blanket. I want to help."

It was the best plan we could come up with. Nappi was adamantly opposed to drugging dogs even if we could have found the right drugs to use. "Too dangerous," he said, as if getting mauled by the beast wasn't dangerous.

A perimeter fence ran around the building. It was only

twenty feet from the structure. Nappi assured me he could manually pick the lock on the back gate while Jerry kept the dog occupied in front. We'd run to the building, and Nappi would then disengage the lock on the back door, enter the building and disable the security system. Assuming we got this far without incident, Jerry would be busy distracting the dog at the front of the building, tempting it with expensive cuts of meat which he would place along the front perimeter. Grandy was our designated driver, remaining in the car with the engine running in case the plan didn't work. If the plan really went awry, she would be the person to drive us to the nearest emergency room for dog bite treatments. Or to the morgue in case the wounds were fatal. This was our plan, and it was a lousy one. It sounded to me as if Nappi and I were the ones in danger of getting mauled while Jerry only risked getting his fingers nipped if he didn't get them out of range of the dog.

"I want to trade places with Jerry," I said.

"Don't you think I can do it?" Nappi asked.

"I know you could break into Fort Knox if given enough time, but this plan is dependent upon how speedy we can be. And how palatable filet mignon and Jerry appear to that dog."

"Don't be scared," said Nappi.

That did it. Eve Appel is never scared. Okay, maybe a few times. Or more than a few. A lot, but I didn't want anyone to think I was scared. I had a reputation to uphold. I was a PI in the making.

"I am not scared for myself. I'm frightened that you might get hurt, and then where would we be?"

Nappi gave me one of his slow smiles. "Silly woman," he said. "Let's go."

Jerry hopped out of the car with enough meat in his hand to open a steakhouse in Miami. As we watched him approach the fence, we heard no barks, no growls, only the sound of soft pads on the dirt as the dog silently approached Jerry at the fence.

Nappi and I were hidden around the corner but could see Jerry bend down and shove a piece of meat under the fence. The dog sniffed it and looked at Jerry.

"I think he's more interested in me than the meat," Jerry said, loud enough so we could hear him.

"Wait a minute," called Nappi.

The dog heard him and raised his head turning it in the direction of Nappi's voice.

"Don't talk. You got the dog's attention. I'll shove a bigger… Yow!"

Nappi and I looked at each other, concerned for Jerry's safety, but didn't want to call out to check.

"He lunged at the meat and swallowed it in one piece. Now he wants more. I hope I have enough to keep him occupied."

"Time to get moving," said Nappi.

Nappi picked the gate lock in just over a minute. We swung it open, hoping it wouldn't make a noise. It didn't. Now we were in the same enclosure as the dog. We sprang to the back door, Nappi had me shine the light on the lock there, and he took a close look at it.

He grinned. "I should tell Ms. Abbot she needs better security."

It took only a few minutes to open it. The security panel was right inside the door. Nappi entered numbers into a hand held electronic gadget, and the lights indicating the panel was enabled went out. I let out my breath.

"You weren't worried, were you?" asked Nappi.

We used our flashlights and spotted the stairs leading to the second floor of the two-story building to our left. We took them two at a time and started down a long hallway. All the offices were on this floor. The HR door was the second one on our right. The door was locked, but that was no problem for Nappi. We entered in less than thirty seconds. The head of HR's desk was in the middle of the room, and file cabinets stood against both walls. I held the light while Nappi unlocked the one marked "Personnel files."

"What are we looking for?" asked Nappi.

"I'm not sure. Maybe some information we can use to put more pressure on these guys, lapses in their employment history, evidence of arrests even minor ones, anything that looks like they played loose with the information on their personnel records or with the law. We're not going to read every file, only those on the list Ms. Abbot made me. They were the employees who were here when Jerry blew Shelley's cover. There are five of them." I began to rethink this idea. What did I hope to find? A note on a file that read, "I'm a sexual predator?"

The door to the office banged opened. I jumped at the sound. Nappi remained focused on the files, while I held the flashlight.

"I thought I heard someone in here. I suppose Ms. Abbot sent you to pry. That's illegal, you know." said the person who entered.

"Well, yes, but so is sexual harassment and kidnapping," I said, gulping back how startled I was by his appearance.

He hit the light switch on the wall by the door. He was slight in build with a comb-over of graying hair.

My accusation seemed to take all the bravado out of him. His shoulders slumped, and he leaned against the wall. "Oh well. It was only a matter of time before the guys responsible for Shelley's abduction flipped. One of them was going to talk to the cops tomorrow, so my lucrative little scheme would have ended soon anyway."

I could hear resignation in his voice and a note of fear.

"Who are you?" I asked.

"I'm George Thayer, Head of HR."

I was surprised he didn't ask who we were. Maybe he assumed we were cops.

"Let me," he said, walking over to his desk and extracting a file from the top left drawer. "I came here tonight to destroy this, but I knew someone would rat me out. This will explain everything." He handed the file to me, then fell heavily into his desk chair and put his head in his hands.

I quickly perused it, "You knew about the sexual harassment here, you knew who the guys were, and you did nothing?" I asked.

He looked up at me with bloodshot eyes. "That's not true. I knew what was going on, so I told the men involved that I wouldn't say anything if they paid me to look the other way. When it appeared Shelley was some kind of plant, probably hired by Ms. Abbot, a few of the guys got nervous and snatched her the other night. Dumb! If they had remained quiet and kept their hands off her and other female employees for the immediate future, this whole thing might have blown over. But they thought threatening her would work. It didn't. So now they're facing kidnapping charges as well as sexual harassment charges, and the whole thing will end up on me. My blackmail scheme is ended, and so is my job. I guess you'll want to arrest me now. The names of the guys are in that file."

He did think we were cops.

"No, we're not going to arrest you. We'll take this file for evidence and give you and your gang of sexual predators a chance to tell your stories to the police. Confessing will make it easier on you," said Nappi.

"I guess that's it then," he said. He pulled himself out of his chair, and we followed him out into the hall. He shuffled down the front staircase, disabled the alarm to let us out of the building, then set it again.

"Uh, you must be friends with the guard dog here then?" I asked, worried the dog might hear us and take a break from his meaty treats.

"Dabney?" asked Thayer, "That's my dog. I brought him with me tonight. He's the worst excuse for a guard dog, no training and little interest in anything except food and naps. I'll probably have to carry him home. He's not much into walks, either."

Thayer called his dog from the far end of the fence. The dog came slowly carrying a piece of steak in his mouth.

"Who's been feeding my dog?" he asked. "You didn't try to poison him, did you?"

"No," I said. "We're animal lovers."

Jerry had disappeared from the fence into the shadows.

"We've got your file and are counting on you to turn yourself in tomorrow or there will be a warrant out for your arrest. Encourage the others to come in also or they'll meet the same fate," Nappi said, keeping our cover as cops.

Grandy pulled up in Nappi's SUV, rolled down the window and said, "What's up?"

"Who's she?" asked Thayer, suspicion in his voice.

"She's our boss. She likes to come along on some cases. Says riding a desk is boring," I replied.

Thayer gave Grandy a longer look, but then nodded and walked off with his dog still carrying the steak in his jaws.

"There goes our late-night dinner," said Jerry, emerging from the shadows and getting into the car.

"There's nothing left of all that meat?" I asked.

"What happened?" asked Grandy once we all had gotten into the car.

We told her about Thayer and his blackmail scheme.

"You guys had all the fun while I sat in the car. You owe me one, Eve. You promised me I could help."

"You did help," said Nappi. "When Thayer saw you, he knew we were legit."

"You think?" asked Grandy.

Nappi nodded.

"Well, okay, but I want to be in on a case where there's some action."

"Next time you can feed the dog," said Jerry.

"But the dog was a pet," Grandy said.

"I didn't know that at the time. That dog was so hungry I thought he would come through the fence and devour me."

"Scary," said Grandy.

"Very," Jerry replied.

I suppressed a laugh.

Grandy sat back in the seat and was quiet for a moment. "You want to drive?" she asked Nappi.

"If you don't," he said.

Grandy hopped out, and she and Nappi switched seats.

"It's been a long night," she said.

"Tired?" I asked, patting her shoulder.

She shook her head. "I'm hungry."

"There's a steakhouse down the street," Nappi said.

"Do they serve fish?" I asked. I had no appetite for beef.

THE NEXT DAY began on a positive note. Jason and Bethany returned in the early morning on foot, towing Lionel's canoe, half in, half out of the water, behind them.

"It's in terrible shape," said Jason.

"Then you'd better fix it," Lionel told them.

"I want to go home. I've had enough of roughing it," whined Bethany.

Lionel gave her a stern look, brow furrowed, eyes cold. "Not until my canoe is repaired."

"I'll do it," said Jason. "Bethany wasn't responsible for wrecking it. That was my doing."

"Okay," I said, "before anyone does anything, we need to hear the story of how the two of you found yourselves out in the swamp."

Sammy laid his hand on my shoulder. "First we should call David and Madeleine and tell them Bethany is back and safe."

"I think Lionel already told David he found the kids," I said.

"Did I? I think I must have forgotten to make that call," said Lionel and turned his attention to the canoe.

"Make it now," I said.

"I'll take care of calling David," Sammy volunteered.

"Dad will be furious when he hears I ran off," Bethany said.

"I thought getting a reaction from him is what your disappearance was all about," I said. Bethany dropped her gaze and wouldn't meet my eyes. "Grandfather will get you some hot breakfast, and then we'll all talk."

David and Madeleine showed up before the kids were finished eating.

David had called Bethany's mother who was also on her way. Jason and Bethany both knew it was showdown time, and they weren't looking forward to it. Neither said a word while they ate.

We all sat at Grandfather's table and let Jason and Bethany finish their food.

"Okay. Tell. We know the two of you met here, but how did you end up with Bethany in the swamp?" I asked Jason.

He gulped down the last of his coffee and said, "She came by here late one afternoon and said she needed a place to hide from her parents. I took her by canoe," here he gave Lionel a look of apology, "and paddled her to the old shack where you and Dad like to picnic and do, uh, other things. I left her there and took out food for a few days, but decided she needed me there, so I joined her. We had decided to leave when the storm came up, but the canoe was swamped, so we left it and took cover until Lionel found us and told us we had to locate his canoe. That's it. The whole story."

Well, it really wasn't the whole story, was it? How friendly had the two of them become? Bethany was two years older than Jason and more sophisticated. What had happened between the two of them? I knew he was smitten with her, but how did she feel about him?

David listened to Jason's story, then asked, "I don't understand why you left the ranch, Bethany. I thought you were settling in there."

Bethany seemed to have lost some of her old teenage outspokenness. Perhaps living in the swamp had taught her some humility.

"You barely spent any time with me, and you took my cellphone away. I missed talking to my friends. And shopping.

I was so lonely. The ranch is great, but I'm not certain I can spend every day there. It's so isolated."

"I know it was difficult for you to adjust. The house was filled with my relatives, but they will be leaving soon. We can work out something so that you work on the ranch during the week and spend some weekends with your mother. We'll find a way to make it work," said Madeleine.

Bethany smiled. "Thanks. I'll try, too. I'm sorry I made you worry about me. I guess I didn't think."

"That doesn't mean there won't be a price to pay for your thoughtlessness," said David.

"What? I thought you weren't mad," Bethany said.

"We're not mad, but what you did was wrong, so as punishment your cellphone time will be limited as will television. You'll have to help Jason repair the canoe. We'll work out the specifics when we get home. Your mother will be here soon. You'll have to explain everything to her," David said.

"I have a question for Bethany," I said. "How did you get from the ranch to here? Hitchhike? Because that's dangerous."

"Oh, no. Mrs. MacAngus drove me here."

CHAPTER 20

———

"Low do you know Mrs. MacAngus?" asked David in an astonished tone of voice.

"I don't, well, I mean I didn't, but when I crawled out my bedroom window and walked to the road, there was a car sitting there. The woman rolled down the window and asked if I knew the people who lived in the house. I said I did, that I was your daughter and I was heading toward town to meet someone. She commented that it was kind of a long walk and asked me if I wanted a ride. I said yes and hopped in."

"What did you talk about?" I asked.

"Mostly about her husband. She said she wanted to talk with him privately, but that someone was always at the house, so it was difficult to get him alone. She acted as if she was anxious to see him as soon as possible."

"I wonder why she was so adamant about talking to Angus alone," David said.

"We can find out right now. She came to visit this morning. I'm betting she's still there. Once she settles in, she stays," said Madeleine.

I thought I knew what Mrs. MacAngus was going to say to Angus. She wanted to confess to him that she and the man she was living with had separated and that she had no money, shoved out of her dream condo to live in a small trailer. I was betting she wanted to beg Angus to take her back. I doubted anyone else was party to the information about her reduced financial situation.

"I'm coming to the ranch with you to say hello to Madeleine. Maybe I can have a few words with Mickey and Angus about the case," I said. "I'll be back here in an hour for a family get-together to sort out what happened with Jason. You still have a few questions to answer, honey, but for now, you look as if you could use a lie down." I put my arm around his shoulder and squeezed. I wanted to throw both arms around him and hug him to me, but I knew he wouldn't like me to do that in front of everyone. He wanted us to see him as an adult. Well, like an adult, he'd be taking the punishment for stealing from Lionel and wrecking the canoe. I considered calling Frida to come out and tell him he was under arrest for theft, but I decided that was too much. Lionel, however, might like it enough to go through with the façade. I kept the idea to myself.

"I'm right behind you," I said to Madeleine and grabbed the convertible's keys to head out to the ranch.

As I parked behind Mrs. MacAngus' car in the ranch drive, another convertible pulled up with David's ex-wife in it.

"Where's my daughter?" she yelled, her face red with anger. "If your son did anything to her..." she began.

I thought about slapping her, but instead did the next best thing: I grabbed her arm and pulled her up the steps and into the house. "Tell your daughter you were worried about her and you're glad she's back," I hissed in her ear.

"What did that Indian boy do to you?" she yelled when she saw Bethany. "Call the cops. I want to press charges."

Maybe it was time for a good slap or a fist to her nose. Instead

Madeleine stepped in.

"Angela, I can appreciate how worried you were, but the kids are both fine. I think Bethany could use a hug, however." Madeleine pushed the girl toward her mother. Before Angela could protest, Bethany threw her arms around her mother and began sobbing.

"I'm fine, Mom. Jason took good care of me. It was my idea to hide out. I thought I could make you and Dad sorry you hadn't treated me better. It was wrong, and I'm willing to make it up to you." She stepped back from her mother, stopped crying and added in a voice more grown up than I'd ever heard from her, "Don't you dare punish Jason for my mistake or think he wasn't a perfect gentleman the entire time or I'll never speak to you again. Forget all your ugly thoughts."

While Bethany and her parents talked, I asked Madeleine, "Where is everybody?"

"Mickey, Dylan, and Darcie are out back with the twins. Angus and his wife are in his room, talking about something important from the sounds of their voices. No yelling, hushed tones."

"I'll go see what going on. I'm making no progress on this case, and it's frustrating me. It appears the attacks on Angus may be connected to his company, but who is responsible is still uncertain, and I'm certain Angus and Mickey must want to fire Crusty and me for the lack of results."

I tapped on the door and stepped into the room. Mrs. MacAngus sat on her husband's bed, her hand on his. She was crying. He patted her hand in sympathy, but his face said that whatever argument she was making, he wasn't buying it.

"I'm sorry things haven't worked out for you and Bruce, but I intend to go through with the divorce. There's no life for us together. How many times do I need to tell you that?" Angus said.

Mrs. MacAngus crying stopped and her face flushed red with anger. "You owe me. I was the little stay-at-home wife all these years while you spent most of your time at the company. I never had any fun, we didn't go out, and our friends were really your business friends. It was no life for me. Bruce made me feel desirable again. But then he showed me the road."

"Why did he do that now?" I asked.

Mrs. MacAngus turned to face me. "That's none of your business," she said, then turned back to Angus and put her hand on his shoulder. "Please, Angus. Let's try again. This time I'll make it work."

He brushed off her hand and shook his head.

"Fine. If that's your final word, I'll have to do what I have to do," she said and fled from the room.

Dylan almost ran into his grandmother as she ran out the door.

"Sorry, honey. I know how much you love your grandfather, but this whole thing has to come to an end." She bent to hug her grandson, then continued down the hallway.

"Hi, Dylan," I said. "I'm sorry your airboat ride ended so abruptly, and you didn't get to see more alligators."

Dylan's face lit up. "Oh, golly. I thought it was so much fun. The storm was so exciting, and I saw plenty gators. I'd sure like to go out again before we leave here."

"I'll see what I can arrange."

On his way to his grandfather's bedside, he passed the bureau on which the cat picture stood. "What happened to kitty?" he asked.

He showed the picture to Angus and then to me. I took it from him and looked closely at the collage of seeds, rice, beans and grasses. There was a bare batch on the cat's fur where some of the seeds were missing.

"It must have fallen on the floor. I'm sure we can fix it," Angus said.

"I think Madeleine may have some dried beans we can use to replace the seeds." I took Dylan's hand, and we left to search Madeleine's kitchen for the beans we could use to repair the picture.

Madeleine extracted a bag of dried pinto beans from her cupboard, and she and Dylan glued them onto the bare spots.

"There," Madeleine said. "It's good as new."

"Not really," said Dylan. "The beans look different."

I looked closely at the picture. Dylan was right. The seeds remaining were more like grains of wheat or oats.

"I think the replacements give the cat's fur more texture," I said.

He seemed reassured, hopped down from the kitchen table and took the picture back to his grandfather's room.

"I'd better stop by the office and talk with Crusty, then peek in on Grandy at the shop," I told Madeleine. I looked around the room, looking for Mrs. MacAngus.

"She left in a fit. I don't think she'll be back," said Madeleine. I could hear the relief in her vice.

"Good. I think she and Angus are finally over. She didn't seem happy about it."

"I think she saw it coming. She seemed upset when she arrived earlier today, and said she wondered why she bothered with Angus. That he was stubborn old coot, but she said she brought the ingredients for one of Angus favorite dishes and asked if she could use the kitchen to finish preparing it. Before she slammed out, she popped into the kitchen. The dish apparently takes some time to complete. It looks horrible, but it's in the fridge if any of the family wants to eat it tonight for dinner. It's like a bag of boiled guts. Ugh."

Angus came into the kitchen with Dylan and heard us talking. He opened the fridge and peeked in. "It is a bag of boiled guts." Angus laughed. "I love it, but no one else in the family does. It's haggis."

"Even the name sounds unappealing. What's in it?" asked Madeleine.

"What I said: calf and sheep offal or intestine and guts boiled in a stomach with oatmeal and spices."

Both Madeleine and I stepped back from the refrigerator as if we expected the dish to jump out at us.

"No sense letting it go to waste even if my wife's dish isn't as tasty as my mother's recipe. It's an acquired taste," he said. "I'll have it for supper tonight."

"The rest of us are having chili," said Madeleine.

"I hate haggis," said Dylan, screwing up his face, "But chili sounds good."

"You seem preoccupied, Eve," said Grandy that afternoon after I returned from talking with Jason.

I sighed. "Almost everything has worked out well. Jason and Bethany have returned, and we know the identities of the sexual harassers at Ms. Abbot's business, but I can't get a handle on who tried to kill Angus. I'm going to call Frida to see if she's tracked down the hunters from Angus' business who came to the ranch the day Angus was shot. It had to be one of them, but I don't understand why they did it or why anyone would kill Angus. He seems so harmless, a charming old man."

I asked the same question of Frida when she answered her cell.

"I'm running out of clues in this case, Eve. It was someone who knew how to handle a weapon, one of the hunters I'd guess, but I'm still trying to track them down. Nappi seemed to think Angus poked his nose into the business too much. Maybe someone was sent to the States to remove him from the picture so the business would operate without the insertion of his ideas, which, Nappi admitted when he went to talk with officers in the business, were rather old-fashioned."

"So out-of-date that the business would suffer financially if he continued to help operate it?" I asked.

"Maybe," said Frida. "It still doesn't track well for me. It sounds as if Angus was an irritant they tolerated, not someone they hated."

"Or maybe it's much simpler than that. Maybe someone in

the family had reason to kill him," I said. "There was plenty of anger and mistrust there: Mickey and his father didn't get along, Mickey and his wife had talked about divorce, Angus' wife left him for his best friend, and then Angus wife was tossed out by the friend and she wanted to get back together with Angus. Very messy, wouldn't you say?"

"I don't know. I've seen families with more troubles. My own is a mess, but no one seems inclined to kill anyone. Don't forget we initially thought Angus was trying to commit suicide, but the shooting put that idea to rest. Unless something was so troubling to Angus that he asked or hired someone to kill him. You know, suicide with help."

"Can you subpoena his bank records to see if he paid out money recently and to whom?" I asked.

"Good idea," Frida said.

We looked at each other, incredulity written on the other's face. Suicide with help? How ridiculous was that?

We were both discouraged. On this case we had cooperated with each other. The old competition was gone, but we still hadn't made progress. For now Angus was alive and surrounded by family, but there was always the chance that someone could come at him again. That someone could be a family member. Since the shooting, Frida and I both had held our breaths and hoped it wouldn't happen or that we would soon get a break and find who attacked Angus. He didn't seem depressed enough to want to end his life, but men handled depression differently from women. They hid behind that masculine façade of being able to handle anything rather than admit they were in mental trouble. Someone was hiding something. Was it Angus, a business associate or a member of his family?

Grandy and I closed shop late because a group of five young women came in to look at our gowns. At the end of June the town would be holding their annual formal dance to raise money for the hospital. Two of the women found the gowns they wanted, but we had nothing for the other three. I told them I would be making a run to the coast in a few days and might have something for them by the end of the week. They promised to return.

Sammy had promised me someone from the tribe to help part-time in the store, but both of us had been so preoccupied with other concerns he had forgotten. So had I, but I was puzzled he hadn't remembered because he had acted as if he had someone in mind. In fact, the expression on his face said he had someone special in mind, someone I would be pleased to hire. I thought over the Miccosukee women I knew and couldn't come up with a name. I'd have to remind him later.

Grandy told me she and Max had been invited to a friend's house for dinner, so I insisted she leave the final cash-up for the day to me. The day's receipts indicated we had done well; sales were up over the past several days, and I was delighted, but I was right to worry about our stock. As my eye traveled over the dress rounds and racks, I thought the shop looked a bit bare. I decided to take a few minutes and rearrange some of the items. I pulled shoes off the shoe racks and removed the lower rack, moving more pairs onto the remaining racks to make them look fuller. I then tackled the household knick knacks which always looked disorganized by the end of the day because customers picked them up and put them back out of order. I didn't mind. I wanted our clientele to feel comfortable handing our merchandise, but I liked to begin the day with everything in order.

When I reached for a picture frame to move it closer to another one, it slipped from my hand and crashed to the floor. I'd have to replace the glass in this one, but before I could get a broom to sweep up the mess, a notion tickling my brain for the afternoon finally became conscious. Those funny-looking seeds in the picture. I couldn't understand how a fall onto the floor could dislodge them. They were small and light. A drop to the floor might knock off heavier beans, yet that wasn't the case. The beans and pasta on the picture remained securely in place. Why did the seeds come off? Unless... someone deliberately removed them. There was something special about those seeds. I ran into our office and sat down at the computer. A few minutes of searching brought up a photo of seeds identical to those from Dylan's cat picture. Who had been in Mr. Angus' room today when he was out? The seeds, Mrs. Angus hanging around the ranch, her anger at Angus, her surprise dish for Angus—it finally came together for me.

I called the ranch and got Madeleine on the phone.

"Have you had dinner yet?" I asked.

"We're about to sit down to it."

"Is Angus having the haggis?"

"Sadly yes," she replied. "He's about to dive into a bowl of that foul stuff."

"Tell him to not eat it. It's been poisoned."

CHAPTER 21

—

WHEN I CALLED Frida and told her my suspicions, she put out an ABP for Mrs. MacAngus, and rushed to the Wilson ranch. Everyone was gathered in the living room, Frida seated across from Angus, her notebook in her hand.

Frida had handed off the haggis to one of her officers to be transported to the state lab in Miami. She was questioning Angus about his wife when I arrived.

I gave Madeleine a hug.

"I can't believe she was the one behind all these attempts on Angus' life," she told me.

"When you put together her appearances here, she's a likely suspect," I said.

"And poison is a woman's weapon," Mickey said. "But my own mother? That's hard to take. I don't think I believe it." He sat on the couch, his arm around his wife.

"Angus said the brakes felt spongy on the way from Miami. That certainly doesn't fit with her appearances here at the ranch," I said.

Angus cleared his throat. "She visited me at the motel in

Miami. I had sent her our itinerary, so she knew where we were staying when we flew in."

"You said nothing about the visit," I said. "What did she want? Why drive all the way to Miami when she knew you'd be visiting her soon?"

"She wanted the usual. She told me she and Bruce had separated. She wanted me to take her back. She doesn't understand the meaning of 'no'." Angus stared at the opposite wall, his face expressionless.

Frida said, "I'm bringing in your mother for questioning at this point and having my officers search for remnants of the seeds that were removed from the picture. We don't know yet if she put them into the haggis."

Mickey nodded. "Good."

Frida turned her attention back to Angus. "Can your wife handle a shotgun?"

Angus's face turned weary with anguish. He ran his fingers through his graying reddish hair. "Yes, she shoots. Her father taught her. She's a good shot."

"Not that good," I pointed out. "She missed."

"Tell me about the picture your grandson made. Did you know there might have been oleander seeds in it? Did anyone know?"

"None of us knew," said Mickey. "My mother suggested one day about a year ago when we were vacationing in Spain that Dylan might want to do a craft project. He was getting bored hanging out on the beach and strolling through the town. You know how young boys are. She recommended a collage made with what we could find outside and in the pantry at the villa we rented. All of us found seeds from plantings around the house and plants growing the fields—sunflowers, wheat and other grasses."

"Dylan loved creating the picture. He gave it to me as a present. I was going to leave it behind at my house in Scotland when we left for the visit to the States, but I decided to bring it with me in my suitcase," Angus said. He spoke as if he was gulping back tears.

"Who knew you brought it with you?" asked Frida.

"Everyone around here. I put it on the dresser. My wife must have known there were oleander seeds in it. She pointed out the bushes behind the villa when we arrived in Spain. I didn't know they were poisonous," Angus said.

Frida looked at Mickey and Darcie.

They shook their heads.

Frida flipped her notebook closed. "That's all for now. We'll know more when we get the lab results back and when we pick up Mrs. MacAngus."

Before she could leave, her cell rang. She talked for a moment, then ended the call. "They found Mrs. MacAngus down the road, at the Biscuit, getting rip snorting drunk. We'll sober her up and see what she has to say." She flipped her notebook shut. "That's all for now. We'll keep Mrs. MacAngus with us overnight and talk to her tomorrow."

"Can I see her tonight?" asked Angus.

"You really want to? After what she has done to you?"

"We don't know that for certain, do we?" Angus said.

"Dad, leave it be," said Mickey.

"She's your mother and my wife!" shouted Angus, his face red, his eyes filling with unshed tears.

"I'll let you see her early tomorrow, after I question her," said Frida. "I'm sorry, but for now, she needs to sleep it off."

"You need sleep, too, Dad," said Mickey. "Let's go." He held out his hand to his father who took it. The two of them headed down the hallway to the bedroom.

Bethany listened to all of this from the kitchen where she leaned against the wall and sipped a glass of water.

"Wow," she said, "This makes Jason's and my little adventure look like a ride at Disneyland."

"To bed, young lady. Your "little adventure" as you call still merits the punishment your mother and I discussed with you earlier."

She shrugged. "Right, but when do I get to see Jason again?" she asked.

Never, I thought, but kept that pronouncement to myself.

I caught up with Frida as she got into her cruiser.

"I guess we're assuming that Mrs. MacAngus left her husband for someone who then tossed her out, then she decided to kill her husband? Her motive seems kind of muddled or unclear," I said.

"Hey, Eve, you were the one who told me she might have put those seeds into that horrid concoction. Now you're not sure?"

"Look, I heard how angry she was the last time they talked, but she had to have been in a slow burn for a long time to tamper with the brakes and take a shot at him, and yet she still begs him to take her back today? How much sense does that make?"

Frida shrugged. "I need to question her. She's our best suspect."

"Maybe there's someone else we should consider."

"Who?" she asked.

"The guy who tossed her away. What was his name? He was supposed to be Angus' best friend."

"So, how does that make him a suspect?"

"I don't know, but he's on my radar as are those hunters. Any word on them?" I asked. I was worried Frida would go a familiar cop direction, turn all her resources onto one candidate and ignore other leads. I wouldn't have said this to her for the world. I respected her too much.

"That's on the back burner for now, but I'm keeping them in mind, and I'm going to add Angus' best friend. His name is Bruce somebody. I've got an address in Naples and a phone number."

Good. I should have known Frida wouldn't let me down.

I tossed and turned that night, sleep fleeting, and arose

when the sun reached out over the field next to my house and inserted its light into my bedroom. Sammy stirred and muttered something about my early rising, then rolled over and fell back asleep. The shower helped me become more alert, but my brain was still foggy from the events of last night. If I pushed it, the pieces fit, but I still had difficulty finding Mrs. MacAngus' anger enough to lead to the murder of her husband.

I made coffee, and the aroma awakened the other members of the house: Sammy, Grandy and Max. The boys and Netty were with Grandfather at the canal.

"You have something on your mind, Eve?" asked Grandy. I shared with the others the story about Mrs. MacAngus and my doubts regarding her guilt.

"But who else could it be?" asked Grandy.

I fidgeted with my coffee cup until it spilled on the table.

Grandy wiped up the spill, and we all were silent, thinking about the situation. Finally, Sammy said, "Sometimes it's better not to push things where they don't want to go. There are plenty of other things that need our attention. There's the house, for example. It's almost finished, and we should have a party when it's ready for us to move into it."

"How soon should that be?" I asked.

"I'd say in less than a week."

"Oh, no. I haven't taken the time to find furniture for it because I've been so wrapped up in these cases. Here I am a consignment shop owner with infinite resources, and I've neglected shopping for the house. We'll all be back to sleeping on the floor in sleeping bags." I jumped up from the table and grabbed my purse. "I've got to take a look at the inventory at the store and in the RV. Sammy, can I borrow your truck to go to the coast today? And, Sammy, where's my help? Grandy, will you mind the shop? Do you think Grandfather will be willing to babysit for Netty today?"

Sammy smiled, and when I caught his grin, I stopped short.

"Oh, you got me, didn't you? I'm so focused on the house I can't think about the MacAngus case. I'll consider that later. Maybe tomorrow. Bye all." I grabbed the truck keys and was off, certain that Sammy and Grandy could handle the shop and the children.

We needed everything for the house from dishes and pots and pans to beds, mattresses and bedding for the bedrooms as well as a table, chairs and living room furniture, and… I needed to make a list. My house was furnished, but Grandy and Max lived in it. If they moved back to Key Largo, it would be part-time, and they would stay in a trailer or motor home. I wasn't going to raid my place for items to use in the new house and leave Grandy and Max with limited furniture and household items.

I found some kitchen items in the store, paid for them as would any client and, as I suspected, realized the store and the RV didn't have what we needed. I also didn't want to deplete our customers' selections. The queen of the secondhand bargain certainly wasn't going to buy new, except for mattresses. Finding what I needed by visiting clients who consigned with us from West Palm was time-consuming and would reduce the inventory I could sell in the store.

I had half-lied to Sammy. The MacAngus case remained on my mind. Because Angus and Mickey were clients of the agency, it was my duty to find out what Carolyn MacAngus had to say this morning. I called Frida's cell.

"Did you learn anything from Mrs. MacAngus?"

"I haven't questioned her yet, but I'm going to as soon as she's had her breakfast."

"I don't suppose I could sit in?" I knew I couldn't, but it never hurts to ask.

"No, but you can talk with her after I'm finished. I'll let you have first shot at her before I allow her husband and son in to see her."

"I'll be right there. Say, you don't have a newspaper from the

West Palm area, do you?"

"Sure. What…"

I ended the call and didn't let her finish what she was asking.

I was seated in Frida's office chair, my feet up on her desk, perusing the want-ads in the paper when she emerged from the interview room.

"Get your size nine ostrich boots off my desk," she said.

"Sorry."

"Are you looking for a job?" she asked, plopping down in the visitor's chair.

"Nope. I'm looking for estate sales, the easiest way I know of to furnish my new house. How's our killer?"

"Sober, and asking for a lawyer."

"You charged her with attempted murder?" I asked.

"Not yet. I'm holding her until I get the lab results back. They should be in this afternoon. It makes the tech's job easier when you can give the lab the kind of poison you're looking for."

"So, can I talk to her?"

"I don't think she'll tell you anything. Go ahead, but hurry. I see Angus and Mickey pulling into the parking lot right now."

Mrs. MacAngus gave me a sour look when I entered the room.

"The coffee is lousy here."

"Here. Take mine. It's my second cup, and I haven't touched it."

"Don't try to pry anything out of me by playing nice. I know you're friends with that detective."

"I am. I understand you want a lawyer. I know some good ones in this area."

"I'll get my own." She sipped the coffee and was silent for a moment. "Thanks for the coffee."

I nodded. "I think you still love Angus even though he doesn't want you to remain his wife. I think you know you made a mistake by leaving him. You found out what kind of man you had left him for."

"I've known what kind of man Bruce was for years, but he put on a good act, promised me the kinds of things I never had with Angus."

"Material things? But I thought Angus was a wealthy man."

She gave a snort of laughter and almost spit her coffee across the table. "Angus had money. His problem was he never wanted to spend it on me. It's as if he knew…"

"Knew what?"

She set the cup down on the table and stared across the room beyond me. When she again met my gaze, she held it for only a moment before she squeezed her eyes shut as if she had seen something so terrifying she wanted to shut it out.

"I need to get out of here."

"I'm sure you do, Here's my problem. If you're not the one who tried to shoot Angus and if there's oleander in the haggis, then these attempts on Angus' life are life threatening. The killer has failed three times. Do you think he or she is finished?"

She shook her head.

"You think you can talk the person responsible out of another attempt?"

She looked at me, but her expression was shadowed. Whatever she knew, whatever she suspected, she wanted to keep it from me. "Thanks again for the coffee, but now I need to go back to my cell and lie down. And think."

Angus and Mickey talked to Carolyn for a few minutes after I left her. That afternoon the lab confirmed that there was oleander in the haggis, enough to kill several people. Frida charged her with three counts of attempted murder, and Angus arranged for a lawyer, a very expensive lawyer. Angus came through for his wife. Bail was set at half a million dollars. Angus paid it. Carolyn Angus was wrong: Angus did spend money on her.

Several days later, Frida and I were sitting on the front porch of Grandfather's small house waiting for a moving van to deliver the furniture I had purchased at an estate sale the day before. "Your case is pretty circumstantial," I said to Frida.

"Do you have any more concrete evidence against another suspect?"

"I understand Bruce was an unpleasant fellow. And what about the hunters?"

"I finally tracked them down in Orlando. Carolyn's former lover and the hunters all have alibis for one or more of the attempts on Angus' life. Bruce was at some concert with a new lady friend. The hunters were in David's sight the entire time they were at the ranch. And no real motive for any of them."

"Even the best alibis can be broken," I said. "Why did the hunters get lost after you questioned them?"

"A miscommunication. They told me they understood I was finished with them. Nappi was probably right that the company found Angus annoying and wanted him out of the picture, but they didn't send men here to do him in."

I nodded. "Yeah, I know. I somehow wanted it not to be Mrs. MacAngus."

"Why? She's more annoying than Angus could ever be."

"She's also probably not guilty."

"Show me some evidence," said Frida.

"You'll never make the charges stick. Yes, she was around for all the attempts, but so were others."

"Now we're back to members of the family including the extended family."

"Don't be silly. You know Madeleine and David had nothing to do with trying to kill Angus."

"I know."

"Here's the problem. If you're wrong about Mrs. MacAngus being guilty, someone out there still has a reason to make another attempt on his life."

She nodded. "That bothers me, but there is nothing I can do about it."

"When I talked to Mrs. MacAngus the morning of the day

you pressed charges, she almost said something about Angus. I know it was important, but then she backed off. I wonder if I should take another stab at her."

"She's all yours, but I don't think she wants to talk to anyone. I've heard she's not very forthcoming with her lawyer."

"It will be months until this comes to trial. Meantime, Nappi has rented Angus and his family a place in those new condos at the edge of town, and Angus footed the bill for a smaller condo for his wife. She told me he was tight with his money, at least when it came to her, but now that she's in trouble for trying to kill him, he comes through with a lawyer and a condo. I don't think this is what Angus had in mind when he decided to travel to the States."

Frida waved her hand dismissively. "The charges against her could be dropped, but then I'm back to the beginning on this case. My boss is thinking he's tired of having tourists from Scotland here in town and even said something nice about winter visitors, and you know how they aggravate him." She paused. "Listen. This is my day off. Can we talk about something other than business?"

"Sure. I was thinking I hadn't seen you in the shop for a while and your wardrobe is looking a bit tired. How about stopping by soon? I'll give you a discount."

"Discount or a bribe of some sort?"

I gave her a playful punch on her arm. "We're buds now, aren't we?"

She ignored my comment but smiled and changed the subject.

"How are the boys and Netty? Excited about moving into the new house?"

I nodded. "My only concern is I wonder if we shouldn't have added another bathroom. Jeremy seems to be into collecting animal and plant specimens, which he likes to house in the tub. He's turning into a real nature boy. Lionel is encouraging him. The two of them have been spending time in the library reading books on zoology and botany." I paused for a moment. "Do you know what Mickey's major was in college?"

Frida gave me a puzzled look. "I assume it was business given his choice of career."

"Nope. Angus told me it was biology. He said that was why Mickey was so bad at the import/export business. 'The boy should have stuck with bugs and plants,' he told me.'"

"So?" Frida said. "Lots of people change their career paths after college. The job market often dictates taking what's available."

"Right," I said, but my thoughts were far away.

"Hey, here comes your furniture."

A large truck with the logo of a wading bird and the name "Tribal Moving" began to back into the drive.

"I've got to go," I said.

I walked toward the truck and waved at the driver. "Keep going. You can back up right to the house. Leave all the stuff on the porch."

"You don't want us to carry it in and place it in the rooms?" asked the driver.

"No time. I've got to talk to a lady about plants."

CHAPTER 22

Frida watched me jump into my car and ran over to me. "What are you doing, Eve? Your furniture's here."

"I know. I'm so stupid."

Frida nodded.

"Not about the furniture. About Mrs. MacAngus. About the family. I've got to see her right away."

"Do you want me to come with you?"

"No. I can't be certain, but I think she might finish telling me what she started the last time we talked, but I'm certain she won't respond well to a cop in the room. I'll be in touch." I waved and pulled out of the drive.

The condos situated on the creek near the rim canal were only a few years old. No one in the area knew Nappi owned them. He kept his ownership to himself, figuring the locals wouldn't take kindly to a mob boss buying into the local economy. Mrs. MacAngus lived in a one-bedroom unit at the end of the first building. Angus and his family occupied a three bedroom a few doors down.

Carolyn MacAngus opened the door after I rang the bell

several times.

"I don't want to talk to anyone," she said. Her hair was uncombed, and she was still in a robe. She looked thinner and older than when I had last seen her. Her face was gray and lined with worry.

"I thought we might share our concern for your husband. You are worried about him, aren't you?" I brushed by her and took a seat in the living room on the sofa. The place came furnished, but the furniture was quality, the artwork was well-executed reproductions. Leave it to Nappi to show good taste even in his condominium properties.

She sunk into the chair across from me. "Of course, I'm worried. I wasn't the person who tried to kill him. His life is in danger, and there's nothing I can do about it."

"I believe you, but I also think there is something you can do. You started to say something the other day about the way Angus treated Mickey. Talk to me about that. Maybe we can find a way through this."

She shook her head and then covered her face with her hands.

"I don't know what to do." She dropped her hands into her lap and twisted the fingers together in distress.

"Tell me."

"I won't betray him. And I might be wrong. I probably am."

"Tell me what you think Angus believed about Mickey. You said to me, 'It was as if he knew...'"

"I've really messed up everything."

"Maybe it's time to unmess things then."

"I can't. I really can't."

"Carolyn," I said. "Angus may die, Others could, too."

She let out a deep sigh. "Okay. Here goes. It wasn't recently that Bruce and I got together romantically. We had an affair years ago. It was a total betrayal of Angus on both our parts. Bruce was his best friend. I was his wife. We realized what we had done, so we broke it off. I was horrified to find out soon after that I was pregnant. I was certain the baby was Bruce's."

"Did you tell him?"

"Yes. He wanted me to get rid of it, but Angus and I had been trying for years to get pregnant. I decided to keep the baby. Bruce said he wanted nothing to do with it, which was fine with me. Angus was thrilled he was going to finally be a father and delighted when it was a boy. But after several months, Angus began to withdraw. He acted as if he wasn't interested in his son. He was distant with Mickey, unaffectionate. He set high standards for the boy and punished him when he didn't meet those standards. Mickey was hurt he couldn't please his father."

"That's what you meant when you said, 'it was as if he knew.' You meant he acted as if he knew the child wasn't his."

She nodded and continued her story. "Bruce rarely came to visit us after Mickey was born. No one thought it strange he was absent because his work took him out of Scotland to Europe and then to the States, but one year when Mickey was around twelve, Bruce was on his way to England, so he decided to stop by. Everyone was very polite, but it wasn't a comfortable visit. Bruce and I had a private exchange in the study. We talked about Mickey and Bruce's paternity. He said he had been wrong to suggest I not keep the baby. He had never married, nor had children. He wanted to admit Mickey was his child, but I said no. It was too late and unfair to everyone. I convinced Bruce how much damage it could do to everyone especially Mickey if he was told his real father was Bruce."

"Did anyone overhear that conversation, do you think?'

"I think both Mickey and Angus might have. The estrangement between them grew after that and continued to increase throughout Mickey's teen years and into adulthood. Angus became even more critical of Mickey even though Mickey had gone into a business which became the business Angus was partial owner of. Mickey seemed to hate the business as well as Angus, and Angus felt the same way about his son. He must know Mickey isn't his. And Mickey has become angrier and angrier over the years."

"You think Mickey was the one who put the oleander seeds into the haggis."

She let out a long breath. "Yes."

"You need to tell Frida this."

"I think it may be too late."

"What do you mean?"

"Angus, Mickey and Dylan rented a boat to go fishing today. They're out on the lake right now."

"We've got to get to them." I took out my cell and called Frida, informing her about the conversation between Mrs. MacAngus and me.

"Can you get a patrol boat out to them?" I asked.

"Our only boat is down in Clewiston being repaired," Frida told me.

"I'll call Max and see if he can use his fishing pal's bass boat."

"That's a huge lake," Frida said.

While Frida and I were talking, Carolyn's cell rang. She answered and talked for a few moments, then held out the phone to me. "It's Mickey. He's frantic. His father was washed overboard."

Mickey had made his move. "Tell him to keep talking. Frida and I will be out to get him as soon as we can. Tell him not to move the boat."

"There's more," said Mrs. MacAngus. "Dylan went overboard with him."

I contacted Max by cell. He and Buddy, who owned one of the fastest bass boats on the lake, were tying up at the docks by the river.

"Things are getting nasty out there with the wind kicking up big choppy waves," Max said.

I told him about Angus and Dylan.

"Okay. Get out here as soon as you can. Buddy says we'll give it a try."

"Frida is calling the marine patrol."

"That won't do much good. They went out on a rescue mission minutes ago. I think we're on our own," said Max.

I heard Frida's cruiser pull up out front. Mrs. MacAngus continued to talk with Mickey, trying to calm him. "He says he doesn't think he can stay put. There are waves washing over the side of the boat."

"Tell him to do his best. There's help on the way. Can he give us a location?" I asked.

"He says someone told him the bass were biting off Barton's Bay. That's where he anchored. He's still there."

"Give me his cell number and tell him I'm calling him," I said. I got the number and punched it in while I ran out to Frida's car.

The wind had picked up, and, like the day Grandfather, Madeleine, the kids and I were out in the airboat, I knew we were in for another of those summer storms that came up without warning around the lake. Frida tromped on the accelerator, and we sped off onto the road leading to the boat landing on the river. We played keep away with the tree limbs that fell onto the road, but it only took us five minutes before we pulled into the parking area and spotted Max on the boat. Frida and I jumped on board, and we were off on another fast ride, this one down the river and into the lake. It was choppy, but the powerful bass boat cut through the waves, throwing cold water on all of us. Max had handed us raingear when we got on board, but I was still shivering from the cold.

"How can anyone survive in these waters? Angus and Dylan will be hypothermic in a few minutes. It's been more than fifteen since Mickey called," I said.

"I see the boat ahead," called Max though the wind. "It looks like Mickey is pulling the anchor to leave."

"Stay where you are. Your boat is almost swamped, and you won't be able to move," called Buddy. "I'm coming along side, and I'll pick you up."

Mickey was clothed in a rain poncho. "Did your dad and Dylan have on life jackets?" I asked.

Dylan nodded.

As suddenly as the storm came up, the clouds began to disperse, and I could see sun behind them.

"I think the storm is letting up," said Buddy. "We can begin a search of this area."

I caught a look of anxiety on Max's face. "You think a search is futile?" I asked.

"No, but I think we'd better hurry. Barton's Cove is not known for bass fishing. It's known as a place the gators like to congregate. See out there?" Max pointed to what looked like debris in the water, large logs among the reeds close to shore. But they weren't logs. They were the reptiles who ruled this lake.

"I'm going to cut into shore and see what we can see. Maybe they made it out of the water. There are some downed cypress and live oak trees over there. They could climb out of the lake and onto them for safety," said Buddy.

Mickey said nothing, his face as cold and still as granite. Was that because of the cold or did I catch a flicker of deep hate there?

"I guess this plan like all your others went sadly wrong. The only reason you called your mother was because your son went in with his grandfather, something you weren't counting on," I said.

"You get a confession out of him now, Eve, and it won't be admissible in court," Frida whispered to me.

"I don't care," I told her. "We need to find out what happened so we can rescue Angus and Dylan."

"You think you have it all figured out, don't you, PI Eve, but you don't know anything." He put his face close to mine and spit out the words at me in a spray of saliva. "Angus treated me like I was less than human because he knew I was Bruce's son, and my mother never let me have a father who could have loved me and been a real dad to me."

"Your biological father didn't want you. If he had wanted to be your father, he would have stepped up, but Bruce isn't the kind of man who does much stepping up, in case you don't know. He let everyone believe what they wanted," I said.

"Then finally he did want me, but my mother sent him away so she could keep up the lie. I hate both of them."

"Yeh, I get that, but you've framed your mother for attempted murder, and you tried to kill your father."

"He's not my father," yelled Mickey.

"I think that's enough of that," said Frida. She pulled her handcuffs off her belt and reached for Mickey's hands. He twisted away from her, shoving her off the boat's seat and into the lake, then he spun around and shoved me in after her.

I thrashed around in the tea-colored waters. My fear wasn't that I'd drown. Mine was that I would become a gator's dinner and Frida would be dessert.

"Frida," I called, twisting and turning in the cold waters to spot her. Nothing.

"Where is she?" I called to Max and Buddy. "Can you see her?" I spit water out of my mouth and turned toward the boat. What I saw was Mickey with gun pointed at Max and his friend.

"Start this boat and get going," he said. Buddy hesitated. "Now, or you're both dead."

Buddy started the engine. I saw him give Max a long look. Max nodded and grabbed the back of one of the seats. Mickey sat on the other seat, gun leveled at both of them. Buddy put the boat in gear, and Mickey waved his gun at me. "I could shoot you, but I'll leave you to the waters or the gators."

"What about your son?" I yelled.

He wiped his free hand over his face, then looked back at me. I could see the pain in his eyes as he said, "I can't worry about that now."

With a flick of his wrist, Buddy shoved the accelerator arm

Jerry and Shelley about why they were together, but the focus was on Angus and Dylan and not on some misguided romance.

Everyone tried to remain upbeat about beginning the search in the morning, and no one wanted to discuss Mickey's role in the situation, but Frida pulled into the drive with Mrs. MacAngus in the car. Their arrival brought Mickey and his misdeeds front and center.

"Mrs. MacAngus is in the clear. As for Mickey, he's not talking much," she said to me, accepting the chair Grandfather offered her. "I asked where he got the rifle he used to shoot Angus and the pistol he pulled this afternoon, but he only said, 'I've got my ways.' I can't think of anyone I've arrested that I dislike more." She shot an apologetic look at Darcie and Angus' wife.

Darcie, staring into the flames, said, extreme sadness in her voice, "There was always something about Mickey. He seemed to get more and more bitter as he got older. I never understood what that was about, but he got me to agree I'd try again with our marriage. I did for Dylan's sake, but now I think I misjudged Mickey. There is little good in that man." Darcie sighed deeply and said, "Right now all I can think of is my son."

"If Angus and Dylan are together, and I hope they are, Angus will protect him. Angus is a good man. He may have some issues, but he's always been loyal to family. He probably knew all along that Mickey was Bruce's son. I know it was hard for him to deal with that, and he was hard on Mickey, but he never let on to Mickey or to me that he considered Mickey anything other than a son, maybe a son he was disappointed in, but his son. And you know he adored Dylan," said Mrs. MacAngus.

Out of the corner of my eye I caught movement from the direction of the canal. I hadn't noticed until now that Lionel wasn't with us, but he stepped forward out of the darkness into the light from the house. He stood there for a moment, then turned and motioned to someone behind him. Two bedraggled figures, one big, the other small, trudged toward us from the canoe he'd beached. It was Angus and Dylan.

"Found 'em wandering around at the edge of the lake," Lionel said, his tone as nonchalant as if he had run across one of his Indian pals hunting in the swamp. "I think they could use some food and a blanket or two. I could, too. What's for supper tonight?"

CHAPTER 23

—

"How could you have known Angus and Dylan went overboard and were out there or where they were?" I asked him.

He looked surprised. "I didn't know. I was out in my canoe taking it for a ride to make certain Jason had done the repairs correctly. The storm came up, so I took shelter until it blew over. I was headed back here when I saw these two huddled on an inlet off Barton's Bay. I didn't think they were tourists on a hike, so I got them into the canoe, and we came back here. Mr. MacAngus said they fell overboard while fishing."

That wasn't quite the truth, but I was happy they were safe and grateful to Lionel for finding them. I walked over to him and put my arms around him. "Thank you."

At first he stiffened at my embrace, but then he returned the hug. "This is no way to greet men returning from a swamp adventure. What's for supper?" he said again.

Darcie was hugging her son and father-in-law and was joined by Madeleine and Mrs. MacAngus. Sammy dashed into the house and grabbed blankets for them.

Lionel let out a humph and started up the steps to the house.

Grandfather joined him and said something to him as they entered the house. All I heard was Lionel saying, "What? Leftovers again?" I made a mental note to myself to bake a pie for our reluctant hero, then remembered how lacking he found my culinary skills. I changed the mental note to read, "Have Grandy bake Lionel a pie."

Everyone soon departed, and, like Lionel, I realized that I, too, was hungry. The family sat down to a feast of peanut butter and jelly. We sent the kids off to bed in their sleeping bags near the fireplace. Netty fell asleep in Sammy's lap, using her thumb for comfort, something she didn't often do. Although today turned out well, she must have picked up the tension earlier.

"You could have slept in your own house tonight on your own furniture if all of it wasn't piled on the porch," said Lionel.

I'd almost forgotten I'd dashed off to accompany Frida in the search for Mickey, Angus and Dylan when the furniture ban arrived.

"We could do it tonight, Dad," said Sammy.

"Absolutely not. Who knows where you two would place it. It's not simply moving furniture around. It's decorating. I'll see to it tomorrow if you want to help then," I said.

Lionel shrugged. "I'm going to decorate that space over there on the floor with my sleeping palette. It's been a long day."

Sammy and I went off to the only bedroom where Netty and I crawled into the single bed, and Sammy took the air mattress on the floor.

"It will be good to have our own place," I said. "I've been thinking we should have an open house celebration and invite everyone. We could have the Biscuit cater it and…"

No one heard me. The house was filled with a cacophony of snores. I rolled over and joined my soprano to the altos and basses.

In the morning, Frida stopped by to tell me a search of Mickey's belongings turned up a spent shell casing with his fingerprints on it. She admitted it was a long shot that there would be any marks on the casing to link it to the shotgun, but it was a possibility and one more piece of evidence to help link Mickey to the attempts on Angus life.

She and I took a cup of coffee out to the porch to talk. Grandfather and Sammy joined us while Lionel and the children spent time together along the canal.

"Mickey also stopped by a gun show in Miami the day the family stayed there. The show was located across the street from the mall where the family shopped. The pistol came from the show, evidence we can use against Mickey," she said.

"The day of the picnic I let him take my car so he could drive Darcie back to the house because she was tired. He must have stowed the shotgun somewhere, perhaps under the seat in Madeleine's van, retrieved it when he left with Darcie, stopped to take a shot at his father, then stashed it in my trunk."

"That's a lot of planning on his part, same with the brakes which he partially cut through at the motel in Miami," Frida said.

"Bad planning, I'd say. He almost killed his wife when she drove the car, and others could have eaten the haggis."

Frida gave a shudder. "Unlikely. Everyone's heard about haggis."

"Still, consider how he treated his son falling into the water after he shoved Angus in. He was about to leave them when we appeared. He couldn't have cared less about Dylan. I think Carolyn's guilt over Mickey's birth father and Angus' guilt over not being a better father to Mickey kept the two of them bound by silence all these years. Carolyn finally told the truth, but Angus is still protecting the son he thinks he failed."

"This is all conjecture, isn't it?" asked Sammy. "Angus hasn't said he was shoved in by Mickey, and Mickey's not confessed to any attempts on his father's life, has he?"

Frida and I looked at Sammy in disbelief. "What do you think he was doing out on the lake?"

"He was trying to kill the two of you. That's attempted

murder of a PI and a police officer," said Sammy.

"If he gets a smart lawyer, he might get off on many of the charges. I think we'll have to offer him a deal to own up to what he did," said Frida, clearly disappointed she hadn't more evidence against Mickey."

Lionel came around the corner of the cabin and heard what Frida said.

"Tell him to confess, or I'll take him out into the swamps and lose him," suggested Lionel.

It wasn't a bad idea, but one not in Frida's bag of police tricks. We all knew that Mickey might be out of prison in twenty years, less than that with good behavior. Given his anger at his father and mother, no one felt comfortable with the thought of him being free, but Frida assured us it was the best the system could offer.

THE NEXT WEEKEND we opened our new house to everyone in the community with a party beginning in the early afternoon and continuing into the evening. This night would be the first we slept in the house, and all the kids were excited to have their own rooms and beds. I wasn't certain how Netty would feel alone in her room because she had spent so much of her life sharing with us, but when I tucked her in and kissed her good night, she curled onto her side and gave me a smile. I turned off the light expecting her to find her way into our room later. She did, but it was after the sun came up, and she touched my arm to awaken me.

"I'm hungry," she said. "Can I go over to Grandfather's house? I think he's already up because I can smell bacon cooking."

"We'll all go over," I said, got out of bed and threw on jeans and a shirt. Sammy dressed while Netty and I went to waken the boys.

I felt some momentary guilt that I hadn't stocked the fridge with supplies to make breakfast here, and I was prepared to apologize to Grandfather for barging in on him, but once I saw the mound of bacon and eggs, I knew our appearance was no surprise. The only one who groused about us was Lionel who muttered something about how difficult it was to "get enough to eat around here because of the neighbors barging in." I knew he was only half kidding.

"It's a beautiful day," said Sammy as he finished his eggs. "Let's take a canoe ride, the two of us." There was that lustful gleam in his eyes, one I hadn't seen for a while.

"Do you mind taking care of the boys and Netty?" I asked Grandfather and Lionel. "I think Sammy needs a break. He put a lot of work in on this house."

The kids looked a bit disappointed that they weren't included in the invitation, but Lionel offered to take them out in his canoe.

"We can paddle out to that old shack that your mom and dad are so fond of," he said.

Sammy and I looked at each other. "No, you cannot," Sammy said. "Find your own spot to picnic."

I asked Grandfather if he needed to call in someone to operate the air boat business today, but he assured me that there were few tourists in the area during these hot summer months. "And if we miss one party wanting to take a ride, it won't break us," he added.

Sammy and I paddled off into the canal. For a summer day in rural Florida, the humidity was surprisingly low. A cooling breeze from the lake pushed fluffy clouds around in a brilliant blue sky. It had been months since Sammy and I had visited the shack in the swamps to be alone with each other and do, well, you know, alone things.

"Someday we may have to consider doing repairs to this place. There's only one corner of the roof that hasn't fallen down," he said as we approached the clearing where the cabin stood.

"I don't see mama alligator. She's usually around keeping an eye on the place," I said, scanning the vegetation that covered both sides of the path.

"She's here someplace," Sammy replied.

She was an unusual reptile. She'd never physically attacked anyone although she had threatened a nasty guy who was trying to harm the family and me.

"She's like having a guard dog, isn't she?" I said.

"I have a housewarming gift for you," Sammy said as we unpacked our picnic basket. He handed me an envelope. I opened it and found a note inside which read, "Noon tomorrow, flight 545, Orlando airport: arrival time for your consignment shop help."

"What does this mean?" I asked.

"You thought I forgot all about my promise to get you help in the shop, didn't you?"

I nodded.

"I promised you a tribe member, but I thought this was one better."

I was still confused.

"My mother is taking off a few weeks from her job in Las Vegas. She said she'd be delighted to help out in the shop."

"Oh, Sammy!" I exclaimed, hugging him.

Sammy's mother was Renata Egret. Netty was named after her. "Netty will be so pleased to see her grandmother," Sammy said, squeezing me back. It had been months, almost a year since Renata had visited us.

"Everyone will be pleased to see her," I said, then hesitated. "Well, not everyone. Lionel will probably hide out in the swamps so he doesn't have to see his ex-wife again."

"Dad has grown up some since she last visited."

Maybe Sammy was right about that. Lionel and I were making progress in our relationship.

"Unless your mother wants to relocate here, and I'm sure she doesn't, I need to address the situation in the shop more permanently."

Shelley was the obvious choice for full-time help in the shop, but would she consider giving up her dream to go to the big city and become a designer? It was worth asking her.

We settled our ground cover cloth under the shade of a palm tree growing in front of the shack.

"It's too hot to crawl in there," Sammy said, "and it's not raining so we don't need the shelter. Here we can catch the breeze…"

Before he could finish the sentence, I pulled him down onto the blanket with me and planted a passionate kiss on his full, sexy lips. For the remainder of the afternoon we ignored everything around us and concentrated on making up for the time we had missed being with each other.

"You don't think the house is too small, do you?" asked Sammy.

I knew why he was asking. "The two younger boys are in one large bedroom, but I'm certain we could fit bunkbeds into any of the kids' rooms. No reason why kids can't share." I smiled up into his handsome face. "We can find space."

THE SUMMER MONTHS rolled by. Jason went to visit his Miccosukee relatives on the ranch. His time with David's daughter in the swamps apparently did not cement their initial attraction to each other. Everyone was relieved they hadn't become an item. From his phone calls it appeared he was working hard and enjoying time learning how to raise and herd cattle.

Shelley continued to work as our tailor. She expressed no desire to change careers to become a PI, but she mentioned moving north to New York City less often. I waited for the right moment to ask her about a full partnership in the shop. Grandmother Renata spend a month with us and helped out in the shop, then returned to her job in Las Vegas. It was good having her with us. Even Lionel behaved himself. He and I continued to have our differences, but fewer now that we'd settled on respectful disagreement and left off overt contentiousness, which we both felt set a poor example for the children. How bad could the man be? He loved my children.

The women from Ms. Abbot's business who had been harassed felt empowered enough to step up and name their accusers, and the file Nappi and I liberated from the HR office helped their case. Kidnapping charges were levied against the men who snatched Shelley, and Ms. Abbot fired them, hiring a new human services director, this one a woman.

Angus, Darcie and Dylan returned to Scotland. Mrs. MacAngus did not accompany them. It appeared the marriage between her and Angus was over for good. Against his lawyer's recommendation, Mickey refused a deal from the DA's office. Meantime he sat in the county jail without bail because he was a flight risk. He was a risk in many ways.

One day toward the end of summer when I stopped at the post office to pick up the mail, there was a letter for me from Angus thanking Crusty and me for the agency's services in finding who had attempted to kill him and a check. In the end, we may have been somewhat instrumental in identifying his own son as his attacker, but Crusty and I had talked and agreed it was impossible to differentiate between billable hours and time spent with Madeleine's family, so the agency never sent Angus an accounting for the case. Angus had paid us a retainer up front. I'd turn the check over to Crusty, but I knew he'd do what I would: tear it up.

The note Angus wrote was short:

> I thought you'd like to see these two pictures. Dylan threw out the kitty picture because we both decided it held too many bad memories. Instead he did another collage made up of only pasta of many shapes. As you can see it's an alligator. The other picture is of Dylan and me.

I knew why he included the picture of the two of them. Although Angus' hair had whitened more since I had last seen him, it still retained the red color of his grandson's. Both had twinkling blue eyes and a broad forehead with a straight nose and a round, dimpled chin.

Angus saw Dylan as his grandson. The picture and the love it showed between the two of them erased all doubt. Others might not be convinced, but it was really a family matter, and I understood how much family meant above all else.

Creations in Fotografia by Rafael Pacheco

LESLEY A. DIEHL retired from her life as a professor of psychology and reclaimed her country roots by moving to a small cottage in the Butternut River Valley in Upstate New York. In the winter she migrates to old Florida—cowboys, scrub palmetto, and open fields of grazing cattle, a place where spurs still jingle in the post office and gators make golf a contact sport. Back north, the shy ghost inhabiting the cottage serves as her literary muse. When not writing, she gardens, cooks, and renovates the 1874 cottage with the help of her husband, two cats, and of course Fred the ghost, who gives artistic direction to their work.

She is the author of a number of mystery series and mysteries as well as short stories. *Mud Bog Murder* follows the first three books in the Eve Appel mystery series, *A Secondhand Murder*, *Dead in the Water* and *A Sporting Murder*.

Visit her online at www.lesleyadiehl.com.